THE WHISTLER OF HUTORIANE

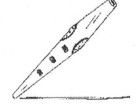

Book One

Written and Illustrated by

Jimmy Eaton

Ivy Shire
Publishing

For my children:

Molli, Brock, Lucas, Layla, Rosalie, and Aria

Special thanks to Alisha for your support and encouragement.

Special thanks to Dallan, Josh, and Justin for your wise insights.

Special thanks to all my early manuscript readers for your important feedback.

PROLOGUE

"Greetings, old soul," said a strange voice.

Draug ignored it and rolled his frail body over onto the right side, atop his scratchy bed of straw.

"Greetings, I say!" the grim voice boomed.

Draug begrudgingly awoke but didn't open his eyes. He answered in a raspy whisper, "Are you in my head? Or are you here? Because my world is black."

"Does it make a difference then, you miserable fool?" the voice asked.

"Why are you interrupting my rest?"

The air in the rock cell swiftly changed from a damp chill to a clammy heat. "You've been resting for over a century. The time has come."

An unexplainable pressure held Draug down on his bed. "How did you find me? And why must you still torment me, Seleman?" Draug mumbled, now gasping for air. "Am I not already damned?"

"You are not damned, but rather in exile."

Draug struggled for his next breath. "Destroy me already! I have nothing. You have stripped me of all power and position. Of everything. You and the others have forced me to live in this miserable state for too long. Destroy me, I beg you!"

"You were unruly and challenged the Council one too many times," Seleman said.

"The factions of the Council all conspired against me!"

The pressure on Draug intensified and the temperature in the room rose to a suffocating heat.

"I come with an offer for you," Seleman said. "Only you. It's an offer you cannot refuse... because well, you can't."

Draug lay on his bed hyperventilating as sweat dripped from every inch of his decrepit body.

"The Council is severely divided," Seleman continued. "Each faction is refusing to compromise. The very existence of Hutoriane is on the verge of total implosion."

Hardly able to make a sound, Draug groaned, "Good."

"You have posterity in the Natural world that can save Hutoriane. I will restore your powers to a portion of what they were, so that you can recruit and employ them to our cause."

The pressure alleviated so Draug could respond. "Destroy me," he said. "I want nothing."

"You are a fool!" Seleman applied immense force again. "Have you forgotten the joy of power? This is a chance to change your legacy!"

Draug was quiet. He had done evil works for most of his existence. Seleman made a point, but Draug hadn't perked up for the same reason. He began to consider his nemesis' offer. Curious and in anguish, he uttered, "Tell me more."

"I have preserved you for this purpose!"

"Liar."

"I will release you from this misery and restore half of your powers if you make an oath with me." The pressure lifted, and the air cooled briefly. Seleman continued to explain the peril of Hutoriane and his proposition along with certain conditions and expectations.

Draug deliberated for a moment. His craving for power was great, but now he figured he had nothing left to exist for. Still, a greater motive nagged Draug.

"I accept, Master."

CHAPTER ONE

"Bean! Grab the mallet and stake down the other side of the tent, please," his father said.

"Yes, Pops!" Bean answered.

The long anticipated buck hunt had finally arrived with autumn. Bean and his father, Hank, were rushing to set up camp deep in the Uinta Mountains of northern Utah before sunset. Ever since Bean could walk, his dad had brought him along for the yearly hunt. But this year was different. It was Bean's hunt. Having finally gained his father's approval, he obtained a hunting license and got his first buck tag.

Hank was an avid hunter, seemingly more committed to hunting than he was to his job. He spent most of his free time researching online best practices for hunting mule deer and studying ballistics to keep up his elite marksmanship. He and Bean spent many hours sighting in and shooting all types of guns, and sometimes even archery. Hank was not a social man. He was pleasant, but not overly friendly or nosy.

Hank loved to take his fourteen-year-old son up into the mountains to observe the wildlife. Hank showed Bean how to use his military grade scope and other optics to uncover hiding bucks. Bean also enjoyed time with his dad. He was not just Hank's only son but also one of his greatest pals. They were thrilled to find out the previous May that they both drew out tags for the buck hunt in their favorite hunting region.

"Bean! Bring your pack over here so we can make sure you have everything you need for the hike tomorrow."

"Yes sir, Pops!" Bean yelled as he finished pounding in the tent stake.

Bean hustled over to an old, root beer-colored pickup truck and climbed up into its rusty back end. This truck was part of the family. As long as Bean was alive, his father drove this truck. Although old and worn, it remained durable and reliable. It had gotten them through so many narrow passages, tight squeezes, steep climbs, thick mud, and over gnarly terrain they never thought possible. This proven and field-tested experience earned it the family name Trusty Rusty.

Bean hollered over to his dad, "Pops, you really still don't trust me? I mean, I put in everything that you told me to weeks ago."

"Let's just check it over again," his dad said. "I know you've had it ready for a while now, but we can never be too prepared."

"I know, I know," he said. Then in unison, they both affirmed, "It's better to be safe than sorry." Hank nudged Bean's shoulder enjoying his mocking humor. Then, like a ravaging wolf devouring its prey, Hank ripped into Bean's backpack, stripping it of its contents, piece by piece.

"Flashlight, knife, water, ammo..." his father rattled off.

"Check. Check. Check. Check," Bean responded.

"Snack bars, poncho, chapstick, gum, jerky, fresh socks, eight one-dollar bills..." he said with some amusement.

"Well yeah," Bean told him, raising shoulders and eyebrows.

His dad continued, "...compass, game bag, toilet paper, matches and lighter?"

"You never know," Bean said.

Hank scoured the backpack. Bean's dad had a clear idea of the proper inventory every backpack should contain when hiking for an extended period, over sketchy terrain, and in unpredictable circumstances. Every item seemed to be present and Bean was confident it would make him proud. But to his dismay, there was a long pause. Hank's slightly chubby, hair-prickled face was grim and serious. His bushy eyebrows slowly lowered over his blue eyes as they glared down at his son.

Unable to withstand this familiar look of disapproval any longer, Bean asked, "Pops, geez. What's the matter? What did I miss?"

"Your whistle. Where is your whistle?" he asked.

"My whistle? That was for when I was younger and inexperienced on the mountain. After years of hiking these hills, I for sure don't need a whistle."

With one eye squinting and a cheek twitching, Hank took a deep breath. "Bean. Seriously. My father gave me a whistle too and insisted that I carry it when hunting or hiking in these mountains. Thankfully, I never had to use it. But I still carry the same whistle. Here, you take it." He reached into his green flannel shirt pocket and pulled out a smooth, engraved piece of hollowed out wood about seven inches long. He quickly shoved it into Bean's pack. "Go get a pen and some paper out of Rusty's console and put it in your pack too."

Bean's positive mood changed. Feeling annoyed that he still wasn't fully trusted, he begrudgingly did what his father asked. "Whistles are for inexperienced hikers who get lost," he said to himself. "I know these rocky paths, hills, and even the tree groves. This is *our* area where we *always* go, year after year. We even came up here a few times earlier this year scouting and trying to pattern some bucks. I know this mountain."

Bean knew his dad would live in these high mountains if his mom Gail would allow it. Hank's whole demeanor seemed to soften with the surroundings of flickering yellow aspen trees, swaying tall pine trees, trickling natural springs, clean air, and breathtaking scenery especially in the fall. Observing the variety of birds and wildlife in their habitats was one of Hank's fondest hobbies. He often commented to Bean on how he longed for the unique serenity, quiet, and peace only the mountains can afford. They had become his refuge and natural sanctuary from his everyday work as a busy real estate appraiser.

"Look, I see headlights coming up the dirt road down there!" Hank yelled over to Bean, pointing halfway down the mountain.

"Is that Uncle Kenny and Bo?" Bean asked, craning his neck to see.

"Let's hope so. I don't want any other hunters coming up here to my area," Hank said, scowling. "Bean, let's get this fire started. They'll need to set up their tent and things when they get here."

"Yes sir! I'll go gather some dried kindling and tinder," Bean said.

Bean put down his backpack next to the tent door and walked briskly to the outer fringe of their campsite. He combed the wild grass and lime green shrubbery for old, broken pieces of wood and dried loose grass. As he did this, he mentally reviewed the route he and his dad had plotted out to hike and reach a secluded bowl-like area about three miles into the backcountry from camp. He rehearsed in his mind how he'd spot the tall tines of a huge buck peeking over some short scrub oak two hundred yards away. He'd set up his shot finding a solid mount for steadiness, like a big rock or tree branch. He'd then carefully determine where to lay the crosshairs of his scope just behind the shoulder of the deer.

"Beany boy!" His thoughts were interrupted by his tall, black bearded Uncle Kenny.

"Uncle Kenny! Bo! You found us!" Bean secured the pile of wood he just gathered and sprinted over back to the campsite by the fire ring Hank had made.

"Found *you*? This is the same place we always come!" Uncle Kenny said. "This is our second home. Even Bo Boy knew where the dirt road turnoff was. How are you, big man?" Kenny's long frame bent over and gave Bean a big hug. "Geez man, you're growing up fast."

Standing five feet and seven inches high, Bean was taller than most of the boys in the eighth grade. He had broad shoulders, big feet, and all the indicators that he too would be as tall as his six-foot-four father and uncle. A good athlete, Bean enjoyed playing football and basketball. In fact, his football coach was disturbed by the idea of Bean missing this week's game to go hunting, wondering who would play defensive end as his replacement.

"These boys are gonna be bigger than us before long," Hank remarked as he put his arm around Bo. "Bo Boy, how old are you now, ten?" he asked.

"Nah, I'm still nine." Bo said with a grin. "But don't worry 'bout me, I can hang with you guys!" All four broke into laughter, happy to reunite for a few days in the mountains.

Bean dropped the wood outside of the fire ring, and then began to set up a small teepee in the center of the fire ring with the small sticks, kindling and tinder he gathered. Bo handed him some bigger pieces of wood and Bean stacked them as if to build a log cabin around the teepee.

"Wow, these boys don't even need us anymore!" Kenny said, looking impressed. Bean then lit the fire with his lighter.

The sun had dipped behind the furthest mountains in the western sky leaving streaks of bright orange, pink, and purple. The once cool and crisp air was dropping to a colder forty-five degrees. The trees cast longer shadows and the dim dusk light invited some brave deer to wander close by and snack on some tall green grass.

"Bean," Bo whispered. "Look, some deer. Get your gun!"

"Bo Boy, relax. Hunt starts at first crack of light tomorrow morning. But let's get a closer look," Bean explained, being the more mature older cousin. He grabbed his binoculars and focused on the three outlined animals.

"What do you see?" Bo asked impatiently.

"Eh, just three does," answered Bean.

"Let me see," Bo said as he reached for the binoculars.

"Hold up, hold up," Bean said knocking Bo's hand down. "Buddy, oh buddy. There's another one. About twenty feet behind the group, to the left. It's a buck," Bean whispered. "It's a buck. It's a three-point!" Bean was hoping to find at least a three-point buck, one with three tines on each side of the antlers. "Quick, go get my dad."

Bo ran over to Hank and Kenny, who had just finished setting up Kenny's tent.

"Uncle Hank! Dad! We got deer!" Bo yelled. All three walked quietly over to Bean, Kenny holding Bo from running.

"What do you see, Bean?" Hank asked.

"Dad, it's a three-point. Right over there, just behind the group of three does, to the left," Bean said, pointing in that direction.

Hank grabbed the binoculars and affixed them in front of his eyes. "Nice. Very nice. I guess we don't need to hike out three miles tomorrow after all. Bean, get your gun." Bean hesitated and looked up in confusion at his dad. His dad nodded. "Go on, get it."

Bean couldn't believe his dad was telling him to do this. They had had so many talks on the rules of hunting and proper etiquette. The hunt officially began in the morning. It was also getting too dark, and the buck wasn't clearly visible...but Bean listened to his dad. He opened the back door to Rusty's cab and grabbed his muzzle loader. He then reached for the black powder pellets, a primer, and a .50 caliber bullet. He quickly returned to the guys.

His dad said, "Okay, load it."

Bean was baffled, but anxious to hunt. He wanted this three-point. He'd waited all year for this moment. But this wasn't right. He knew it and he knew his father knew it. Obediently, he loaded the gun, jamming the bullet down into the barrel with the ramrod. Once ready, he sneaked over to the back-end corner of Rusty's tailgate and pulled the gun up in shooting position with the buck faintly in his sight. Hank, Kenny, and Bo crept up behind him. As Bean began to cock his gun, a firm grip engulfed his trigger hand and gently lowered the gun a few inches.

"Bean, are you kidding me?" his dad asked in total disappointment.

Bean gently set the gun on the ground, leaning it against the tailgate in confusion. "Dad, you told me to grab my gun."

"Yes, I did."

"And I looked at you unsure, but you nodded for me to continue anyway."

"Yes, I did."

"And I was thinking it wasn't right. I thought you thought so too, but..."

"Is following me more important than doing the right thing?" Hank asked. "When does the hunt actually begin? Isn't it getting too dark?"

Bean began to understand. While he couldn't bear his father being so condescending, he felt ashamed for letting his father down again. He was also embarrassed that Hank chastised him in front of his Uncle Kenny and Bo. He quickly grabbed the gun, took out the primer, and returned it to the truck. Then he walked over to the tent and shut himself inside.

Kenny said, "Well, Bo Boy, let's go get dinner started. I'm hungry!"

"Bean, come out and eat," his father said after a few minutes. "Your mom made us some delicious chicken dinners."

Bean didn't respond. His thoughts went to home and his mom, Gail. She was a strong-willed and opinionated woman. She was fit, pretty with long blond hair and was above average height, but slightly shorter than Bean. She had a passion for local politics and community involvement. She loved to network with people, gossip with friends at lunch, and even had a group of women she ran with every morning. She didn't have a full-time job but was always very busy with Bean's two younger sisters, eleven-year-old Haley and eight-year-old Madison. They were both quite involved in dance, soccer and piano lessons.

Gail didn't deal much with Bean other than overseeing his homework and nagging him about chores. Her actions often annoyed Bean. He was especially bothered with her constant posting on social media of everything she did multiple times a day. He once asked her why she had to take a picture of herself in workout clothes simply to post it with the caption, "well today isn't going as planned." Bean was suspicious of her motives for attention. She justified the post to him explaining that people wanted to know the real you. Bean just wanted to know the *real* her. Before Hank and Bean left, she did take time to prepare some chicken and vegetable skewers for their dinner and a couple tinfoil-wrapped hash browns.

After a few minutes, Hank repeated, "Come out bud. I'm sorry. I shouldn't have tested you like that."

"Beany boy! Come on, we have to make our plan for tomorrow," Kenny said. "You need to show me where we're going. Did you bring a map?"

After a long pause, Bean responded, "Yeah. I'll get it." He grabbed the map, slipped on his shoes, put on a sweatshirt, zipped up the tent, and slowly walked over to the guys. He crashed down on a camping chair next to Kenny, immediately slouching. Bean didn't want anything to do with his dad. He opened up the map of the Uinta mountain range and showed Kenny where they were and where they were heading early in the morning.

"Here, Bean." Bo set a plate full of food on Bean's lap.

"Thanks, Bo," Bean said. Bean began to shove each piece of chicken in his mouth as if he hadn't eaten in days, but didn't touch the cooked onions, green peppers, red peppers, and mushrooms on the other skewers. The chicken was so delicious, Bean quickly forgot he was even upset. "Did we bring any barbecue sauce?"

Hank pointed over to the cooler. "You guys know we've come up here for years now. I remember listening to all the wild hunting stories Grandpa Carl would tell Kenny and me around the campfire. Psssh, he even told us of a run-in he had with some transient Indians."

"Seriously, that story is crazy," Kenny said. He began to laugh. "Hank, they weren't transient. He said they supposedly lived around here."

"Well, he described the one like he was an old bum off the street or something," Hank said.

Interest piqued, Bean spoke up. "Come on. No Indians live around here. They were here maybe two hundred years ago, but..." Bean assumed they were telling a fib.

"I'm scared," Bo said.

"We haven't even told the story yet, Bo Boy!" Kenny said with another chuckle. "Sorry guys, I guess the story will have to wait until next year."

"Wow, what's that?" Bean asked Uncle Kenny, pointing to a furry thing on his lap.

"Why, that's my lucky cougar paw," Kenny said. He handed it over to Bean. "Check it out." Bean was impressed as he examined the large paw. Kenny turned his attention over to Hank. "Hank, did you bring your guitar?"

"Yeah, he did," Bean said before Hank could say no. "Actually, I brought it for him." Bean glared over at his dad with a look of redemption. "I'll go get it." Bean loved to hear his dad sing. Even more, he loved to sing along with him. Hank didn't play the guitar super well but played enough to entertain a campfire gathering. Bean tried to learn the chords his father played in his spare time at home. Hank did know a bunch of oldies. Bean's favorite was "Stand by Me."

"Here, Pops," Bean said, carefully handing Hank his old six-string acoustic.

Hank began to tune his guitar while Kenny and Bean collaborated on the plan for the next day. They decided they should awake at 5am and get hiking at 5:30am. Bo sat quietly, shivering with a light blanket wrapped around him.

Hank sang, "When the night has come..."

Bean finally joined in, "I won't be afraid, just as long as you stand by me."

CHAPTER TWO

The next morning arrived too soon. The chill, the anticipation, and the hard ground made it easy for the hunters to awake and arise. Each dressed warm with multiple layers that they could eventually shed as the sun heated the day. They planned to be out all day, from dawn to dusk. These were the prime times for deer activity as they'd be moving around, visiting a watering hole, eating, and resituating their position. If for some reason the hunters didn't harvest an animal, they would head back around 6:30pm, keeping an eye open for a big buck on the return trek.

Hank had gotten up a little earlier to rekindle the fire and heat up some oatmeal for the guys. After the bunch was fully dressed and equipped, Kenny offered a short prayer expressing gratitude for the time together and asking for safety and success for the day's hunt. Bean admired his uncle's faith. Kenny didn't have a tag, but he was there for tradition and to help haul out their potential kills. Hank wasn't religious but did attend church each Sunday with the family to keep peace with Gail. Gail wasn't exactly religious either, but she wanted this to be part of their family's image. The hunters wolfed down their hot breakfast. After they secured their tents, locked up the trucks, and put out the fire, they set out hiking on an immediate incline in a northeast direction up the mountainside.

The elevation was approximately ten thousand feet above sea level. The morning mountain dew dampened the ground, making it slippery in some areas. The crisp air woke their senses quickly. They fastened LED flashlights to each of their heads. In the open areas, they marched hastily, one after the other, like an army troop heading into battle. In the areas of thick brush, Hank led the way, bushwhacking and trailblazing where needed, while the others followed a few feet behind. But their course was mainly unobstructed.

While not an exact science, Hank had taught Bean that there were many factors to locating an optimal hunting spot. They needed an area where they could hunker down and have their camouflaged clothing give them some advantage. There, they would blend in with the shrubbery or tree line while being able to observe a hillside or open meadow where deer could be grazing. Determined to find the right spot, they aimed to be sitting quietly in place before first light. However, the further they went, the louder and slower Bo got. The youngest was now lagging behind by forty yards.

"Bo Boy," Kenny loudly whispered. "Get on it!" He motioned with his right arm to catch up with Hank and Bean. Bo picked up the pace until he approached his dad.

"I don't feel good, Dad," he said.

"Oh man, what's the matter?" Kenny asked annoyed.

"I don't know. My stomach or something," Bo said.

Bean and Hank stopped. They were all relieved to have a much needed water break, but no one really wanted to confess so.

"Boy, you promised to hang with us. Here, drink some water. You'll be fine." Kenny handed his son a bottle of water.

The once overly dark-blue sky was now lightening over the east. The sun was still about twenty minutes from bursting onto the night sky. Stars dimmed gradually, but the southwest moon kept its brilliant aura. The hunters' eyes had adjusted now to the darkened surroundings and could see remarkably well. They agreed to turn off the flashlights. Hank explained they had just about fifteen more minutes until they'd arrive in the general vicinity he wanted to hunt. While Bo refreshed, his dad lectured him on how important it was to walk as quiet as possible so as to not spook the deer. On alert, they persisted on following Hank's lead.

Hank came to a sudden halt. Bean, looking off to the left, caught himself before he crashed into his father in front of him.

"Shhhhh." Hank raised his right index finger to his lips. With the same finger, he motioned it over to the right of the group and pointed out a magnificent sight off in the distance about a hundred yards. To what seemed to be a bush shaking or doing a jig, the wide antlers of a bull elk were moving up and down and side to side with a natural rhythm. The animal's gigantic silhouette was outlined and cast against the cool grayish-blue sky.

Kenny whispered, "You only see that during the buck hunt."

Hank and Bean smiled and knew this sighting was rare to behold during the elk hunt.

Shortly after, the group trudged up a gradual draw between two expansive hillsides. They stayed in the treeline and were as stealthy as they could be. They knew the sun's light would be illuminating the area soon. Deciding on a couple rocks to rest on and behind a fallen tree, the hunters gently set down their packs and gear. Kenny hastily unloaded and set up his spotting scope, as did Hank. Bo grabbed his water bottle and took a few sips. Bean and Hank loaded their guns and propped them up on their shoulders. They all sat quietly, finally affixed in their hunting spot and waited.

The sunlight from the east brightened up the opposite mountainside and an opening four hundred yards across from the hunters. They were nestled down in the shadows, with much more gray and dull lighting in their immediate surroundings. Early birds chirped, busy squirrels raced across branches, and an occasional rustle of crispy leaves on the ground disrupted the silence. Kenny glassed the left side of the hillside; Hank watched the right; and Bean used his binoculars to scan the entire area. Bo kept checking behind the men as if they were actually the ones being hunted. Restlessly, he unzipped his sack for a granola bar.

An hour passed rapidly. Hank knelt next to Bean and whispered in his ear, "Remember, hunting is a sport of patience."

Bean nodded with his binoculars still in both hands, keenly viewing the same area to detect any movement at all. His father tore some grass out of the dirt and tossed it in the air. To his consternation, a slight breeze carried the grass out forward directly in front of them. "Oh dang," he said. Kenny and Bean soon realized what he was doing, and their faces went bleak. Bo nonchalantly finished his granola bar.

"Can they smell us?" Bean asked.

"Maybe," his dad said. "When a buck smells, hears, or sees something out of ordinary nature, it will retreat deep into the woods for cover. The distance that it takes a normal man fifteen minutes to travel, a startled buck can go for miles."

Bean knew his dad had high expectations for a buck this year. A huge, alpha male with wide five-point antlers or more was what Hank intended to slay. Hank understood this type was expertly aloof and survived long enough to grow up into a highly desired specimen. He'd told Bean how some impatient and inexperienced hunters could harvest a two- or three-point deer, but that few hunted well enough to slay a four-point buck. The hunters furtively huddled up twenty feet behind where they were observing. They needed to regroup and come up with a new plan of attack.

"We may have been scented," Hank said. "It seems that we are far enough away, but I've read that our scent can carry a few hundred yards or more. Heck, we aren't even sure if there is anything over there. But if there was one, I don't think he's there now. At least not a nice one."

"Hank, I can pack up my scope, and hike down across that ravine," Kenny said. "That way, I can get us another set of eyes on the general area and hopefully flush out some deer in the process."

"That's a good idea," Hank said. "I'll head down to the left and then come around just below you. I'll leave my spotting scope here with Bean."

"Wait, Pops, you're gonna go too?" Bean asked hesitantly.

"Yeah, bud. You stay here with Bo," his father said. "Don't worry. You have a whistle if there is an emergency."

"Dad! I'm not staying here!" Bo nearly shouted.

"Bo Boy, quiet!" Kenny said. "Don't complain. If you come with me, that's more walking. And wherever you are, you must remain quiet."

"I'm going with you!" Bo said.

Hank didn't object. Neither did Bean. Bean liked the idea of having it completely silent anyway. But he did feel uneasy about his dad and the others leaving him there alone.

"How long do we want to try this strategy?" Bean asked Hank and Kenny.

"Bean, it's okay...as long as necessary," his father said. "We're hunting. This is the hunt. I need you to watch and be patient. This could work out really well for you. You could get a good look at a buck."

"Yeah, Beany boy, Bo and I will be over on that hillside above the ravine to the south by that rock formation," Kenny said. "You will be able to see me and I'd be able to see you too if your camouflage wasn't so good!" Kenny's joking eased Bean's anxiety. "But seriously, let's plan on returning here in two hours, at approximately ten AM."

Bean squared up his shoulders and took a deep breath. That's what he was looking for. "That time sounds great," he said.

"Yep, perfect," Hank said. He turned to Bean and hugged him with his right arm and pulled him in tight. "Buddy, you'll be fine."

Bean nodded, still feeling a little apprehensive.

The hunters each took a long drink of water. Kenny and Hank removed their camouflage jackets. Instead of adding bulk to their backpacks, they left them with Bean for when they returned. Both Kenny and Hank strapped on their packs and Hank grabbed his muzzle loader. Finally, they gave each other a quick fist bump before they parted ways. To Kenny's surprise, Bo had already started down the hill, heading toward a small patch of aspen trees to the right. Bean watched through his binoculars as his dad embarked down to the left side of the mountain. Gradually, his father disappeared into the distant trees and brush. Instantly, a fearful feeling came over Bean, but he reassured himself, "I'm a real hunter. I know this mountain."

The stillness and eerie silence were unbearable to Bean. While he shared his father's love of the outdoors, he could only endure this moment of solitude for so long. He was hoping to hear the bustling of Bo behind him unwrapping a candy bar. Bean looked at his watch and thirty minutes had already gone by. He looked through his binoculars down to the left to check up on his dad. As he sat there, something was maneuvering down to the right of where he thought his dad had gone.

"Dad?" he wondered out loud. He focused his optics on an area to the right, close to a large moss colored rock and two red berry bushes. The bushes started to tremble and shake. Some dark shadow moved behind them. Bean held his breath. Suddenly, two deer popped out into the open.

Bean's heart was racing. "How far away are they?" he asked himself. He grabbed his range finder and discovered they were about three hundred yards out. Out of range for his muzzle loader, he was only able to hit two hundred yards accurately, at best. Bean replaced the range finder with his binoculars again. To his disappointment, he confirmed they were does. Remembering last night's experience, he wondered if there was a buck hovering close by in some of the sage brush. He scrutinized the area roundabout, but nothing. Bean sat in the calm of nature and watched the does for a long time.

Growing very impatient, Bean set the binoculars down and glanced at his watch. It read 9:12am. "Only about forty-five more minutes," he told himself. His stomach rumbled, so he opened up his backpack. He went to grab a candy bar when he noticed the wooden whistle his dad inserted. *That dumb whistle*, he thought, knowing he was too big to need it. He tore into the candy bar and took a few big bites. Bean felt like he was being watched. Just then, the crackling of wood and leaves behind him made his heart jump. He turned abruptly to find a rabbit skipping through the trees and disappearing within seconds. He decided to give the spotting scope a try as it already sat on the tripod.

"Uncle Kenny and Bo should be right up over there," he said to himself as he lowered the scope to his height. He turned the scope to his right, took his eye off the scope to get his bearings of the vicinity he wanted to observe. A tall, precipitous rock outcropping stood about thirty feet high, and stretched for about a hundred yards wide. Some darker spots looked like small cavities in the rock.

If I were Uncle Kenny, I'd set up right in that area, he thought. But after twenty-five minutes of glassing, Kenny and Bo were nowhere to be seen. He rationalized that they must be on their way back, crossing the ravine.

He zoomed back in and focused again on some of the dark spots of the pink rock formation. Bean looked over about five different holes which he estimated were at least three feet wide.

"Those would be a good place to explore or hide out," he said to himself. "I'll have to ask Uncle Kenny if he got up close to them. Wait, what time is it?"

Bean looked down at his watch. It now read 10:23am. Terrified, Bean grabbed the binoculars and started to scan left to right, up the hill and down, and right back to the left in a controlled, yet panicked motion. There was no sign of his dad, Kenny, or Bo.

~~~ CHAPTER ~~~
THREE

"How could they be late?" Bean asked with some aggravation. "They knew I wasn't totally happy about being here alone. Did they underestimate the travel time to cross the hill and ravine? Can they both be lost?" Bean began to pace twenty yards to the left, then fifty yards to the right. He'd alternate with his naked eye, and then lift up the binoculars to scour every visible opening space. He was tired of this area and sick of seeing the same repetitive images. But now the jitters and angst of not having his dad return on time aroused his interest and vigor to look with more determination. He was now venturing seventy-five yards to the left, and then tracing back the same distance to the right. His watch read 10:51am.

Twenty minutes late was unacceptable to Bean. But an hour late was unfathomable. "Should I whistle for them?" he asked. "No. I'm not the one who's lost. Should I call for them? If so, I'd totally scare off any deer in the area. Heck, I've been here almost four hours. There aren't any bucks around here anyways."

Bean cupped his hands around his mouth and hollered, "Daaaaaaad! Kennnnnny! Daaaaaaad!" To his dread, there came no response.

Bean knew what to do when you get lost. "Stay put," he told himself. "After all, they *left me* here. They'll know where to find me. I'm not going anywhere. But where are they? Are they okay?" He remembered Kenny's prayer before they left, asking for safety and success. "Of course, they're okay." He called out again in his loudest voice and waited for a response, to no avail. He grabbed the paper and pen he packed and wrote a little note:

> *Dear Pops - Where the heck are you? The time is now 12:34pm. You said we'd meet back here at 10am. This is freaking me out. Kenny and Bo haven't returned either. I am taking a little walk to the right, south side of the hill toward the big rock formation. I hope to find you there. I think Kenny set up over there too. Please stay here until I return. Love, Bean*

Bean stuffed the note in the right pocket of the jacket his dad left earlier. He adjusted the note so Hank could see it sticking out, bright and white. Then he laid it on the highest rock where they all were settled. Bean then tied Kenny's jacket as high as he could around the closest, thinnest aspen tree. He hoped this would stand out if they were looking for the spot.

He picked up his backpack, the scope, and his gun, and hiked to the right in a southward direction and staying close to the tree line. The sun now hung high at its zenith and its warm rays pierced through the branches onto Bean's freckled cheeks. Bean quietly hummed the tune of "Stand by Me" as his mind swam with concern for his dad. Then a tear popped up in the corner of his right eye and made its way swiftly down his smooth baby face. One tear turned into many as the once brave hunter became overwhelmed with fear, confusion, and despair. He continued on until he found a good spot that his dad would've chosen.

Hunger sharply struck his teenage body. Bean knelt under a tall, thick, evergreen tree and pulled out the ham and cheese sandwich his father made. Unsure of how long he'd be alone, he wisely ate just half of the sandwich. He inserted it back into the plastic baggie and put it back in his backpack. Bean noticed the curious whistle again. This time he chose to inspect it.

The whistle was about an inch and a half in diameter, but it narrowed down to a half inch at the top and bottom. The hollowed-out hole running through the center was the size of a pea. The color was an orangish-bronze hue. There was one small hole in the back toward the top, and three wide slits stacked an inch apart toward the middle of the whistle.

As he rotated it in his left hand, Bean noticed a worn engraving that looked similar to a compass. The circle wrapped halfway around the tube-like body with an "x" crosscutting the center of it, creating four pizza-like sections. Inside the circle, in the left section made by the "x," was a curiously inscribed symbol that had four tiny dots. In the upper middle section was a star symbol. In the right section was a sideways lollypop looking mark. And in the bottom section was the cursive letter "M." A loud clarion call disrupted Bean's examination of the whistle.

He'd heard this sound before. He stood up, stuffed the whistle in his right pocket, and went out from under the tree to observe the new bright-green meadow below. Bean didn't need the scope. Nor did he need the binoculars. Standing enormous at just fifty yards away was a chocolate-colored, royal bull elk staring back at Bean. Its loud bugling call penetrated Bean's ears like the bell ending class at his school.

I sure wish I was back in school today. The thought surprised Bean. Was this the same bull that Pops pointed out earlier that morning? Probably. Bean walked backward, aware of the animal's strength and power, finding cover behind the same tall evergreen tree. *Could my dad and Kenny hear it too? Maybe it will draw them close.* He waited there for a while, but there was no sign of either of them. Hesitant to know, he decided not to look at his watch.

Bean set up the tripod and mounted the spotting scope. After watching the bull elk close up until it eventually migrated down into the brush, he decided to examine the rock outcropping again. The rock cavities interested Bean, and if he wasn't in such a precarious predicament, he would've loved to explore them. The scope lens gave him a mild headache, so he decided to look around without it. As he was gazing at the base of the rock formation, he noticed a swift movement a little higher up. Bean jumped to his feet, hoping to identify what it was through the scope. Slowly, he turned the scope to the right and up an inch. He focused in.

Astonished, Bean discovered a large, tan mountain lion napping on the second shelf of rocks, not too far from the top, but lying beneath an overhang that shaded the cat from the light of day. Its tail swayed up and then rested back down every few seconds. That's what had caught Bean's naked eye. His dad would be proud. In awe, Bean watched the cat for a few more minutes. Suddenly, adding horror to the moment, the lion stood on its four legs, stretched, and then nimbly made its way down the rocks and onto the grass beneath. Bean, now terrified, promptly packed up his gear and headed back to the original hunting spot.

The terror of an actual predator so potentially vicious and close by consumed Bean's mind. His brisk walk turned into a jog. It was difficult to jog with the weight of a backpack, along with holding both a big scope and gun.

Did the cougar see me? Bean wondered. *Am I being too loud? Is it even after me?* Panicking, he decided to ditch the scope, tossing it into the woods to his left. The scope's metal frame hit a rock on impact and rang out too loud for Bean's comfort. He accelerated into a run, approaching their first hunting spot.

Hoping his dad or Kenny would be there, he yelled for them. "Daaaaaadddddd! Kenny! Daaaaaaadddd!"

He remembered why he was running in the first place. "You idiot," he told himself. "If the cat didn't know you were here then, he does now with the ruckus you're making."

Out of breath, Bean stopped running and came up to the tree where he tied Kenny's coat. It was still there. He glanced over at the big rock, and to his disappointment, the white note still protruded from the pocket as he had left it. Just then, wood cracked in the trees behind him.

Bean looked over his shoulder and rotated to his right, glaring all around him but not seeing a cougar. Adrenaline still pumping, he decided to make a dash down the left side of the mountain following his father's path. As he rushed down the hill, he stumbled over some small rocks and fell into some thorny shrubbery. He gashed his knee, tearing his pants and scratching his left cheek too. He didn't have to time to sulk. He got back to his feet and continued descending a little more carefully.

Bean felt justified leaving his post. *Maybe the lion will sniff out their jackets up there and think we left a long time ago.* He limped about two hundred yards down the hillside and into a stony area sheltered by hundreds of yellow aspen trees. The daylight wasn't bright anymore. Breathing more than his lungs could handle, he stopped and hid down in a shallow gully about four feet wide.

Totally parched, Bean reached into his backpack for water. He gulped until his thirst was quenched. With just a few drops left, he finished the bottle. Bean's watch now said 5:26pm. His heart still pounding, he cried out, "Where are you, Pops? I need you. I'm gonna die!"

While nearly hysterical, the thought of his tough father mustered up some strength and courage. It occurred to him that he was the hunter, not the cougar chasing him. He abandoned the gully and made his way up to a small boulder that rose to his waist. Bean checked his gun, mounted it on the rock, and waited behind it for the encounter.

"Come on out, little pussy cat!" he called out. "I know you see me!"

With so many different emotions overwhelming his young mind, Bean surrendered his ego and decided to pull out the whistle. It was his last hope. He was desperate and felt unsure of his ability to shoot a fast-moving target. He placed it between his lips and blew as hard as he could. No sound exited the tube, just air.

"Oh my gosh." Bean gasped. "This piece of crap doesn't even work." He tried again. This time, a soft, fluting tone resonated through the thin mountain air. He attempted again, and a low-pitched trombone sound blared through the trees.

As he waited, Bean peeked up the hill about forty yards. He was able to make out the shape of the sleek cougar ducked down in some tall wild flowers, looking ready to pounce. He pointed the gun in the direction but couldn't find the cat in his scope. *Dang. Dad, where are you?* he wondered. He blew the whistle one last time. No sound left the pipe, but a powerful wind blew through the gully and rushed up at Bean. The gust knocked him off his feet about five yards back, causing him to drop his gun by the rock.

Raising his dizzy head, Bean heard a man's voice yell, "Bean! Quickly! Come this way!"

Bean looked over his to his left, just on the other side of the gully thirty feet away. A bare arm extended out of a cave-like opening and a hand waved for him to follow. He glanced back at the lion, now only twenty-five yards away. With the whistle in hand, he catapulted himself into the gully, climbed up the other side, tripped, and then darted for the cave opening. He dove into the cave just as the cat bit at his scratched leg. The rock opening shut instantly behind him.

Bean breathed violently, unable to believe what he'd just escaped, yet very relieved to be alive. The cave was pitch black, total darkness. The air was damp and musty. He couldn't think. He couldn't see. He was feeling claustrophobic and still very paranoid.

"Dad? Are you there?" he mumbled between breaths. "Uncle Kenny? Dad?" There was a long silent pause. The only noise in the cave was Bean's rapidly beating heart. "Dad? Who's there? Help me...please..." Bean's speech slowly slurred as the state of shock now crippled his body. Bean closed his eyes and fell into a deep sleep.

CHAPTER FOUR

With a wet cloth cooling his forehead, Bean came to. He slowly raised his right hand to his head and pulled off the wet rag.

"Where am I?" he asked out loud. Laying on his side, he sat up, feeling the weight of his backpack still fastened to his shoulders and torso. "Dad, are you *here*?" With his eyes wide open, the blackness remained too thick to see his own hand in front of him. He remembered his lighter and began to unzip his pack and feel around for it.

"Bean," an old voice grumbled, startling Bean. Bean jumped to his feet, pain jolting his knee.

"Who's there?" Bean asked as he continued to locate the lighter. He remembered it was in the small front pocket of the backpack.

"Don't be frightened," the voice said, now a little closer. "But I am not your father."

"Who are you? Stay back!" Bean found his lighter and frantically tried to light it.

"Bean. You don't know me. I've been watching you," the voice said.

Bean didn't know how to respond. After five attempts, the lighter held a flame. Just then, a quick breath of air blew it out.

"Not yet, Bean. You aren't ready to see me."

"Please, don't hurt me," Bean said, sensing how close the voice was. "What's going on? Do you know where my father is?"

"I am here to help you. Did I not rescue you last night?" the voice asked. Bean, remembering the terror he survived and, sensing he had slept for a while, began to trust the person behind the voice a little.

"That was you waving to me?" Bean asked.

"Yes. And who do you think placed the damp rag on your forehead and bandaged up your knee?" the old voice continued.

Bean bent over to feel the bandages wrapped around his left knee. He was feeling consoled and more certain he was not in danger.

"Well, who are you then? And why have you been watching me?" Bean asked.

"I will tell you soon enough," the voice replied. "First, you must make some promises to me."

"How can I make a promise to someone I don't know or can't even see?"

"Young boy. The first promise is not difficult. I need you to promise that when you see me, you won't be scared and lose the trust we now have."

Bean's instant courage surprised himself. He quickly responded, "I'm not scared, I promise. Do you need my lighter?"

Suddenly, a torch lit up on the earthy rock wall to Bean's left. Then another mounted torch lit up behind him. With the area half lit, Bean's eyes gradually adjusted. Two more torches lit up across the room, with a wide ladder running up the wall in between them. The area to his right remained dark. Bean began to observe his surroundings and get his bearings.

The room was about twelve feet by twelve feet wide. A bed frame stood behind him, made of log stumps, still with bark on the sides of the posts. A thick and matted light brown animal hide covered the top platform with layers of straw lying evenly underneath. It was fastened down at the corners by some hemp rope. The floors had the appearance of dark brown cement. The walls were darkish green with some scattered gray rocks breaking up the surface.

Not seeing anyone yet, Bean looked above him. The light from the torches stretched up about twenty feet high, but the ceiling was still not visible. The wooden ladder attached to the wall across from Bean ascended beyond the light and faded into the darkness above. Other than the bed, the torches, and the ladder, the room was apparently empty. Bean pivoted to his right and stared into the shadowy darkness ahead of him. He was anxious to put an image to the voice.

"Bean," the voice said. "Are you okay? Why the long silence?"

"Just checking things out. And I still don't see you," Bean said.

Shuffling a few steps forward, a short, haggard being with long, stringy white hair emerged from the shadows in front of Bean. His sagging and wrinkled eyelids completely covered his eyes and the loose skin rested on his defined cheekbones. His mouth was wide and drooped down at the corners. His bottom lip was enveloped by his upper lip. The old man had white whiskers of different lengths sprinkled over his cheeks and down to his pointy chin. His skin was a light gray.

The elderly, frail figure wore a dark brown elk hide, which draped down to his ankles. A short necklace hung off his hunched neck. It was a thin silver chain and had a wide circle ring dangling at the bottom. The hide was tied around his waist with some hemp. Only his bare arms and feet were visible. He held a long, curved staff that Bean figured was once an elk shed. At the top of the staff was a long tine that bowed and came to a sharp point. Below his hand on the staff, were a few nubs spaced about a foot apart that seemed to be cut off tines. His left hand held a thin, yellow leather scroll.

"You're not that scary," Bean said.

"Haha, very well then," the old man chuckled. "My name is Draug. As you see, I am blind."

"Then how have you been watching me?" Bean asked.

"You carry binoculars and even used a spotting scope to see, correct?" Draug asked.

"Yeah."

"Well, I have my instruments and methods too," Draug said. The answer appeased Bean.

"Come with me, Bean." Draug slowly turned and led Bean into the black space. As they advanced, new torches were lit and the ones they left behind went out. They entered a new room like the last one, but twice as big. It smelled mildly foul and smoky, having hints of burnt sage brush. He led Bean to a large, rock table with a flat, smooth surface. The rock table was a rectangle three feet wide by seven feet long.

"You must be very hungry," Draug told Bean. "Sit down." Bean noticed the tree stump behind him to his left and sat on it. "Your knee is okay now. So is your cheek. Remove the bandage and I will grab you some stew." Draug set a leather scroll on the rock table and then vanished into the dark.

Bean, bewildered with his new reality, took a seat on the hard stump and gently passed his fingers over his left cheek. He didn't feel a scratch or anything. He looked down at his left knee, bandaged by a thin red cloth. He began to unravel the cloth once, then twice, and finally three times around his knee. To his astonishment, his pants weren't torn anymore. He pulled up his camo pants and there was no trace of a scratch or even a bruise on his leg. He lifted his knee and extended it straight out in front of him. Feeling no pain, he lowered it just in time for Draug to lean over and set down a bowl of hot stew in front of him along with an oversized wooden spoon.

"Badger-herb stew will perk you right up," he said.

Bean grabbed the spoon and stared into the bowl of warm, mustard-yellow stew in front of him. His hunger made it easy to ignore Draug's comment. He dipped his spoon into the stew and lifted it back up to his mouth. Then he stalled.

"Did you say badger... stew?"

"Yes. It is my favorite," Draug said with a wide grin.

Bean didn't want to offend him. After all, Draug had saved his life. He gave him a bed. He healed him. Draug now wanted to nourish him. And Bean was starving. Bean swallowed the first spoonful. To his pleasant surprise, the stew tasted similar to his mother's beef stew. Bean's thoughts went to home and his missing father as he ate up.

"This is good, thank you," Bean said gobbling up the soup. "I'm worried about my dad. And Kenny and Bo. I need to get back outside and find them." After a long pause, Bean looked up at Draug standing beside the table. Draug's face was still and difficult to read with his eyes permanently shut. "Wait, can't you see him like you saw me? Can't you tell me where he is?" he asked urgently.

"I sense your father is in serious danger," Draug said. "But I cannot see him anymore."

"Oh no." Bean's breathing sped up again. "You can't see him anymore? What do you mean?"

"I followed Hank for a long time, for most of his life," Draug said. "But when he handed the whistle to you, I was cut off."

"The wooden whistle? Why?" Bean asked.

"I watched your grandfather too for much of his life," Draug said. "He was a good man. Your father was a good man. And you too."

"Whoa, whoah, whoah. Hold up." Bean peered up at him. "I don't understand. Why are you watching us? And *how* are you watching us?"

"You need to make another promise with me first," Draug said. Bean stared at Draug, narrowing his eyes further and trying to really understand what he was saying.

After a quiet moment, Bean said, "Thank you for taking me in. Thank you for fixing my knee and now feeding me. But I need to leave now. I need to go find my dad." He stood and took about eight steps to the right. Not seeing any door, he circled back around toward the room he slept in, but it was too dark. He didn't see any way out other than the steep ladder he recalled back in the first room. "Where does the ladder lead to, and how far up does it go?" Bean demanded. With no immediate reply, Bean turned back to the rock table. Draug was gone.

"Draug?" Bean called out. Feeling helpless and frustrated, he walked back to the rock table. He pushed the empty bowl of stew and spoon aside. He then propped up both of his elbows on the table's thick edge. *Who is this guy?* Bean wondered. *He isn't normal.*

Bean peered over at the leather scroll rolled up tightly on the table. He noticed the red bandage cloth there too. Bean looked down at his watch: 9:03am. "Draug, come back. What do you want from me? I need to go!" he yelled. Bean put his head in his hands, with both elbows still resting on the table.

After a long pause, Draug said, "I am here to help you, Bean." He suddenly reappeared to Bean's right. Bean lifted his head up and looked at Draug.

"Okay. Well, I'd like to go find my dad, especially if you think he is in serious danger," Bean said. "That's how you can help me."

"Your father is alive," Draug reassured Bean. "But he seems to have been overtaken and is now a slave to something very evil."

Bean sighed in grief. Then holding back the tears asked, "Who captured him? Why do they want him?"

"There is a lot I must tell you, but you need to make an oath with me."

"What's that? A promise?"

"Yes, but a special one... sealed with your blood," Draug grimly added.

Bean's heart sank. He didn't want to make any promise, much less one requiring his blood. But he wanted to save his dad.

"Tell me what you want, and I'll tell you if I'll make an oath with you," Bean said.

"Your grandfather Carl hunted my mountain for many years. One rainy day, while pursuing an elk, he slipped off the side of a steep trail, and fell fifty feet. The fall knocked him unconscious and he broke his leg in two places. I took him in and completely healed him. I saved his life." Bean leaned in, intrigued. "The next morning, we made an oath right here at this same table. He was to never tell anyone about his encounter with me. I gave him that wooden whistle now in your pocket. Always keeping it safe, he made an oath with me to pass it on to his son."

"You gave my Grandpa Carl this whistle?" Bean asked while he dug in his left pocket. He pulled out the wooden whistle. "This was yours?" Bean held the whistle up in front of Draug's shut eyes.

"Yes, I gave it to him. But no, it was not mine." Draug's reply confused Bean. "The whistle belonged to my tribe that migrated from the south centuries ago. It was only blown in times of trouble, to call in our warriors to defend or to warn our band to prepare for bad weather. It has been passed down through many generations."

Bean was in awe. He gazed at the whistle with a new respect, turning it in his hand. "Are you an Indian? And why did you give it to my grandfather?"

"Yes, I am Uinta," Draug said. "So, he would pass it on to his son, your father. Of which, he did do. He kept the oath."

"Why did you want my father to have it then?" Bean asked.

"Your father carried it, but never blew the whistle." Draug quickly answered.

"Okay. But why did you want him to have it?" Bean persisted.

"He is a great hunter. I will tell you more in due time," Draug said, dodging the question. "But your father is in imminent danger. Are you ready to help him?"

"Yes. Yes, I am ready," Bean said eagerly. "What do I need to do? Just carry the whistle?"

"No, much more than carry the whistle." Draug pointed to the red cloth on the table. "Put that red cloth in your backpack. It will help you if you are injured again. Grab the wooden ladle. Put it in your backpack too."

Bean stood up, set the whistle on the table, and then did as Draug instructed. "Now what?"

"Now, untie the knot and unroll the scroll," Draug said.

Bean obeyed and gently began to open the scroll. As he did, a light orange glow shone through the background, highlighting the lines and images on the scroll. Bean couldn't believe his eyes as the scroll appeared to come alive by some natural energy. He set the bowl onto the left side of the scroll and held down the right side with his hand.

Bean didn't understand the images on the worn, ancient leather scroll. Within seconds, he did notice a circle-X symbol in the lower left-hand corner, like a compass. He picked up the wooden whistle with his left hand. Turning it to reexamine it fully, he now recognized the circle-X emblem on the whistle matched up the same with the one on the map.

"What do you see?" asked Draug.

"What is this circle with an X in the center? I noticed it on the whistle, and now I see it again on this scroll." Although interesting, he wasn't sure how the scroll was going to help him find his father.

"Ah. That is the sacred emblem of Hutoriane," Draug said. "What else do you see?"

"Whoah, hold up," Bean said. "What is...hunterland...did you say?"

"No. Hutoriane. H-U-T-O-R-I-A-N-E." Draug stressed each letter. "It is the real name of this planet on which we live, encompassing all of its complexity and total design." Bean was silent and fascinated. "You live on the surface and know the physical or natural part of earth. But there are realms, dimensions, and layers to this entire sphere that you never knew existed and may never experience."

Bean analyzed the scroll more intently. "I see more strange images in this middle area, maybe it's a map. And there is some old writing on the right side," he observed. "Does it say where my father is?"

"No," Draug responded abruptly and began to cough. He cleared his throat. "The images each tell a story and, yes, together are a map that reveals how to get what I need. But I've shown you too much. We need to make our oath now. We can't waste any more time and jeopardize the mission."

Bean didn't understand, but sensed Draug's urgency. And he too wanted to start finding his dad. He gulped. "What do I do?"

"I saved your life last night," Draug said. Bean nodded, still unsure about what Draug wanted. "Now you need me to help you liberate your father." Bean didn't know where his dad was and wasn't sure Draug knew either. "But right now, I need you to be on my errand. If you succeed, your father will be released, and you will have your life back."

Bean began to feel manipulated, not having much of a choice. After all, he felt he couldn't *really* leave and like he owed Draug something too. "What is the errand?" he asked. "And why can't *you* do it?"

"I am much too old and blind. Your mission is to restore my people to their rightful power and inheritance," Draug declared. Bean could hardly grasp what Draug was saying. He was thinking of his dad in dire need and wondered if Kenny and Bo were okay too.

"Wow," he said. "The errand sounds too big for me."

"I intend to help you help me. Then I can help you get your father back." Draug explained.

Feeling compelled, indebted, and exhausted from the confusion, Bean was ready to act and so he promptly accepted. "Okay. I'm ready. Whatever it takes. I'll make the oath."

With a broad, sinister grin, Draug grumbled, "Let us begin. Please, roll up the scroll. Set the bowl on the ground. Remove all the items off the altar."

Feeling nauseous, Bean cleared off the table. Sick to his stomach and dizzy, the herbs and chemicals in the hot stew Bean consumed for breakfast were now in full effect. Bean started to stand, but suddenly dropped to the ground like a heavy sack of potatoes. He was still conscious, but his body was completely numb. While still able to see and hear, Bean lost his sense to feel and couldn't move any muscle.

In a low, nefarious melody, Draug began to sing and chant in a foreign language. With his right arm, Draug gradually raised his elk staff high above his head. With his left hand, he pointed down at Bean, and then turned his palm up. He flicked his fingers in an upward motion. Bean's limp body languidly lifted off the ground, rising to about five feet in the air. Draug waved his same hand to move the body slowly over on to the rock altar.

Bean was more terrified now than when he'd been pursued by the mountain lion. He felt betrayed by Draug. Helpless and hopeless, he had no clue what exactly was about to transpire—and he couldn't do a thing about it. With his body now limp on the altar in a fetal position, lying on the left side, Draug used the hook-like tine at the top of his elk staff to pull Bean's left arm out and hang it off the edge of the table. Bean watched in horror as he couldn't resist.

"If your filthy white man's blood has not completely diluted your chosen Indian blood, then I will have a newness of life and power," Draug mumbled. Bean heard it but was too scared to try and understand. Draug moved the wood stump over beneath Bean's arm hanging off the table and set a pint-sized silver grail on the stump. He lowered his elk staff to Bean's arm. With the sharp point of the top tine, he carefully slit Bean's left forearm, up close to his elbow. Bean didn't feel any pain, but he did see the steady drops of blood now dripping from the small laceration down into the silver grail.

When the grail was filled to the brim, Draug wrapped up Bean's forearm with the red cloth bandage to stop the bleeding. Then he lifted the silver grail full of Bean's blood to his mouth and eerily sang four times, "An angel falls when demons rise, extend my life, oh father of lies."

Draug drank. Bean wished he could shut his eyelids. Witnessing this evil séance, Bean tried fervently to cast his thoughts back to his father and home life. Fortunately, the loss of blood caused Bean to black out for a long period of time with his eyelids still open.

～～ CHAPTER ～～
FIVE

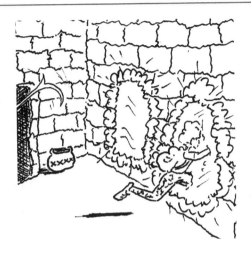

"Bean, for the last time….!" his mother Gail shouted.

"Mom, I'll clean my room in a minute!" Bean responded. He continued messaging his buddy about their upcoming football game while he finished some chips and salsa.

"You have no respect for me, Bean!" his mother complained.

"You know I love you," Bean answered in a mocking tone. "Just one sec, geez," he said under his breath.

Gail stomped down the stairs and into the kitchen. "I don't care how big you think you are, I will always be the boss and you will always be my little angel, Bean!" she said as she kissed his cheek. She squeezed his left forearm and began to pull him away from his snack.

"Ouch, Mom!" Bean cried out and grabbed his left arm with his right hand.

"Bean, Bean, I am not your mother," Draug said while unwrapping the red bandage on Bean's left forearm. Bean awoke from his dream.

"What? Where am I?" Bean said, bewildered and rubbing his eyes. He looked at Draug nursing him. He moaned. "Not you again. I want to go home."

"Your arm is all healed," Draug said.

Bean, still on the rough hard surface of the rock table, inspected his arm and found a small scar about an inch long with a tiny circle at the end. It looked like a lollypop turned sideways. He came to and recalled the evil ceremony he was subjected to.

"Dang, Draug!" Bean yelled, jumping off the table. "You scared me. What was all that chanting? Why did you drink so much of my blood? I thought you would just prick my finger or something." He eyed the silver grail still sitting on the altar.

"Keep calm, Bean. It's all okay," Draug said, trying to settle him down.

"Really? It's all okay?" Bean shouted. "My dad has been missing for over a day now, captured supposedly. I was almost eaten by a lion. Now I'm a prisoner to an old witch-vampire guy who drank my blood!"

"You are not a prisoner. You are not here against your will," Draug said in a calm, low tone. "If you want to leave, climb the ladder back in the bedroom."

Bean felt silly for not trying the ladder back when he thought of it. "I yelled out for you and asked where it led. But you didn't answer."

"I am not a witch and certainly not a vampire," Draug said. "I am a healer. Some call me a *medicine man*."

"A medicine man? What's that? Are you evil?"

"Everyone has some evil in them. I am a healer, like what I've done for you. I have other spiritual powers, too." Draug explained.

"Like what?" Bean asked, both intrigued and annoyed.

"Have you not observed any of them while visiting with me?" Draug answered.

Remembering the rock door instantly shutting, the torches lighting up, the healings, the vanishing acts, and the horrific altar experience, Bean finally asked, "Okay fine, but why did you have to drink my blood, especially if you think it's a filthy white man's?"

"The white man introduced smallpox to my people and created an epidemic that killed thousands. They took our lands, starved our people, and shot our people. They forced the Tumpanawach, Pahvant, San Pitch, Uinta, and the Ute tribes to live in one restricted area." Draug said bitterly. "This is just part of the story. That's why their blood is filthy."

"Whoah." Bean hung his curly blonde head in shame. He perked back up. "Then why did you want *my* blood? For revenge or something?"

"Many, many moons ago, I had a son named Semme. He was my only child. He fell in love with a white Mormon settler, and abandoned me and our people. They had six children, four daughters and two sons. Although he wanted nothing to do with me, I observed him from afar and his posterity down to the present day. Your grandfather Carl was my great, great, great, grandson. You Bean, are my great, great, great, great, great grandson."

"You're kidding me, right?" Bean replied in disbelief. "*We're* related? How are you still alive then? And how old are you anyway?"

"My spirit is eternal, so is yours," Draug said. "But mortally, I was forty-three when my son left in eighteen sixty-one."

"Holy cow," Bean said, amazed. "You're ancient."

"I'm still alive as a mortal being because I too made an oath with a powerful entity and have a work yet to complete," Draug said. "And drinking the blood of any male in my posterity revives my body and replenishes my power. The one who donates their blood to me must do so willingly. And Bean, your blood is not filthy."

In a weird way, Bean felt proud. He began to understand a little more. Overwhelmed with the answers to his questions, Bean blurted out, "Our oath! What did I promise you again? Just my blood?"

"Your blood sealed your oath with me. You committed to helping me restore our people to their rightful power and inheritance. I will aid and protect you on this journey," Draug reminded Bean. "In return, I committed to helping you find and liberate your father. And answer some of your questions along the way."

"But how long can my father hold out?" Bean asked.

"Your father is in a state of comatose, my intuition and sources tell me," Draug solemnly responded. "He's not in pain, just captive. He will last if you complete my errand successfully."

"Oh no, Pops," Bean muttered. *I'll save you,* he thought. "Are you sure I can even help you?" Bean asked.

"Yes. Your sense of duty, your purity, your determination, your hunting skills, and your blood tell me you are chosen. Our people have been waiting for you," Draug said, instilling a sense of purpose and nobility in Bean. "We must act now. There is a very old woman named Ramona you must meet with in South America. She is of the Pemón people in the Great Savanna. She is expecting you. She will instruct you on how to complete your mission."

"Huh? South America? How will I know where to find her?" Bean asked as he looked down at his watch. It read 1:14pm.

"Here. Put this in your pocket. These are the directions to her habitat." Draug handed him a beige cloth with writing on it. "I stocked your backpack while you were knocked out.

You have all the essentials and supplies you'll need for the journey, including the leather scroll."

"Wait, how do I even get there?" Bean asked, adrenaline stirring in him.

"I am the Guard of Hutoriane, gatekeeper of the portals," declared Draug. "I will send you."

"Who? Wait. What portals?"

Suddenly, two blurred openings appeared to Bean's right. The window-like openings were cast on the far stony wall across the room.

"Hurry, Bean!" Draug said as he held his elk staff above his head, both hands trembling. "Take the orange portal on the right."

In awe at the sensational display of energy before him, Bean threw his backpack over his right shoulder and walked tentatively over to the glowing portal.

"But, Draug?" Bean looked back in trepidation.

"Use the whistle if you need!" shouted Draug. "And protect the scroll!"

With no idea of his destination or what awaited him, Bean leaped into the orange blurry portal.

CHAPTER SIX

In a flash, Bean crashed to a hard surface, dropping his backpack just behind him. Blinking and clearing his eyes, he rose to one knee and grabbed his backpack. Like a newborn baby seeing for the first time, Bean tried to examine and identify his surroundings. Still dark but it was not as pitch black as Draug's lair. As his eyes adjusted, he could make out two ledges four feet high running parallel on either side of him. He could hear a low buzzing sound, and even slightly feel its vibration. Subtle light reflected off some long iron rails on the ground running parallel to him as well. Off in the distance, faint light gleamed ahead of him.

"I'm in some sort of tunnel," Bean told himself. "I should head toward the light over there." As he took a few steps, he got tripped up by the inconsistent floor beneath him. "These are railroad ties. These are railroad tracks. This is a subway!"

Bean had never been in the subway but had seen some in movies. The steady hum started getting louder. *I better climb up to the side quick.*

The loud sound of a subway train drew closer. As he staggered over to the right, he secured his backpack and pulled himself up. The ledge on either side was not wide.

Whoah, I can hardly stand on the side here. The sound of the train seemed to vibrate the tunnel. Bean hustled toward the light he saw in the distance ahead, opposite of the approaching train. As he got closer, he could tell it was just a flood light or something. The train roared, and its headlights appeared around the bend behind him.

"Geez, Draug," Bean said. "Why did the portal drop me in here? You trying to kill me?"

He was sure the powerful draft the passing subway cars would cause would spin him off the shallow tile wall and into the train. Bean started to run as fast his legs could carry him, all while trying to keep his balance on the ledge. He could see the next flood light twenty yards ahead. The train blew its thunderous horn, approaching fast. Bean raced forward and could now see a brighter opening a hundred yards ahead. He knew he couldn't get there before the train did.

Coming up to the light on the wall, he saw there was an inlet to a utility door or something. Bean jumped to his right and found the door knob. The door was locked, but he held on to the door knob firmly as the train loudly raced by just three feet behind him. Catching his breath, he stepped back to the side and continued rushing after the train. It slowed to a stop seventy-five yards in front of him. Hundreds of people began exiting the train. Bean started to sprint.

Bean caught up and soon found himself in a herd of people moving in all different directions. Some headed up the stairs to the left, some to the right. Others tried to squeeze by while others pushed through. Bean read the words on the wall: *La Estación LOS CORTIJOS.* He looked back at the train and saw the words *Metro de Caracas* on the side of each train car. *These words look like Spanish to me,* Bean figured. He thought back to an Introduction to Spanish class he had the previous year. Bean decided it would be fun to ride the train. He jumped aboard.

There were two seats available and Bean had to make a prompt decision. One was next to a sharply dressed businessman in a black suit, white shirt, and red tie. The other vacant seat was next to a chubby middle-aged woman in a yellow floral shirt. To Bean, she seemed a little more pleasant. He quickly shed his backpack, sat down next to the lady, and snuggled his backpack on his lap. The train sped off.

Now at ease, Bean began to watch the people. Some were talking, but most kept to themselves. Many were quietly reading, listening with headphones, or playing on their smartphones. Bean missed his phone. It was back at camp, inside Trusty Rusty and under the front seat. He missed his comfortable life. He missed his mom, his little sisters, and his dad. Bean wanted to call his mom and ask if she heard anything from dad. But he didn't want to get Hank in trouble for losing his son. They left to hunt on a Tuesday. They planned to return the next Sunday evening.

"Excuse me, miss," Bean piped up. "Do you know what the date is?"

After wiping the sweat off her forehead, the lady next to him slowly turned her head toward Bean. "Cómo?"

Bean wasn't sure she heard him clearly. "Do you know what the date is today?" he repeated, enunciating slowly and clearly.

The lady nodded and smiled but didn't answer him. She turned away from Bean.

Bean thought she might be deaf, and he didn't want to rudely ask her again. He tried to remember any words from Spanish class, but nothing was coming to him other than "hola" and "me gusta." He began to feel like some passengers were noticing him too. *Did I say something too loud?*

Seated across from him was a younger girl about his age, dressed in a blue uniform of some sort. As Bean inspected her outfit, she looked up from her phone and locked eyes with him. Her big brown eyes were magnified through her thick glasses. Her black wavy hair was parted in the middle, wrapped around her round cheeks, and hung just above her shoulders. She smiled and then looked back down at her phone.

The train's conductor announced over the intercom, "La Estación LOS DOS CAMINOS." The chubby woman left her seat and a balding older gentleman with reading glasses and a swirly mustache replaced her. Bean wasn't sure where he was headed but was enjoying the train ride. *That girl smiled at me*, he thought, feeling uneasy. *She seems friendly, I guess.* He glanced up at her and he was stunned to see her looking at him again. Flushing, she looked back down at her phone.

"Excuse me, sir," Bean tapped the gentleman next to him on the shoulder as he was reading a newspaper.

The man tilted his head, so his eyes could see over his glasses and asked, "Sí chico, qué quieres tú?"

"Do you speak English?" Bean asked.

"No te entiendo." The man went back to reading.

Wow, I guess that's strike two, Bean thought. He noticed another guy with a tight gray shirt and bright yellow jogging pants glaring at him now, standing in the aisle holding the overhead bar. Bean was starting to feel some discomfort.

He was also very hungry. He remembered his half-eaten sandwich in his backpack. He opened the pack with some caution, realizing it had some important contents he was supposed to protect. Rummaging through the pack, he breezed over the binoculars, the scroll, the now-useless ammo, a compass, some beef jerky, the wooden spoon, and other items. To his delight, he found the sandwich and took it out along with the beef jerky. He zipped up the backpack and took a bite out of the sandwich.

"La Estación PARQUE DEL ESTE," the train intercom informed the passengers of the next stop. As it coasted to a stop, many passengers left while new people entered and shuffled around. Bean was intently eating his late lunch when, out of his window, he observed a family hugging each other with joy and shedding tears. He was envious of their obvious reunion and prayed that it would be him and his father soon. The train door automatically closed, and the train continued on.

Bean finished his half sandwich and had one piece of jerky left. As he stuffed the last big piece in his mouth, he started to chomp on it and turned his head away from the window. To his utter embarrassment, the girl that was once seated across from him now sat next to him. Her face turned to Bean at the same time, and she greeted him, "Hola, cómo estás?"

Chewing a mouthful of tough jerky, Bean answered, "Hola." Bean's pale, freckled face turned tomato red, and felt he'd ruined any chance of a good first impression. She giggled.

"What's your name?" she asked, with a thick Spanish accent.

Caught off guard again by the girl's English and friendly tone, Bean swallowed the jerky. "Bean."

"Bean? As in 'frijol'?"

"Well, yeah, but..." Bean answered thinking now of how funny his nickname must sound translating it into Spanish. "What's your name?"

"Eva." She lifted her right hand to shake Bean's. "Good to meet you."

Bean wiped the jerky crumbs off his right hand and shook her clammy hand. "You too," he said with a smile.

"Where are you from," Eva asked Bean in a slow, thought out manner.

"I'm from…" Bean started to answer, but then had a quick recollection from his Spanish class. He started again, "Soy de Utah."

Eva gave him a blank look and tilted her head. "Where is Utah?"

Giving up on his Spanish, Bean answered, "It's in the United States. America." More heads now turned, seeming to tune in to their conversation. Trying to ignore the attention, Bean asked Eva, "Where… dónde… are you from?"

Now seeming a little more reserved, Eva answered softly, "Aquí, de Caracas."

Bean sensed her discomfort but didn't understand the sudden change in Eva's demeanor. "Are you okay?" The man in the black suit Bean once considered sitting by was now looking their way.

"Yes. It's okay."

He continued to ask questions. "So, are we in South America? I'm looking for a place called the Great Savanna."

"La Estación ALTAMIRA," the train intercom alerted the passengers as it arrived at the next stop. Many passengers debarked, and new faces entered the train car. Bean waited patiently for Eva to answer his ignorant questions. She pulled out her notebook and scribbled some words on the paper. She slipped Bean the note.

"Estamos en Venezuela, un pais de Sur America. Caracas es la capital del pais," the note read. Bean understood the words "Venezuela" and "Sur America," and was satisfied with her answer.

Bean wrote, "Gracias. Dónde is the Great Savanna?" He passed the notebook back to Eva.

Eva wrote back beneath Bean's question on the paper, "Great Savanna is Sabana Grande." Then she pointed up at the map of the subway stops on the wall above his window. She showed him that they had just passed ALTAMIRA, and SABANA GRANDE would be coming up in three more stops.

Bean smiled and said, "Gracias." Then he wrote, "You are very nice. Do you know what day it is today?" He figured it was Thursday, but his time in Draug's cave felt like a long blur.

"Hoy es jueves," she noted. Then she wrote, "You are nice too. I like your blue eyes."

Bean read her message. He was uncomfortably flattered. "Thank you. Where are you going?"

"Home. CHACAO is my stop," Eva wrote. "You have email?"

Bean jotted down his email, and then penned, "What's yours?"

Eva wrote in the bottom right hand corner of the paper:
Eva Sophia Cruces
ES.cruces@rgallegosesc.com
+58 212- 4582848
2080 Av. Francisco Solano, Edif. 4, Apt #329
Caracas, Distrito Capitál, Venezuela

She then tore off that corner of the paper, folded it, and gave it to Bean. Bean was surprised to read all the personal information she gave. He put the note in the front pocket of his backpack. The train intercom informed the passengers, "La Estación CHACAO."

Bean looked at Eva, and asked, "Your estación?"

"Sí, amigo. Fue un placer. Escribeme cuando puedas," Eva responded warmly as she stood up and departed.

Bean waved goodbye and yelled, "Thanks again!" He didn't understand what she said but felt her sweet sincerity. He watched as Eva disappeared into the crowd exiting the subway. Bean looked for her out the window but couldn't find her. He lamented seeing her leave, as he thought of how she was the only normal person he had spoken to in the last two days. But he was glad she told him where to get off. *Draug will be proud,* Bean thought.

"Hello, my friend," a raspy voice said, interrupting Bean's daydream. Bean looked to his left to find the guy with the tight gray shirt and yellow jogging pants seated next to him. The man seemed college age, was dark, and had muscular arms. He had a smooth face, except for a tiny patch of hair just under his bottom lip. His eyes seemed black. His hair was dark brown and very short.

"Hi," Bean answered pleasantly, and began to play with the zipper of his backpack. There was an awkward silence.

"Para dónde vas?" the man inquired.

Bean tried to interpret his question, but to no avail. "Uh, I don't speak Spanish," he said apologetically.

"Es okay," the man said. "Entonces, you gringo?"

Bean hesitated, not positive of what he asked. Bean answered, "I'm Americano."

The man stared at Bean with his piercing dark eyes. Then he said to Bean in a low, gritty tone, "Sí eres gringo." He looked away and didn't ask Bean any more questions. Bean felt some tension he couldn't describe. He tried to ignore the anxiety and thought of his dad. He looked down at his watch to see it was 2:47pm. It occurred to him Venezuela was probably not in the same time zone as home. He was curious to know the correct time but didn't want to ask the guy next to him.

"La Estación CHACAITO," the intercom sounded. Holding his bag firmly, and still feeling anxious, Bean leaned his head back and closed his eyes.

Just one more stop and I'm there, Bean told himself.

~~~~ CHAPTER ~~~~
SEVEN

"La Estación SABANA GRANDE," the intercom blared to the passengers as the subway train floated into the station. Many scurried, grabbed their things, and Bean followed them off. All the directional signage was in Spanish, so Bean flowed with the herd of people to the left stairs and ascended. Fortunately for him, he stood about the average height among the crowd and could see in most directions. As he began the next flight of stairs to the street, he glanced back and noticed the man in the gray shirt was behind him a dozen people or so. Not wanting to make eye contact, Bean quickly turned around and was instantly greeted with warm rays of sunshine as he approached ground level.

Mmm, sunlight. After spending almost two days in dark, subterranean environments, Bean craved the natural light. He paused for a long moment to soak it in. As the people scattered in different directions and headed to unknown destinations, Bean found himself spinning in awe at the tall buildings and hotels surrounding him. *I thought South America was third world, or behind the times,* he wondered, puzzled. Caracas was impressively large to Bean. But its size and all the people began to intimidate him.

How does Draug expect me to find Ramona, among all these thousands of people? He glanced across the busy street and saw a large clock above the entry doors of what looked like a bank. It read 6:21pm. Bean was shocked at the time difference. He walked out of the current flow of people and changed his watch forward three hours up to 6:21pm. *It's already evening here, and I have no idea what to do and or where to go.*

Suddenly, something tugged on his back pocket. He turned around to find a small girl in dirty clothes holding her hand out.

"Chico, por favor, dáme dinero," she said.

"Hi, sorry I don't understand. Do you need something?" Bean replied.

The little girl batted her eyes and nodded her head, shaking her ratty hair. She appeared sickly and starving. Bean held both of his hands to his mouth as if pretending to bite a cheeseburger, and then asked, "Are you hungry?"

The little girl shook her head again. "Sí."

Bean guessed she was about eight or nine years old. He looked around for a parent but couldn't identify one. The little girl grabbed Bean's hand and led him over to a narrow storefront with the words "Empanadería" inscribed outside on a sign. Then she pointed into the glass food warmer and showed Bean what she wanted. The store attendant made his way over to them.

"Qué quieres?" the short male attendant with a worn navy apron asked Bean.

Remembering he only had eight dollars, Bean cautiously asked him, "Cuánto for..." He pointed to the empanada.

"Cien bolívares," the worker said.

Bean didn't know what that meant. But he unzipped the front pocket to his backpack and indiscreetly took out his eight one-dollar bills. He handed the attendant one dollar, hoping it was enough. The man hesitated for a moment, seeming to calculate something, and then took Bean's money. He reached into the food warmer and pulled out two empanadas. Relieved it was enough for two, Bean thanked him and handed the girl her empanada. She swiftly ran off and Bean watched her escape into the hordes of people.

Bean's eye caught the same man in a gray shirt and yellow jogging pants sitting on a bench, watching him. Bean tucked his money away and took a bite out of the empanada, pretending not to have seen him. I think *that dark guy from the subway is following me.* He fought down panic while eating his food.

"Wow this is delicious," he said out loud, as the taste distracted from his concern. The store attendant looked up and smiled. Bean was glad his accidental compliment pleased the man. *I need to lose this guy, but where and how?* Bean wondered. *I also need to get online somehow. I need to look up the word "Pemón."*

"Amigo," Bean called for the store man's attention.

The man set down something in a fryer and walked over to Bean. "Qué pasa chico?"

"Internet? You have internet?" Bean asked slowly.

The man confirmed, "Internet?" in a low voice.

"Sí, sí!" Bean answered in excitement as he bit into his empanada again.

"Ah, okay. Hay un cibercafé por allá." The man pointed off to his left. Bean looked in the direction he was showing, unsure of what he was saying. "Queda como dos cuadrados y pico por allá."

"Dos?" Bean asked as he pointed in the same direction as if he understood everything the man said.

"Sí chico, suerte!" the attendant finished.

Bean finished the empanada, tightened up his backpack, and headed toward where he'd been directed. He was glad to have a place to go but was beginning to doubt the whole mission.

What am I doing here? Bean asked himself. *I'm in the middle of a busy city of a foreign country, and on another continent. This is a whole other world. I don't even speak Spanish. This better be worth it. I hope my dad is okay.* Bean picked up his pace and checked each storefront for the words "cibercafé," all the while trying to zig-zag through people, hoping to lose the man in the gray shirt.

Similar to an outdoor mall, there were storefronts on both sides of the wide cobblestone walkway. Aggressive street vendors called for Bean's attention, like those at a flea market. Obscure statues and art monuments occasionally obstructed his path. On the buildings were billboard advertisements of food, drinks, shows, and other products Bean had never heard of. He noticed extra-long lines of people waiting for the bakeries and grocery stores. He enjoyed the aroma of sweet pastries. As Bean passed others, he felt their curious eyes watching him and many heads turned his way. He finally became aware that he was one of the very few blonde, pale humans in the vicinity among thousands of dark-haired, tan-skinned people.

There it is! Bean mentally yelled as he saw the cybercafé up on his left. Anxiously, he looked back to his right and left to see if the man in the gray shirt followed him. Relieved to not see him, he forged ahead. He arrived at the entrance and threw open the door to the internet café. Luckily, the place wasn't overly crowded. Bean looked around and tried to figure out who was in charge.

"Buenas noches, chico," a quiet voice greeted Bean.

"Hola," Bean answered, now noticing a young woman with long black hair stand up and walk his way.

"A la orden, en qué te puedo ayudar?" she asked Bean politely as she approached.

The soft light reflected off the girl's straight black hair and created a mild glow around her face. Her big, hazel eyes sparkled, perfectly outlined with long, curved black eyelashes. Her cheek bones were high and lightly colored with hints of pink. Bean was completely captivated by her beauty and could not speak for a moment.

"Um, do you have the internet here?" he asked slowly, hoping she'd understand.

The girl responded in perfect English. "Certainly! Just find a computer kiosk and help yourself. We charge two hundred bolívares each hour."

Bean could not think straight; the girl was so pretty. But he tried to calculate the cost in dollars thinking back to the empanadería shop. "So, two dollars per hour?"

The girl giggled, then saw he was serious. "No, amigo. That would be about fifty cents per hour."

Bean thought about what he paid the store worker for the empanadas and frowned for paying him so much extra.

The girl asked, "Is everything okay?"

"Uh, yeah," Bean said. "I'm so glad you understand me too."

She looked pleased and asked, "Are you American?"

"Yes, how did you guess?" Bean asked with a straight face.

"Well, you kind of stick out...a lot. Curly blonde hair, blue eyes, white skin, and you only speak English." Light laughter shook her shoulders.

"Oh right," Bean agreed. "My name is Bean, what's yours?"

"I am Adriana," she said. "Did you say your name is 'Bean', as in frijol?"

Embarrassed for the second time at how silly his name sounded, Bean replied, "Haha, yes."

"Ah, well good to meet you, Bean," Adriana said as she escorted him over to a vacant kiosk.

"You too!" Bean said, revealing a little too much excitement. As she walked in front of him, he could smell her sweet floral perfume and couldn't help but notice her long hair extending down above her tiny waist.

"I'm sorry to pry, but what brings you here?" Adriana asked while she gracefully leaned down to turn on the computer for him.

"Here to the internet café, or here to Sabana Grande?" Bean asked.

"Um, both."

"It's a long story, but I'm here trying to find an old woman named Ramona." Adriana looked up at Bean as if sensing there was more to his vague story. He continued, "She has something for me and she lives here, in the Great Savanna. She is of the Pemón people."

To his astonishment, Adriana started to giggle again, putting a hand up to her mouth to cover the sound.

"What'd I say?" Bean asked, a little embarrassed.

Adriana collected herself and said, "This is Sabana Grande, meaning Large Savanna. It's just a popular retail, mall-like area with a bunch of outdoor shops. But it is not the Great Savanna or 'Gran Sabana.' That is where the old native Pemón Indian tribe lives. It is part of a huge national park called Canaima National Park."

Bean was confused and getting frustrated. "On the subway, a nice girl told me the Great Savanna was Sabana Grande, saying it was coming up in just a few more stops," Bean explained in a defeated tone. "She must have misunderstood me."

"It's okay. She probably thought that's what you meant. So why does a young American teenager need to talk to an old woman in Canaima National Park?" Adriana asked.

At that moment, it occurred to Bean that he wasn't even sure. "Um, I'm actually trying to find my father," Bean mumbled. "I'm not exactly sure how, but I'm told Ramona can help me." It all sounded weird to him as he said it out loud. He was starting to feel embarrassed.

"Are you here alone then?" Adriana asked.

"Yes."

With a straight, stern face Adriana asked, "Bean, do you know how dangerous it is here?"

"Not really. What do you mean?"

Looking to her left and right, as if to not be overheard, Adriana explained softly, "Venezuelans don't like Americans. Our government has brainwashed most of the citizens to believe the U.S. stole all of our oil and prevents other countries from doing business with Venezuela. Our TV and newspapers are constantly talking about the bad things the U.S. does to Venezuela. Venezuelans blame Americans for being so poor and having such a bad economy."

"Really?" Bean answered, feeling more than a bit ignorant. Bean still wasn't sure what it meant for him.

"Yes. And Caracas, this city, is extremely dangerous. There are 'malandros' or thugs and thieves around every corner preying on any weak target. Our people are starving, and they too will do anything to get what they need to even eat. If anyone finds out you're an American, your life could be in serious jeopardy."

Bean remembered the long lines he passed of people desperately waiting to get food. He wasn't just nervous about trying to figure out how to find Ramona and save his dad; now he was worried about his own life. He was very scared.

"Honestly, I'm surprised you've made it even this far without being mugged," Adriana said.

"Geez...well, what should I do? I need to get to the Gran Sabana," Bean asked, not wanting Adriana to sense his mounting fear.

"The Gran Sabana is hundreds of miles away. And the whole park is a gigantic region, like twelve thousand square miles big. Do you know what part you need to get to?"

"I guess wherever the Pemón people live," Bean responded.

"Ah, right."

The computer was now on. Bean pulled up two chairs and they went to work. Unsure of where the settlements for the Pemón tribes were, she began to search "Pemón" Indians. Bean was delighted to have someone helping him figure this puzzle out. It reminded him of the math tutor he had in study lab preparing him for a difficult test.

As Adriana researched, Bean watched her, mesmerized. Then he asked, "So how come you speak English so well?"

"I lived in the States for a few years, just outside Phoenix, Arizona," she calmly replied as the search results popped up on her screen. She clicked on a few links, and perused them for a few moments, one at a time.

"Oh cool. I am from Utah," Bean said.

"Nice. You been to Phoenix?" Adriana answered with half of her attention.

"Not yet."

"It's a cool place. Okay...it looks like there are a few settlements in the Kamarata Valley, just southeast of Salto Ángel." Adriana showed Bean.

"What is Salto Ángel?" asked Bean.

"Angel Falls. It's the highest waterfall in the world," Adriana said, sounding shocked that he hadn't heard of it. "It is like fifteen times taller than Niagara Falls."

"Wow, that'd be awesome to see," Bean said. He remembered the cloth note he had in his pocket that Draug gave him. It had some kind of directions written on it to find Ramona. He quickly pulled it out.

"Can you read what this cloth says?" Bean asked. The note read:

"Ramona se encuentra en una churuata escondida, rodeado con árboles de mere y justamente afuera de Kavak"

With more interest, Adriana read the sentence to herself and then out loud for Bean. She began to ponder while she researched the word "churuata," and then the word "Kavak."

"Okay, it says 'Ramona lives in a hidden palm hut, surrounded by cashew trees, and just outside of Kavak' which is a very small settlement south of Kamarata," Adriana said. "I will jot it down for you."

"Hmm, so Kavak is a small Pemón town?" Bean confirmed with Adriana. Adriana sat quiet again, deep in thought. After a long pause, Bean looked at Adriana and asked, "What's the matter?"

"So, is your dad *really* missing? How did you even get to my country?" Adriana asked doubtfully.

"Adriana, thank you for helping me, I mean it," Bean said, looking her in the eye. "Yes, I don't know where he is. He went missing a couple days ago when we were hunting. I need to go find Ramona, and then I think she'll be able to help me. But I can't tell you more than this."

She frowned but seemed to accept this. "I don't know how you've made it this far, but you still have a lot further to go. Do you have a way to get to Canaima?" she asked.

"No," Bean answered.

"You need to try and get a taxi ride down to Ciudad Bolívar," suggested Adriana. "That's like seven hours away from here. But it's the closest city to the national park. And then from there you'll have to take a plane or dirt road for a few more hours to the town of Canaima it looks like." She examined the map online and showed Bean.

"Okay, that's what I'll do then," said Bean. "I'll figure it out. How much do you think the taxi will cost?"

"Probably a hundred dollars, maybe more. Remember, it's a seven-hour trip," Adriana said. "Do you have enough?"

"Dang, I only have seven dollars," Bean said. "And I owe you fifty cents." Bean was feeling nauseous and overwhelmed. He began to wonder what else he had in his backpack worth money. "Adriana, can I use your restroom?"

"Yep, it's in the back to the right," she directed him past her desk.

Bean passed a few rows of computer kiosks and found the bathroom in the back hallway. He was tired and very worried, ready to give up. He shut the door to the bathroom and removed his backpack. He walked up to the mirror and stopped, stunned. He couldn't believe how filthy, and shabby he looked. His camouflaged clothes were all dirty. "I can't believe I look like such a bum meeting a girl so cute," Bean gasped. Bean turned on the water, wet his hands, and ran his fingers through his dirty curls to improve his appearance. He thoroughly washed his hands and face.

He didn't want to give up on his dad, but he was losing hope. Bean didn't want to call on Draug either. After all, he seemed like an evil, old man. *I don't care if he is supposedly related to me,* Bean thought. *It feels like I'm helping an evil man do something very wrong. He never even told me who Ramona is. Just that I needed to meet with her. How did I get caught up in all this?*

In that moment, Bean recalled the night before the hunt when his dad rebuked him. He heard his father's voice ask again, "Is following me more important than doing the right thing?" Bean fought back the tears and repeated the phrase again. Remembering his blood-binding oath, Bean answered, "Yes I hope so. I'm gonna find you dad."

Bean savored the privacy, quiet, and safety in the bathroom. For the past two days, he had been in constant danger and around strangers. This brief moment of refuge gave him courage and replenished his strength. He unloaded his backpack and examined the contents as his father Hank would do. He wanted an exact accounting of what he had.

"Flashlight, knife, a snack bar, poncho, chapstick, gum, fresh socks, seven one-dollar bills, compass, lighter, red cloth bandage, map scroll, wooden spoon, and the whistle," Bean said out loud as he checked off each. "I need to add some food and water." Bean put everything neatly back in the pack. He put the knife and whistle in his right pants pocket. To his dismay, he didn't see anything of real value he could sell to get money.

Clack, clack, clack! Loud knocks on the door startled Bean. "Bean, are you okay? I need to close now, and you need to get going," Adriana said. Bean fastened his backpack and exited the bathroom with a fresh determination.

"Here, this should cover your taxi fare," Adriana said while handing Bean a stack of large bills in Venezuelan currency. "These bills are called bolívares. It is one hundred fifty dollars' worth of Venezuelan money."

"Adriana, wow. You shouldn't. Isn't this a ton of money here?" Bean asked.

"It's okay. My father still lives in Phoenix and sends my mother and me money each week," she said. "Really, take it. Pay me back when you can. But be very careful. There are malandros all over."

"You are a real friend, Adriana. Thank you so much," he said. "Will you give me your email and phone? I'll certainly repay you when I get back home."

Adriana wrote her information down on a little note pad. "Listen, when you walk out of here, go left and walk straight down to the street to the corner. There will be a few taxis lined up ready to go. Give one of them this note." She handed Bean both notes with Spanish writing.

"Oh, okay. I will." Bean stuffed the money and notes in his left pants pocket.

"Also, I have an aunt in Ciudad Bolívar. I will call her right now after you leave. She speaks a little English and she'll be waiting for you at your drop off," she added. Bean smiled in awe at all Adriana was doing for him.

"And put this hat on," she said as she handed him a Leones de Caracas baseball hat. "Your hair is gonna give you problems. Be safe. Don't stop for anyone."

"Okay, I won't. Seriously, thank you so much." Bean put the hat on and hugged her. "I'll thank you properly when I can."

"No, don't worry about it," Adriana said as she hugged him back and then gently kissed his right cheek. Bean's heart suddenly stopped. There was a long pause. He stared back at her for a few seconds and they both smiled.

"Good luck, Frijol!" Adriana joked as she pushed Bean out the door.

CHAPTER EIGHT

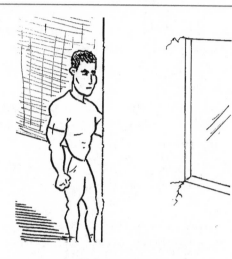

Nervous and on edge, Bean quickly scoped out the area and found the street corner Adriana was referring to down to the left and about a block up. He started to walk at a face pace. The time was now 8:06pm and it was dark. The cobblestone walkway was dimly lit by electronic store signs and overhead lamps about every hundred feet. Bean moved quickly along the right side of the cobblestone walkway to stay out of the main traffic. He came up to another long line of people waiting to enter a small grocery store. As he got closer to the line of people, he didn't want to catch anyone's attention. He decided to backtrack a little and swing around the line rather than cut through. That's when he noticed a few sketchy teenagers approaching fast behind him.

Bean tried not to make eye contact with any of them. Moving laterally to his left, Bean then headed in the direction of the street corner again. Three guys had now begun to keep pace next to him, two on his left and one on his right. Bean pretended not to notice them and kept on walking even faster. The boys started to laugh and taunt as one skipped out in front of Bean.

"Épale chamo, párate!" demanded the one in front, who came to a sudden halt. He had dark eyes, a shaved head, and wore a tight white tank top with holey jeans. Bean quickly sidestepped him to the right and began to trot. There were less people around now. Bean was frightened and trying to think how to escape the situation. He felt the outline of his wooden whistle on his right pants pocket as he jogged. Then with perfect timing, the boys seized Bean all at once right where the light faded between the streetlights. There was a photography shop just behind them, but it was closed.

One meaty teenager with shaggy, long hair grabbed Bean's left arm tightly. Another taller guy in a red t-shirt pinned Bean's other arm back. Bean didn't resist much. Their leader in the tight, white tank top examined Bean slowly up and down. Terrified, Bean kept his head down, not wanting to look at him at all.

"Chamo, chamo," the leader repeated. "Por qué corrías?" He waited a second for Bean's reply. Impatient, he asked Bean again, "Por qué corrías? Tienes miedo?"

"No hablo español," Bean said.

"No, no hablas?" the leader mocked Bean. "Odio a los gringos!" he said with his teeth closed. Suddenly, he smacked Bean across his face. He kept his hand raised in the air next to Bean's head.

Bean's cheek burned. He slowly tilted his head upward, feeling defenseless and anticipating another strike. The malandro leader ripped the hat off Bean's head and waved it in Bean's face.

"A ti te gusta este equipo?" the gang leader taunted. "Yo también," he answered as he put the hat on his own shaved head. Bean couldn't believe what was happening and wasn't sure how to respond.

"Dáme tu reloj y tu bolsillo, ya!" the thief demanded. The chubby thug holding Bean's left arm now let it loose. Bean didn't understand what he said. The taller malandro grabbed at Bean's backpack, but Bean held on firmly. The action jerked him to the ground. The other thief reached for Bean's left arm and tried to take off Bean's watch. With his eyes closed, Bean tightly grabbed the right backpack strap with both of his arms and hung on for his life.

The thugs' leader took a few steps back as if to wind up and kick a penalty shot in soccer. Bean embraced for impact.

Thunk!

Loud hits echoed.

Smack! Smack! Clank!

Bean opened his eyes to see the gang leader on the ground with a man on top of him, throwing hard punches. The chubby malandro left Bean and tackled the guy pounding his leader. With a swift jerk of Bean's head, the tall assaulter pulled Bean's hair back and tried to strike the top of Bean's head with his elbow. Bean raised his left arm to block it.

With quick moves, twisting limbs and jarring blows, Bean watched his defender knocked out the fat malandro. Bean now recognized the mysterious fighter helping him. In his gray shirt and yellow jogging pants, it was the dark guy who followed him from the subway.

The tall attacker suddenly let go of Bean and squared off with Bean's new bodyguard. The thug whipped out a butterfly knife and Bean's defender held his fists up. Both moved around to the right in a circular motion, then counterclockwise, trying to gain position. Bean noticed the leader on the ground, coughing up blood. The meaty attacker was out cold.

Bean was confident he could escape now but felt cowardly for running while his defender still fought. Bean's face throbbed from the slap, and he felt like taking revenge.

He reached into his right front pocket to pull out his hunting knife, but hesitated.

The tall attacker took a swipe at the man in the gray shirt but missed. He tried again, but Bean's defender quickly moved inside and got entangled with the attacker's right arm. Suddenly, he bent the tall attacker's arm and a gross crack made Bean wince. The attacker dropped the knife and wailed in severe pain. The thug leader was getting up on his hands and knees. Bean jumped to his feet and he snatched up his Leones hat. Bean thought about kicking the injured leader in the face while he was down, but he didn't.

The man in the gray shirt yelled to Bean, "Go gringo!" With another jiu-jitsu move, he flipped the attacker onto the ground, slamming his head on the cobblestone. The malandro grunted and Bean's defender hit him two more times in the nose to finish him. Bean ran off and his fearless bodyguard pursued him to the street corner.

"Gringo!" the man yelled. Bean kept running and didn't respond. "Espérate!" the man called out. Bean turned the corner and could see the row of taxis all lined up on the right side of the street just as Adriana explained. The mysterious man finally caught up to Bean and grabbed him by the shoulders.

"Gringo, es okay," the man said as Bean shrugged him off. "Tranquilo, tranquilo."

"Don't hurt me!" Bean said, emotions running wild. "Don't hurt me!"

"Shhh, calm down. I protect you," he whispered. "My name is Toni. I can explain."

Bean stopped resisting and tried to take some deep breaths. Bean decided to listen to the man who just saved his life. Bean noticed he was bleeding on his left bicep.

"You're bleeding." Bean pointed to the man's arm. Toni looked down as if surprised to see any harm was done to his body at all. He quickly removed his gray shirt, revealing his defined, muscular physique. He ripped up the shirt into a few long strands, and tightly wrapped his wound.

"Who are you? Why have you been following me?" Bean asked between exhales.

"First, we need to get you out of here fast," Toni said.

"I know. I need a taxi to take me to Ciudad Bolívar," Bean said pointing over to the taxi cabs.

"Ciudad Bolívar?" Toni winced and touched his wounded arm. "I'm going with you. Wait here."

He quickly turned and approached the first taxi in line on the side of the street. After a short conversation, Toni looked back at Bean as the driver turned him down. Toni went to the next taxi driver. Same thing occurred. Toni walked over to the third driver. Bean was feeling urgent, thinking of his surroundings or that his attackers could be arriving any minute. He remembered the note Adriana wrote and took it out of his left pocket. He ran it up to the first taxi driver and showed him.

"Qué es eso?" the man asked. He took a minute to carefully read the note. He looked at Bean, then back down at the note. Bean pulled out his wad of money and showed the driver. Now suddenly convinced of the note's truthfulness, the driver said, "Súbete!" Toni looked over and saw Bean opening the backseat door.

"Espérame, voy también!" Toni yelled. He ran up to the front taxi, an old light blue 70's model Cutlass Supreme. He climbed into the deep, ripped velvet back seat and slammed the door shut. As the driver started his car, Bean could see one of his attackers limping around the corner. Bean showed Toni.

"Apúrate amigo!" Toni shouted to the taxi driver.

The taxi sped off. It swerved in and out of traffic through the congested streets and in between the tall buildings of Caracas. Each turn felt like a boat swaying on large wakes. The driver raced onto the freeway heading in a southeast direction toward Ciudad Bolívar. Gradually, a huge sense of relief and calm set in for Bean. He was proud for protecting his backpack and whistle. Bean had narrowly escaped another life-threatening moment, thanks to Toni. But this time he was injured with a swollen right cheek and a throbbing forearm.

He remembered the red cloth bandage in his backpack that Draug used to heal his knee. Anxious for some relief, he hurriedly fumbled around in his pack and found the cloth bandage. As he took out the cloth, he glanced over at Toni whose gray shirt bandage was now almost saturated in a dark purple from all the bleeding.

"Here, man. Use this red cloth for your arm. It will heal you," Bean told Toni. Toni held the cloth up, trying to examine it as the taxi drove under street lights every few seconds. "Trust me, wrap it around your bicep."

Grimacing, Toni finally accepted Bean's offer and wrapped his arm in the red cloth.

"Qué pasa chico? Pensé que eres sordo o discapacitado?" the conductor interjected as Toni bandaged himself.

Toni glanced at Bean with a puzzled look. Bean shrugged, having no idea what the cab conductor said. Bean wondered what Adriana had written in the note that convinced the driver to take him in so quick.

"El chico? Sí, pero a veces dice cosas que no tienen sentido," Toni responded to the taxi driver explaining the boy just mumbles things sometimes.

The cab driver readily accepted Toni's answer. "Ah, está bien," the cab driver said as he turned up his old analog car radio to some salsa music. The taxi driver was older, plump, and stout. He had dark-reddish skin with curly gray hair, and he had a matching gray mustache that extended down the sides of his mouth to his jaw, stopping at his pelican-like double chin.

"Cuántas horas para llegar a la Ciudad Bolívar? Toni asked the driver.

"Toma como siete horas y pico," replied the driver.

"Gracias." Now with his arm tightly wrapped in the fresh red cloth, Toni leaned over to Bean and whispered. "He thinks you are deaf and can't talk. Don't talk anymore. Let's just get some sleep. He said we will be there in the morning."

Bean had a bunch of questions for Toni, but he agreed to stay quiet and tried to get comfortable. He had a pounding headache and his young tired body was exhausted. As he watched out the air-fogged window, he thought of Adriana's soft kiss. He even thought of playing soccer with his little sisters before falling fast asleep.

CHAPTER NINE

The peaceful car ride felt all too short for a seven-hour trip. Bean opened his eyes as the warm brightness from the morning sun hit his face, having slept all night. He stretched both arms in front of him, let out a long yawn, and glanced over at Toni. Toni was awake, looking straight ahead with a stern face. He didn't look like he'd slept well. *Maybe he'd been awake most of the night*, Bean wondered. Bean took a deep breath to speak, but remembered he wasn't supposed to. Bean reached over and tapped Toni's left forearm.

"Ya están despertando?" the cab driver asked noticing some movement in the backseat. "Estamos llegando a la dirección que me diste."

"Muchas gracias, señor," Toni said.

Toni looked over at Bean, who made up some sign language, pointing to Toni's arm to ask him if his arm felt any better. Toni stared at him until he eventually understood Bean's body language. "No se," Toni answered. Bean persisted and tried to signal to him to remove the red bandage. Toni ignored him.

As it neared Ciudad Bolívar's city limits, the light blue Cutlass Supreme embarked over a long suspended bridge. Bean looked out the window and gasped at the water beneath that stretched infinitely in both directions. "Holy cow!" Bean let out unable to hold in his excitement. Toni quickly tapped Bean's left knee to hush him up.

The taxi driver looked up into his rear-view mirror. "Que bonito, no? Allá está el Río de Orinoco. Aquí estamos en la parta más angosta, pero este puente todavía es 712 metros largos," he said.

Bean and Toni listened as they each kept their attention out the window, though Bean still didn't understand a thing. Toni translated to Bean that the cab driver just said they were crossing the narrowest part of the river, but it is still 712 meters wide. Bean raised his eyebrows impressed.

As they entered the city, instantly there was a much slower vibe and feel than the bustling mammoth city of Caracas. The buildings were much smaller and had more of an older Spanish style. The tiny homes in town were made of cemented blocks, and were connected to each other, one after the other. Bean noticed the different bright pink, blue, yellow, and red colors of each home. The taxi found its way through the narrow streets. It came to a stop in front of a grandiose yellow cathedral with colonial architecture, white ornate trim, and a tall clock tower on the right side of the structure.

"Llegamos amigos," the plump taxi driver said, looking tired.

"Cuánto cuesta el pasaje?" Toni inquired.

"82,000 bolívares justo," the driver responded.

Toni looked over at Bean and whispered, "Do you have money?"

"Sí... cuánto... necessita?" Bean whispered in his best Spanish with a little humor. Then he reached into his pocket and pulled out a thick wad of bolívar bills. Toni looked surprised to see Bean had so much money in Venezuela's official currency. Toni proceeded to count off eighty-two thousand bolivars and handed the rest back to Bean. Bean was glad to see some money left over, although he wasn't sure how much. Toni handed the driver the money.

"Suérte chamos. Que les vaya bien!" the driver said as they climbed out of the sunken back seats. Bean shut the door and walked over to Toni's side between the car and the cathedral.

"Igualmente, gracias por la cola," Toni said. Bean listened to how Toni responded.

The sidewalk wasn't as busy as Sabana Grande. There were a few dozen people around lingering on the corner and eating breakfast across the street at the panadería, while others whizzed by walking to an early appointment. Bean had no idea what Adriana's aunt looked like, but he began walking trying to identify a woman who could be curiously looking around for him too.

"Gringo," Toni said in an annoyed tone. "What are you doing?"

"I'm looking for Adriana's aunt. She said she was gonna be here when the taxi dropped us off," Bean explained as he peeked at his wristwatch. The time was 7:17am, Friday.

"Who is Adriana?" Toni asked.

"She's the girl I met in the internet café who gave me the money for the taxi," Bean answered as he continued to scan the area. "Who are *you* by the way?" Bean asked now remembering the questions he had for Toni.

"Me? I am here to protect you," Toni replied.

Bean stopped. "Why? Who told you to protect me? Draug?" Bean asked. He looked directly at Toni, who was a few inches taller, much broader and stronger.

After a short pause, Toni said, "No, I don't know the name you just said. If I am here to protect you, does it matter who I am and who sent me?"

Bean considered his point. "Yes, it matters to me." Bean was done being the gullible and ignorant teenager. "But I do feel more comfortable with you here. You speak Spanish and you punch hard. Who told you to protect me?"

"A medicine man. He can see the future and told me of your arrival," Toni said.

"Did you say medicine man? What medicine man did *you* talk to?" Bean asked, wondering if he knew Draug after all. "What did he tell you about me?"

Toni didn't quite know how to respond. Suddenly, the two were interrupted by a middle-aged brunette, just shorter than Bean, and with short hair down to her shoulders. While she wore no makeup, she was thin, and naturally pretty with big brown eyes and full lips. Her yellow sundress with small white flowers and trim nicely matched the cathedral they stood in front of.

"Con permiso, te llamas Bean?" she asked in a pleasant, soft tone.

Bean was caught off guard and hesitantly answered, "Si, I am Bean. Are you Adriana's aunt?" Next to Bean, Toni adjusted his posture, pulled back his shoulders and flexed his bare stomach as if he were in a bodybuilding competition.

"Que bien. Sí, yo soy la tía de Adriana," she responded holding her hand out to shake Bean's. Bean felt an instant warm connection with her as he shook her calloused hand. "Mi nombre es Isabel. Tienes hambre?"

Toni translated for Bean. "She's Adrian's aunt. Her name is Isabel. She wants to know if you're hungry."

"Good to meet you! Sí...tengo...hambre," Bean responded with a grin.

Isabel smiled back. "Él anda contigo?" she then asked Bean, gesturing to Toni.

Bean understood her signal and replied, "Sí."

"Muy bien," Isabel said and invited them both to follow her.

She escorted them through the ten feet-high, arched brown doors and into the grand cathedral. Bean admired the beautiful stained-glass windows along the walls and gothic images. It was interesting, but quite different from the rather plain building he attended church in every week. Three aisles of pews ran the length of the structure up to a golden, elaborate altar.

A bronze statue of Jesus Christ hung on the cross set on the far wall behind the altar, facing the front of all the pews. Bean reverently paused to examine the sight. Then he looked up at the ceiling. It had murals of angels swirling around a light blue painted sky with scattered clouds.

"Bienvenido al Catedral de Santo Tomás, por aquí por favor," Isabel said noticing Bean taking it all in. She led Bean and Toni into a short hallway off the main chapel and into a spacious kitchen. "Les gustan arepas?"

"Sí, claro," Toni replied. Bean wasn't sure what arepas were, but he heard "gusta" and knew it meant "to like something" in English. He was ready to eat too.

"Siéntense por favor," Isabel said, signaling for the two guys to sit down at a long maroon table. Bean set down his backpack next to him and took a seat on the opposite side of the table from Toni. Within seconds, Isabel placed a plate of warm food in front of each of them. The arepas were palm-flattened balls of white corn meal fried into a disk shape. Each had two on their plates. The arepas were sliced and stuffed with white cheese, shredded chicken, and butter. Their breakfast also included fried platanos and sweet rice pudding. Isabel poured them each a tall glass of guayaba juice. It was silent as Bean and Toni savored each morsel.

"This is the best breakfast I've ever had!" Bean declared as he swallowed more of his juice.

"Gracias por este desayuno tan sabroso Isabel," Toni said as he took a bite of his platano.

Isabel seemed to understand English but couldn't speak it. "Que bueno chicos. Me alegra. Quieren más?"

"No, thank you," they both answered simultaneously.

"Adriana me dice que estás tratando de llegar a la Gran Sabana, por Kamarata?" Isabel struck up conversation as she cleared their plates. Toni listened and then looked at Bean to see if he understood. Bean looked back blankly, so he translated.

"She says Adriana told her that you want to go to the Great Savanna, by Kamarata. Is this true?" Toni asked, looking interested as well.

"Yeah. I'm trying to find an old Indian woman in the small settlement of Kavak, which I think is close to Kamarata and Angel Falls," Bean said. "Adriana was so sweet to help me get this far," he added, thinking of how pretty she was too. "Thank you for meeting us."

"Claro, de nada," Isabel answered. "Sabe que yo tengo un amigo que es un piloto. Él lleva turistas por excursiones en Canaima."

Again, Toni translated to Bean. "She has friend who is a pilot and he gives tours of Canaima."

Bean perked up with excitement but wasn't sure if she was offering the pilot's services.

"Adriana no me dijo que tendrías un compañero contigo," Isabel continued, now suspiciously glaring at Toni.

Toni translated again, "Adriana didn't tell her that I'd be coming with you." Bean squinted back at Toni for a second, trying to figure out the best way to respond.

"Toni is...my bodyguard," Bean answered. "He helped me escape some malandros trying to steal my backpack last night after I left Adriana. I got punched in the face. Toni got cut. In fact, how does my face look now?" Bean stood up and walked over to a mirror above the sink to check it out.

"Él dice que yo soy su guardaespalda," Toni said to Isabel.

Isabel walked over to Bean and examined the left side of his face. The swelling had gone down, but it was still a little bruised and discolored.

"Toni, take the bandage off your arm now and show Isabel," Bean said, wanting to break the tension he could sense between him and Isabel.

Toni obliged and slowly unwound the bandage from his right bicep. He looked shocked to see the laceration had completely healed and now there was a clean, thin, three-inch scar.

"Le cortaron anoche y ahora esta curada completamente?" Isabel commented, sounding suspicious.

Toni looked at a complete loss for words.

Just then, a tall, bald man entered the kitchen dressed in all black with a white band around his neck. He was slender, and his long face was clean shaven. Bean and Toni observed him as he slowly passed by without acknowledging them. He walked toward one of the two small windows in the kitchen and peered outside for a long moment. Bean sat back down at the table. The room was silent.

"Where are you men from?" the skinny man asked in a very low voice, still glaring out the window.

"I am from the United States, the state of Utah," Bean said. He looked over at Toni, waiting for him to speak up.

"I am from Caracas," Toni said.

"What is the purpose of your visit to my cathedral?" the man inquired in clear English.

"Les invité a ellos a desayunar. Van para Canaima," Isabel responded for the guys.

The tall priest turned around and walked slowly to the table where Bean and Toni were seated. He stared down at Toni for a minute as if to see into his soul. Uncomfortable, Toni looked away. The priest then glared over at Bean. Bean innocently looked up into his eyes and gulped. *He doesn't seem like a good man of God,* Bean thought. Finally, the priest peered over at Isabel who was still standing by the sink.

"You have invited something evil into our holy sanctuary," the priest said to Isabel.

"Padre, perdóname," Isabel begged. "Qué les pasa? Sabe ud?"

"They need to leave now," the priest commanded.

Isabel turned to Bean and Toni. "Lo siento pero..." Before she could finish, Toni stood up. Toni handed Bean the red cloth and Bean put it back inside of his pack. "Déjame ensenarles la puerta."

Bean wondered what the priest was sensing. He felt more suspicious of Toni. He thought of how Toni found him in the subway and followed him. Bean began to question Toni's motives in defending him and why he was determined to protect him. Bean followed Toni and Isabel out. They opened the big doors, and Isabel walked outside with them for a minute.

"Disculpe, pero tengo que obedecer. Él es mi jefe. Trabajo aquí como cocinera y criada," Isabel said.

Bean and Toni were grateful to have been fed well. "No problema," Toni said. "Muchas gracias."

"Está bien," Bean said. "Muchas gracias."

Bean and Toni started to walk down the sidewalk in a southward direction. Isabel watched them go, but then hollered. "Bean, por favor, ven acá!"

Bean turned around and saw Isabel motioning for him to come back. He checked with Toni.

"Can you wait here a second?" Bean asked Toni. Toni agreed and watched closely as Bean took a dozen steps back to Isabel.

There was a look of terror in her eyes. "Bean, Adriana... told...me...you...look for your papá, sí?" Isabel said in slow, broken English.

"Yes, sí," Bean answered, feeling her concern.

"I think...you...in...danger with him," she said in a quiet voice, referring to Toni.

"But he saved my life last night," Bean said, confused.

"Y por qué...why?" she asked.

Bean didn't know. He paused and looked into her big brown eyes and said, "I don't know. I will find out though."

"And...Father Sinombre...felt...the evil too," she continued.

"Yeah, he was scary," Bean said.

"Father Sinombre? I am talking about Toni," Adriana said confused.

"Oh okay. Well Toni says he wants to protect me...and he did save me."

"Here...es mi...numero. Call me...if you...have problemas." Isabel slipped Bean a note.

"Gracias. Um, will you tell Adriana thanks again for me too?" Bean asked.

"Yes. My...mi pilot friend. His...name...es Alejandro Sevilla. Take...el bús to Tomás de Heres airport." She hugged Bean and kissed him on the left cheek as if he was her own son. "Suerte, Bean!"

Bean felt invigorated from her caring support. He went back to Toni and told him what she said about taking a bus to the airport. They continued to walk away from the cathedral and both looked around for the next bus stop.

"I don't trust that priest," Toni spoke up.

"Yeah, he was scary. But he didn't trust you either," Bean said.

"Neither does Isabel apparently," Toni said.

Bean didn't respond. Toni stewed beside him and neither spoke for a few minutes. Bean sensed he wanted to talk and question him more.

The problem was, Bean didn't know if he'd have any good answers. Bean looked down at his watch, which read 8:24am.

CHAPTER TEN

"Gringo," Toni said, breaking the silence as they walked down the row of cement buildings.

"Why do you call me gringo, man?" Bean asked, a little annoyed.

"Gringo is a term around here for North Americans," Toni explained. "We need to make a plan."

"I have a plan. I need to catch a plane down to Canaima and find Ramona," Bean said.

"You think we can just walk onto a plane? Do you have enough money? Do you know what to expect in Canaima?"

"It will all work out," Bean said. "It has so far. You do need a shirt though," Bean said, sarcastically. Toni didn't laugh.

"The medicine man told me that if I found you, you'd lead me to the platinum '*kuakilla*'," Toni said. "That is why I need to protect you."

"Platinum '*kuakilla*'?" Bean repeated. "What is that exactly?"

"This is why we need to talk now and make a real plan," Toni said.

They stopped walking, and Bean studied Toni, a little intrigued. A larger restaurant stood on the right with some metal tables outside on the sidewalk. Bean decided it was worth it to sit down, hoping to figure out Toni's motive to protect him. They sat down at one of the tables, off in a quiet corner section where there weren't many people around.

"When I was about your age," Toni said, "I lived in a small town up in the Andes Mountains of Ecuador, near the Colombian border. My family tribe was the Muellama. We had a very rich and powerful history, but we've now dwindled and diminished to a few dozen people. We were very poor, but were excellent weavers and produced quality textiles, wooden instruments and articles of precious metals."

"Okay," Bean said, listening.

"The people of our village combined their resources, sold their products along with their most prized possessions, and saved enough money to send me to Caracas to get educated in the modern world. My grandfather, who raised me, came with me to Caracas and insisted that I learn to fight expertly. I am their last hope to restore our people to their proper heritage."

"Whoah, that's cool," Bean said, though still not sure of how it all related to him. "Anything else?"

"Yes. My grandfather was our tribe's medicine man," Toni added. "He could see the future and understood our people's unique past. He taught me about our ancient heritage, and how I need to preserve our knowledge of how the natural world operates. The last couple years, he has marked my body in preparation to receive the fullness of power," Toni said as he pointed to a scar on his chest. "He even told me of you. He said that you would lead me to the platinum kuakilla."

"Wow, man. That's a lot to understand. So, what is the platinum kuakilla?" asked Bean.

"Kuakilla means moon in my language. Just like the moon controls the tide of the ocean and defines the shorelines on Earth, the platinum kuakilla can affect the hearts of men and define the rules of the planet. My grandfather has taught me of our right to possess and control the platinum kuakilla. He who obtains the kuakilla will have the power to run the world."

"That's crazy," Bean said, humoring Toni. He wasn't sure he could believe all Toni told him.

"Thousands of years ago, my people mined platinum in the modern-day region of Choco, Colombia. Some men found a perfectly shaped platinum sphere about three inches wide and delivered it to our tribe's medicine man. The medicine man was Ampu, the most powerful who has ever lived. He engraved holy symbols onto the kuakilla and blessed it. Every chief of the Muellaman people thereafter donned a platinum necklace around his neck, holding the platinum kuakilla at the most sacred rituals."

Bean thought quietly, trying to take in all Toni was saying. He was surprised to hear Toni talk so much. "So, what happened to this platinum ball, this kuakilla?"

"When the Inca civilization expanded northward in the late fifteenth century, several Ecuadorian tribes fought fiercely but eventually were subdued. The Muellaman chiefs rarely wore the kuakilla in fear of it being discovered and taken. Also, in fifteen thirty-one, the first Spanish conquistadors landed on Ecuadorian shores and shortly conquered the Incas. They wanted our lands and treasures too. More chaos, diseases, and bloodshed ensued from the white man that killed millions of our people."

I'm white, Bean thought.

"The medicine man of our tribe at the time was Chulu. Chulu knew the Spanish desired our treasures, so he had the platinum kuakilla tightly woven, wrapping it up to protect it from sight and to protect the engravings. The tribe's medicine men kept it hidden for two centuries and our people thrived. But finally, one wicked medicine man removed it and wanted to relocate it along with a few of the tribe's best warriors. They were never heard of again and my people have dwindled since." Toni looked down, somber.

Bean's mind was now overloaded with information that didn't seem pertinent to him. He thought for a long moment and stared off at the people passing by. Where he was and who he was with was so strange, he just wanted to escape. He just wanted to be back home, shooting guns with his dad or hanging out with friends.

Bean came around. "So, what was the name of the bad medicine man?"

"I could be cursed to even say it out loud."

"Geez. And you think I'm the one who is supposed to lead you to this platinum kuakilla?" Bean asked again.

"Yes," Toni quickly replied.

"How did you even figure it was me in the first place?" Bean asked. He was starting to feel the urgent need to find a bus to the airport.

"Earlier this week, my grandfather called me into his bedroom. Lying on his bed very sick, he told me you'd be arriving soon. He said I would recognize you. A few days later, as I was heading to my jiu-jitsu training, there you were on the subway sticking out as obvious as can be," Toni said.

Bean chuckled.

"He told me to protect you and to not leave you until I obtain the platinum kuakilla," Toni explained. He paused for a minute. "Then he took his last breath and said, 'don't let the demons rise.'"

Bean's smirk disappeared. He stared into Toni's dark eyes. Toni had no emotion, just an intimidating, fierce focus. The phrase he just said sounded familiar to Bean. He suddenly remembered Draug's séance and him saying "angels fall when demons rise." Bean's head was spinning.

Bean tried to review everything and make sense of what he was hearing. Toni was meant to restore his people. Draug said Bean's mission was to restore his Uinta people. Then the words came again to Bean's mind. "Angels fall when demons rise..." Bean pondered for a second longer and then it was clearer. He remembered Adriana translating the huge waterfall in Canaima, Salto Ángel, to "Angel Falls" in English.

"The waterfall...Angel Falls!" Bean exclaimed.

"In Canaima? Salto Ángel?" Toni asked.

"Yes! I know we are going to the right place!" Bean said.

"You sure?" Toni asked, still looking doubtful.

"I'm positive. What do we need for our journey?" Bean spoke hurriedly.

Toni squinted over Bean's right shoulder. Bean heard some excitement and scurrying about a hundred feet behind them. He turned to look, seeing approaching figures. Three men in blue uniforms hastily walked their way with assault rifles.

Bean turned back to Toni, who now looked deeply concerned. "What? What's up?" he asked.

"We need to go now. We need to hide!" Toni sharply whispered. Bean looked back over his shoulder and saw the policemen approaching fast. Hunched over, Toni stood up slowly and told Bean to follow him. They rapidly weaved through the restaurant tables and headed south on the same sidewalk.

"Toni, what did we do?" Bean asked.

"Not sure, but they are looking for something out of the ordinary," he answered between breaths. "If they see you, they will treat you worse than the malandros did last night."

They spotted a pharmacy a few places up on the right. They rushed inside, snuck through the aisles, and found themselves in the back of the pharmacy.

"Señor, señor!" they heard a voice shouting in their direction.

They knelt down as to not be seen. Bean froze in terror, his heart beating fast. He began to observe the contents of the aisle they were in. A toothbrush, toothpaste, deodorant, and soap all never seemed so desirable to the growing teenager. Toni slowly peered up and over the aisle shelf to get a better view.

"Señor, necesitas una camisa!" the man said behind the counter.

Toni sighed and said to Bean, "He wants me to put a shirt on." Turning back to the store attendant, "Sí, ya voy a ponermela."

Bean was relieved that it was just the store clerk yelling.

"No se vende camisas aquí?" Toni asked.

"No señor. Se vende por allá en la tienda de ropa," the store worker said, pointing to the clothing store across the street.

Leaning over and whispering to Bean, Toni said, "They don't have shirts here. He said there is a clothing store across the street."

Just then, the iron store door swung open with a clank. Bean and Toni looked over the highest shelf in their aisle to watch. A single police officer entered the pharmacy.

The police officer stopped at the front counter to speak with the store clerk. Their voices were audible, but the words indecipherable. Behind Toni and Bean, a back door stood cracked open. The two hunkered down to talk.

"We have to get out of here fast," Toni whispered. Bean nervously nodded in agreement. Toni glanced at the back door and his eyes lit up with an idea. "Actually, I'm gonna grab a few things and distract the policeman. While I do this, go to that back door and hide somewhere. I will come get you in ten minutes or less."

Bean remembered the last time he had to wait for someone to return for him. He didn't love the idea, but it seemed like his only option. "Okay, got it," he said. "Oh, and buy a toothbrush, toothpaste, and deodorant, please."

Toni stood up, and moseyed over toward the next aisle, picking up a box of brown hair dye as he went.

"Párate ya," a harsh voice commanded Toni. "No te mueves."

Bean watched in between the products on the shelf as the policeman advanced rigidly toward Toni with his fully automatic rifle pointed at Toni's head.

"Levanta los brazos arriba de su cabeza," the officer said.

Toni slowly lifted his arms above his head.

Bean glanced over at the back door. He needed to act. On all fours, he carefully crawled over to the door as to not catch the attention of the policeman nor the store attendant.

"Gracias señor!" Toni yelled back at the store clerk sarcastically.

Bean squeezed through the back door and into a dimly lit storage room. He could faintly hear Toni's exchange with the store clerk.

"Llamó a la policía porque no tengo una camisa? Que mulléja."

"Cállate!" the policeman yelled at Toni. Bean heard some loud thumps and products hitting the floor. "Tírese al suelo!" *I hope he doesn't kill Toni,* Bean thought. Bean crawled back and watched carefully from inside the cracked-open door.

The iron store door slammed open again with two more policemen rushing in. They yelled in a rage and Bean could sense Toni was in serious trouble. Bean wanted to help, but knew he needed to protect his whistle and the scroll in his backpack. He decided to hide. He felt his way around some stacked boxes of extra inventory and could see a small window allowing some daylight in to shine on a large desk full of papers. Suddenly the back door creaked open behind him. In a panic, Bean tucked himself under the desk and pulled a chair in close for cover.

Boxes began to fly across the room. Bean knew they were looking for him. He could still hear the frantic shouting in the store front. A wooden shelf crashed to the floor. Bean could now see his pursuer's feet coming closer. It was only a matter of seconds until he was found. Bean reached into his right pants pocket and pulled out the wooden whistle. While he dreaded to see Draug, he refused to be taken captive and have his backpack seized.

"Chico, yo sé que estás aquí," a man's voice taunted.

Putting the whistle to his lips, Bean blew. No sound came out. Bean remembered back on the mountain that it took a few tries to get it right. Taking a big breath, he blew it again. A high pitch, soft flute melody left the whistle. His pursuer now identified the direction where the noise came from. As he started to close in on the desk, Bean blew the whistle again even harder. A low, yet powerful trombone tone vibrated the room, causing the policeman to stumble. In a wild frenzy, Bean blew the whistle one last time.

No sound came out, but the small window above the desk shattered, spraying shards of glass in every direction. A mighty gust of wind swirled into the storage room like a small tornado. The policeman had cuts on his exposed face and arms as he was thrust back into the boxes.

"Bean! Quick! This way!" Draug called out.

Bean fumbled out from under the desk and tried to locate Draug. Another policeman kicked open the storage room door.

"Duck!" Draug yelled to Bean as a large stone flew over Bean's head, hitting the other cop squarely in the nose.

Bean saw the blurry opening in the far corner of the room and made a dash for it. With two policemen dazed on the ground, Bean narrowly escaped into the portal.

CHAPTER ELEVEN

Bean lay flat on his back on the hard cement floor of Draug's lair. Again, he breathed in the musty air in total darkness. "Draug?" Bean said. "Will you light the torches so I can see, please?" After a few seconds, the surrounding wall torches lit up. "Thanks. Why do you like it so dark anyway?"

"The natural world is always dark for me," Draug said as he stood above Bean. "Do you have a report for me?"

"Oh, right," Bean said, remembering Draug was blind. "Uhhh, report?" Bean sat up, crossing his legs.

"Yes, how is the mission coming along? Are you getting close?" Draug asked.

A lot had happened since Bean was dropped into the subway the day before. Bean wasn't sure what all Draug knew or could sense. He decided to put it back on Draug.

"Didn't you say you can see me in your own way? That you watched my dad and Grandpa Carl for years?"

"If the whistle is close, I can sense your emotions whether they be fear, confusion, sadness, excitement, joy and even love," Draug said. "I know that you've experienced all of those emotions in the last twenty-four hours."

Bean was a little embarrassed, feeling like he didn't have much privacy. "Really? Love too?" he asked.

"Yes, a few different kinds of love. You felt gratitude from something. You felt longing for something. You felt infatuation. You felt comfort from someone or something," Draug said.

Bean could recall a few of the moments Draug referred to.

"Wow," Bean remarked. "But you don't necessarily see who I'm talking with or know what I'm talking about?"

"No. Do you have something to tell me?" Draug asked like a concerned parent.

Bean thought for a second. "I don't think so. But things were going really well. I was feeling like I was on track and getting closer to finding Ramona and then the police came."

"The police?" Draug asked.

"Yeah. They are pretty dangerous and mean in Venezuela. I'm not sure why they were following us, but..." Bean started to explain.

"Us?" Draug asked. "Are you traveling with a companion?"

"Kind of. I've had to meet and interact with a lot of people. Each has helped me find my way, give me resources, and get a little closer."

"You need to be very careful, Bean. No one should know where you are going or why you are going," Draug said.

"Well that's easy...because I don't even know where I'm going or why I'm going," Bean chuckled. "I just want to find my father."

"You have grown more confident, and slightly disrespectful," Draug observed. "Come, let us examine the scroll." Draug slowly turned and drifted into the dark.

Bean followed Draug over to the rock table where he had breakfast the day before—and where he gave his blood. Bean had questions but didn't want to tell Draug everything he knew. He thought a lot about Adriana and her sweetness. He was also concerned about Toni, and he wasn't sure if Toni's goals would interfere with Draug's. He was confused as to why a sense of loyalty or sympathy was developing for Toni. He unzipped his backpack and pulled out the leather scroll.

"You have questions for me," Draug stated.

Bean thought about it and then asked, "Yeah, why did the portal drop me in the middle of a subway?"

"Without you blowing the whistle, I can't summon definitive coordinates for the portal's destination. I knew the direction you were to go, but I did not know the exact distance or point of arrival," Draug said. "If I had known exactly, I would have dropped you at Ramona's door."

"Will you be able to send me more accurately now?" Bean asked.

"Yes, for a few more minutes while my signal is strong and recent," Draug replied.

"Then we should, hurry, right?" Bean said as he unrolled the leather scroll. He set his binoculars down on the right side of the map and held the other side down with his left hand. The map was a little more familiar. He saw the circle X symbol in the lower left corner again.

"What is the name of this symbol again?" he asked.

"You are drawn to it?" Draug wondered.

"I guess."

"It is the sacred emblem of Hutoriane," Draug reminded Bean. "The great ones have referred to it as the Esfera Platina."

"Esfera Platina?" Bean echoed.

"Yes. It represents all of Hutoriane in its many dimensions. It means Platinum Sphere in English," Draug said.

Then it occurred to Bean. *Platinum? Sphere? Like a platinum moon? Could it be the same platinum kuakilla Toni was searching for?* He looked closer at the circle-X symbol. There were small images in each divided quadrant.

"Do you know what the tiny images are in each section of the circle?" Bean asked.

"They are Indian pictographs. I don't know what each means, but I do know they represent the four dimensions of the earth: Under, Outer, Inner, and Natural realms," Draug said. "That writing is in some ancient Indian language." Draug pointing to the right side of the scroll. "I'm hoping Ramona can translate and divulge the message of the scroll in its entirety to you."

Bean stared at the circle-X, the map's images, and the Indian writing on the leather scroll. Parts of it seemed clearer. *But what are the dimensions Draug referred to?* He was very intrigued by the puzzle in front of him. It felt urgent to continue the quest to meet Ramona and find out what she had to say. The challenge of the mission now motivated him. But he didn't want to lose sight of his original purpose in finding Hank. He caught himself.

"How's my dad, Draug?" Bean asked, lifting his head from the scroll.

"I suppose he's still in a coma, unaware of time or anything," Draug answered, seemingly uncaring.

"Don't you care about helping me find him?" Bean asked. "Isn't he your great, great, great grandson or something?"

"I am obligated to help you find him, as long as you fulfill your obligation to me," Draug said coldly.

Bean was reminded of their oath. Helping Draug was the only thing that mattered to Bean. Although Toni and

Adriana had helped and were on his mind, they were not part of Bean's main purpose. He couldn't let himself get distracted. He needed to resist thinking of them as a part of the equation to solving the map. The visit with Draug not only rescued Bean, but newly motivated him to save his father as soon as possible.

"Okay, Draug, I'm ready to go back!" Bean declared as he carefully rolled up the scroll.

Draug nodded. He bowed his head as if to find his power and took a deep breath. Slowly raising his wrinkled head, he lifted his elk staff high above his head with both hands declared, "I am the Guard of Hutoriane and gatekeeper of the portals!"

Awestruck, Bean watched him shake and tremble. Suddenly, two portals appeared on the stony wall behind Bean.

Bean was all set in a football stance ready to jump when the quarterback yelled hike. "Do I take the door on the right?" Bean asked with his game face on.

"Yes, Bean!" Draug cried. "Good luck!"

With his backpack fastened tightly to his body, Bean took a few steps and dove into the portal.

~~~ CHAPTER ~~~ TWELVE

Bean was more alert this time as he passed through the portal. He flew at a high speed over the Earth's terrain, with bright blue, green, white, and yellow streaks swirling all around him. He felt free, refreshed, and strong. A powerful force started to yank on his ankles and he felt like he descended through clouds and then into a smoke-filled orange tunnel.

With a poof, Bean landed on his feet, stirring up a plume of dirt from the gravel road beneath him.

Bean looked around, trying to get an idea of where he'd come out of. But there was nothing familiar in the air or in the ground. He gazed down the straight, rural road as far as his eye could see. The reddish dirt road thinned into the distance, surrounded by rolling green hills. He could not get his bearings and wasn't sure which direction of the road he should travel.

"Dang, Draug!" Bean complained. "You've got to get better at this portal thing."

What if I'm not even in Venezuela? Which way am I supposed to go? he asked himself.

Bean remembered he had a compass and rummaged through the pack until he found it. He held it flat in his hand and the red needle found its way north. North was to Bean's left as he faced one direction of the road. Behind him, the road stretched in the opposite direction. *At least I know the road runs east and west, but how does that help me get to an airport?* He looked down at his watch. It read 1:32pm. *I guess I'll go west. It will make me feel like I'm going home.* Bean turned around and headed that way on the red dirt road.

He marched for an hour, observing the lush landscape. Clusters of trees would spread for a half mile, and then a clear opening of tall grass and scattered bushes would go for another mile. Every plant and shrub were a different shade of green. Growing up in Utah's dry climate, all the green was new and beautiful to Bean. But the scenery got old and he was tired of walking. It began to drizzle light rain. He quickly thought of his white poncho and dug into his backpack. Bean unfolded the poncho and draped it over his clothes. He continued on, thinking of the times he and his father would go shooting. He started to hum the song "Stand by Me."

The rustling of his poncho was loud as he walked. Its hood covered his ears, so Bean barely heard the truck approaching. Bean jumped to the side just in time when an old yellow pickup truck pulled up beside him. In the truck's cab sat two dark-haired boys and their black-bearded father at the wheel. The older boy rolled down his window. Music blared, and Bean could tell they had been having a good time.

"Hola amigo!" the father said, putting an elbow up on the steering wheel and turning down the music with his other hand. "Para dónde vás?" His boys stared out at Bean with their messy brown hair and brown eyes.

Bean was oddly happy to hear Spanish again and understood the words "hola" and "donde." He walked up to the window and smiled. "Hola! Um...Ciudad Bolívar?" The rain had stopped.

"Bueno, súbete!" the father responded, waving for Bean to climb in.

Bean quickly took off his poncho and shook off the raindrops. He rolled it up and opened his backpack. He didn't want to get the leather scroll wet, so he shoved the poncho into the front pocket instead. He zipped up the pack, scrunched into the cab, and could hardly shut the door. Bean guessed the boys were eleven and nine years old. Bean, the two boys, and their medium-sized father were all crammed into the truck's cab. The man turned up the music again and they continued happily down the dirt road toward Ciudad Bolívar. Bean was relieved to be traveling faster.

After twenty minutes of travel, Bean took off his Caracas Leones hat and wiped his forehead. The motion caught the two boys' attention. Their mouths dropped as if they'd never seen someone with such bright yellow, curly hair and blue eyes as Bean's. Then the father looked over. He too was awestruck and looked back at the road right away with eyes wide open.

The father turned down the music. "De dónde eres tú, amigo?" the father asked.

Even though Bean could sense these guys were humble and nice, he knew the "United States" wasn't a safe answer. He carefully responded, "De norte," and gestured to his right with his thumb. The compass came in handy after all. Bean put his ball cap back on.

"Del norte? De Cumaná o de Barcelona?" the man asked Bean, giving him two choices.

"Sí. Barcelona," Bean said having heard of this city before. The man nodded, but Bean could tell his mind was spinning and wanted to ask more questions. "Me llamo

Frijol," Bean spoke up. The boys started to giggle. Bean did his best fake laugh along with them.

"Cómo? Tú nombre es Frijol?" the man asked.

"Sí," Bean answered with a straight face.

The man seemed even more surprised but accepted it. "Bueno. Ese hijo se llama Miguelito y el otro más pequeno se llama Juancito. Mi nombre es Juan," the father said, introducing himself and his two boys.

"Hola," the boys said in unison.

"Hola, y gracias por la cola," Bean answered, remembering how Toni thanked the taxi driver for the ride.

"De nada," Juan replied turning up the music again.

Bean sighed in relief getting through the brief conversation.

They passed sporadic cattle ranches. Other farms had livestock of sheep, goats, chickens, horses, and even llamas. The properties seemed to get smaller the closer they got to town. The houses were made of large red bricks, cemented together. Some had clothes hanging out on a line to dry in the sun. The homes were painted white, blue and light brown. None of the roads were paved. Suddenly, a small airplane buzzed overhead.

"Airplano?" Bean asked, trying to say airplane in Spanish.

"Avión? Sí. Hay un aeropuerto aquí cerca," the man replied.

Bean was excited and hoped he understood correctly. After a few minutes, another one flew overhead. He started to think of how he might even get on to a plane destined for Canaima. Is *this even the airport where Isabel's friend works?* he wondered. He recalled the warning from Adriana of how dangerous Venezuelans could be with North Americans. He glanced over at the boys. They both looked back at him and smiled.

He thought of Toni and their violent run-in with the police a few hours previous. *Did Toni get captured? Of course not. Draug and I took out two of the three policemen. Toni could've easily taken one out.* Bean knew if he didn't get arrested, Toni would certainly be looking for Bean. *Should I go back to town or to the cathedral to find Toni? No. That is not my problem. I need to go straight to the airport.* With an unlikely stroke of recollection, Bean thought of the airport's name, it being similar to the cathedral's namesake.

"Está...aeropuerto Tomás de Heres?" Bean asked, hoping the father understood his bad Spanish.

The bearded driver looked over at Bean suspiciously. He must've started to hear Bean's accent more clearly and could tell his Spanish wasn't good. "Sí," he answered fast. "Pero tú no eres de Barcelona. Tampoco eres Venezolano."

Sensing the mood change, Bean tried to interpret all he said. He thought he understood "no Venezolano." Airplanes passed overhead loudly and more frequently as they got into town and were now on a paved road.

"Gracias amigo," Bean answered. "No hablo bien el español," he admitted.

"Entonces? De dónde eres tú?" the man asked again.

Bean answered bashfully, feeling caught, "...el norte. Soy de Norte America." The two boys stared at Bean astonished, and the man kept driving, visibly perturbed and quietly looking straight ahead.

After a few long minutes, the father finally spoke up, "Escúcheme bien, chico. No me gusta su país. Pero a mí no me gusta nuestro gobierno tampoco. Me gusta mi familia solamente."

Bean understood the last part and thought of his own family. He waited a minute to respond because of the tension levels raising in the crowded small cab of the truck. He responded, "Me gusta mi familia también." Then he reached into his pocket and pulled out three hundred bolívares. He waved it over to the father and offered him the money.

The father looked at the money. "No es necesario. Guárdalo."

Bean answered, "Muchas gracias por la cola." They were coming up on the airport turnoff. "La parada por favor." Bean remembered the term from the subway announcer.

The truck pulled off the road, gradually coming to a stop. Bean unzipped his backpack and pulled out the new pack of gum. Giving it to the boys, he said, "Here, for you, chicos." The boys smiled ear to ear. He thanked the father again, threw his backpack over his shoulder, and got out.

The father looked at Bean for a moment and then said, "Suerte, chico. Qué te vaya con Dios."

Bean understood the word "Dios" to mean God and gave the father a thumbs up. The boys and their father continued on.

~~~ CHAPTER ~~~ THIRTEEN

Bean was grateful yet anxious to arrive at Tomás de Heres airport. As he walked along the roadside in the grass, a few buses and cars slowly passed him, heading to a passenger drop off area. He watched as mostly smaller planes would land and take off through the barbed wire airfields. The air traffic control tower stood off in the distance, along with three large plane hangars. The airport's main building was a white rectangle shape, but not a big structure.

As passengers got off the buses or out of cars, Bean mixed in with the flow of people and followed them into the building. There were two counters with clerks checking people's bags and confirming their flights. The lines weren't very long. Bean didn't have much money and didn't speak Spanish well. He knew standing in line only to talk with a booking agent wouldn't work out well, and maybe even call the attention of the authorities. Bean walked over to a row of chairs in a waiting area below some big windows. He sat down a few seats away from two men in their twenties with one girl around the same age. Bean tried to be as inconspicuous as possible.

Bean's watch said 3:16pm. As he sat in his chair, Bean tried to observe all he could of his surroundings. To the far left, lines of people got checked in at the counters. To the right of the counters, there was a wide hallway where the passengers seemed to enter and disappear after they checked in. In the small baggage claim area, a dozen people congregated, awaiting their luggage. There were a few managerial offices to the right of the baggage claim and then the bathrooms. Lastly, Bean noticed there was another short counter. It too only had a few people waiting in front of it.

The sign above that last counter area to the right read "Excursiones Especiales." Bean figured the line was for customer service or something. He observed the people's behavior. While few stood patiently in line and were casually interacting, others were scurrying around. The small group closest to him was laughing a lot, seeming to be excited for their destination. Bean could tell they were speaking some foreign language, but confidently knew they weren't speaking Spanish.

Feeling like he was losing valuable time, Bean started getting antsy. He couldn't see any other way to board a plane other than to see if Isabel's pilot friend would allow him on one of his flights. He mustered up the courage to go to the customer service line on the far right side. He pulled his Caracas Leones hat as far down as it could go, and he tucked his blonde curls in at the sides. Bean headed over to the counter. As he got close, there was no one left in line. He took a big breath and stood as tall as he could.

"How can I help you, sir?" the skinny woman asked in a professional tone. Bean was surprised that she spoke English.

"Hello, can you please tell me if Alejandro Sevilla is available?" Bean asked as politely as he could.

"Alejandro Sevilla, the pilot? Captain Sevilla?" the lady clarified.

"Yes," Bean answered, glad to hear she knew the name.

"I don't think he is available. He is boarding his passengers as we speak. What is this in regard to?" the woman asked.

Thinking as fast as he could, Bean stuttered "It's an emergency. Please call him. Tell him it's regarding Isabel."

The lady was now visibly put out, but said, "I can try to get a hold of him." She got on the desk phone and made a call.

"Hola, Captain Sevilla?" the attendant asked. Bean tried to overhear his response, but it was all jumbled and hard to hear.

"Sorry, but we have an emergency that needs your attention," she continued with the sound of the plane's propellers whizzing around loudly in the background. "Yes, an emergency. It is regarding Isabel. There is someone here that needs to talk to you," she said as she glared at Bean. She listened to the captain's response. "Okay, will do."

She hung up the phone and called another person on her radio. "Alfredo, por favor, necesito su ayuda en frente."

Bean couldn't totally understand her Spanish and wasn't sure what was happening. The lady looked down at her papers and jotted down a few things. Bean stood in suspense. She was quiet and stayed occupied for a few more moments. Anxiously waiting, Bean had to speak up.

"Miss?" Bean asked respectfully.

The lady looked up. "Can I help who is next?"

The small group of three cut in front of Bean. Bean couldn't believe she ignored him and was ready to help

the next people in line. A heavyset man in a white uniform
appeared behind the counter, taking a bite out of a half-
eaten sandwich. "Just one moment, please," the lady said to
the group of three.

"Puede usted llevar a este chico con la gorra para afuera
cerca de los terminales al lado este? Él Capitán Sevilla va a
reunirles con ustedes allá. Es una emergencia," she explained
to the man in the uniform.

The man signaled to Bean and Bean followed him. The
lady tended to the next group, not missing a beat.

The man walked so fast, Bean could hardly keep up.
He'd open a door, take a few steps down a hallway, and then
open another door to another hallway. He didn't say a word
to Bean, but just chomped on his sandwich. As they hurried
through the maze, Bean considered what he'd say to Captain
Sevilla. The heavyset man opened a final door to the outside.
There were only four planes at the terminals. Bean and the
man walked to the last one on the east side and waited.
About a hundred yards away, a small yellow airplane had one
propeller spinning on each wing.

Bean saw a woman and a man step up a couple stairs
and into the plane. Another tall man shut the door behind
them. He picked up a few bags on the ground and stuffed
them into another compartment in the side of the aircraft.
Then he turned and started Bean's way. Bean's escort in the
white uniform waved to the man as he finished his sandwich.
Bean figured the guy must be Captain Sevilla, who trotted
toward them.

Captain Sevilla wore a dark blue captain's hat and a
tight, tan, button-up shirt. His eyebrows were dark brown
and thick like fuzzy caterpillars. His sideburns extended down
to the bottom of his ear lobes. His face was square, with
each feature prominently defined. His nose was exceptionally
long. He was tall and fit. As Captain Sevilla got closer, he
towered over Bean and Bean's escort.

"Qué pasa?" he asked Bean.

Trembling, Bean said "Um...Isabel...es your amiga?"

The man stared down at Bean sternly for ten seconds. Bean began to cower. But to Bean's astonishment, Captain Sevilla let out a huge laugh. He extended his big arm to shake Bean's hand. Bean timidly reached out his hand and the captain shook his arm firmly.

"Alfredo, gracias por tu ayuda," Captain Sevilla thanked Bean's escort. "Estamos bien ahora. Puedes regresar." Bean didn't understand what was going on.

Turning to Bean, Captain Sevilla commanded, "Vámonos ya!" He put his arm around Bean's shoulders and led Bean to the airplane in a brisk walk. About halfway to the plane, Captain Sevilla switched to English, "I was expecting you earlier today. What happened?"

Still nervous but happy with the warm greeting, Bean responded, "I was on the way, but had a little trouble. So, you knew I was coming?"

"Why yes! Isabel called me and told me. But it is a good thing you didn't, because I didn't have any extra seats on the morning excursion," Captain Sevilla said. Bean smiled with gratitude. "The afternoon flights aren't as full. In fact, I have you sitting next to me as the co-pilot."

As they walked up to the plane, Bean's eyes got bigger. He had been on a large commercial jet twice, but never had he been on a small propeller plane like this before.

"Here, hand me your backpack," commanded Captain Sevilla.

Hesitant to not have it close in his possession, Bean reluctantly handed it over to him. Captain Sevilla opened a storage hatch and threw it in with the other passenger luggage. But Bean kept his whistle in the front pocket of his pants.

Captain Sevilla quickly led Bean past the other four passengers all seated and waiting for takeoff. He helped Bean get situated into the plane's small cockpit next to him. He placed some headphones over Bean's hat covering his ears. The Captain put on his head phones and welcomed all the passengers aboard his plane. Within forty seconds, the plane was speeding and then soaring off the ground.

~~~ CHAPTER ~~~ FOURTEEN

Bean watched out the window as the cars, buses, houses, big trees and parcels of land all began to shrink beneath him. Bean was in a small propeller plane, with a strange crew of people, flying over a foreign land somewhere in the southeast of Venezuela. For a brief moment, he had forgotten why he was on the plane and was blissfully enjoying the adventure and the exhilaration of flying. His eyes were wide with amazement. The plane's engine and propellers were very loud, but the captain could talk to Bean clearly with their radio and headphones.

"Isn't it beautiful, Bean?" Captain Sevilla asked, noticing Bean's awe.

Bean looked around and then over at the captain. The captain repeated with a smile, "Isn't it beautiful?"

"Yeah. This is amazing!" Bean said.

"Have you ever flown before?" the captain asked.

"Yeah, but not like this...in the front seat," Bean answered. "Have you flown for a long time?"

"Yes. I originally got my pilot's license in the United States about fifteen years ago," the captain said. "I've been flying these tours to Canaima and Angel Falls for about eight years or so now."

"Wow, that's a long time." Then it occurred to Bean where he was heading. "So...Isabel told you I needed to get to Canaima then?"

"Yes. Actually, she said you needed to get to the tiny settlement of Kavak, just south of Auyan-tepui," the captain answered. "Is that right?"

Remembering his research with Adriana, Bean replied, "Yeah that's right. Isn't the whole park called Canaima? And what is A...yan...teepee?"

"The largest town in Canaima National Park is called 'Canaima' too," the captain explained. "Let's talk more in a minute. I need to give my spiel to the other passengers now."

"Okay."

"Since three of you are from the Netherlands, one from Venezuela, and one from the U.S., I will speak mainly in English for the tour," Captain Sevilla began. "In about forty-five minutes, we will be entering one of the most exquisitely beautiful parts of planet Earth. Canaima National Park, established on June 12, 1962, is the sixth biggest park in the world. It is roughly the size of the country Belgium or the state of Maryland. The park encompasses most of the land known as the 'Great Savanna' or La Gran Sabana. It has one of the most unusual landscapes in the world, with meandering rivers, huge waterfalls, gorges, caves, stretching valleys, and impenetrable jungles."

The word "jungle" sent Bean's mind back to his last family vacation. In fact, the last time he was on a plane, his whole family was heading to Disney World the previous year. His family wasn't wealthy, but Hank made a good middle-class income. He and Gail made it a point to take the family on one big trip each year. Bean remembered how hysterical his mom was when his sister Haley went the opposite direction after a ride and got lost from the family. They searched the jungle part of the Animal Kingdom Park everywhere, but left Bean alone by the ride in case she returned there.

After ten minutes, Haley returned to where Bean was. His parents didn't get back to Bean until forty-five minutes later though. Gail called Bean a little angel for caring for his sister. But Bean never felt like he was a priority to his mom. *Mom might not worry too much about me, but what will she do when she finds out her husband is missing?* Bean thought. Bean was deeply concerned about his dad but was now getting worried about his mom if he failed the mission.

"At each altitude, the vegetation type is different. And in each region of the park, Canaima has a very diverse fauna with lots of different animals to see," the captain continued. "In the sky, you can see the red-shouldered macaw, the harpy eagle, the dusky parrot, and toucans. In the grasslands, you'll see giant armadillos and giant anteaters. By the rivers, you might spot the giant otters," he added. Bean was now tuning back in to the captain's monologue. He was feeling uneasy at the thought of encountering any one of these *giant* animals.

"In the trees of the jungle, you'll find neat monkeys like the white-faced saki or the brown-backed saki. There are opossums and sloths too. The jungle is crawling with reptiles like the green iguana, the yellow-banded poisonous dart frog, and the largest viper snake in the world, lachesis muta," Captain Sevilla said. "The lachesis is similar to a rattlesnake in the U.S., vibrating its tail when alarmed, but it makes no sound. Its victims don't have any warning before it strikes."

Bean hated snakes and was now terrified of the environment he'd soon be entering.

"My personal favorite is the mighty jaguar," Captain Sevilla continued. "The dense rainforest is the big cat's preferred habitat. Like the tiger, it too enjoys swimming and has an exceptionally powerful bite. It has the unusual killing method of biting directly through the skull of its prey between the ears."

"Oh geez!" Bean gasped along with a couple other passengers in the back.

"Ha, sorry everybody," the captain said, chuckling. The rest of the passengers all laughed with him, some obviously faking it.

"What can you tell us about Salto Ángel?" a man asked in the back with a low, serious tone.

"Angel Falls? I'm glad you asked," the captain responded. "The most popular attraction in the park is that of Angel Falls, the world's highest waterfall." Bean started feeling anxious with anticipation as he knew he'd be seeing the waterfall shortly. "It was long known of by the Pemón Indian tribe who still inhabit the region today. But it is named after Jimmie Angel, the American aviator, who crash-landed his plane atop Auyan-tepui. Angel and his small crew were forced to descend the tepui on foot, taking eleven days to get back to civilization. News of their adventure spread fast and now the falls are named in his honor."

"Auyan-tepui is the table top mountain where the waterfall drops from," Captain Sevilla continued. "Auyan-tepui means 'mountain of the God of Evil.'" Bean opened his eyes wider and listened more closely. "The waterfall is located in an isolated jungle, only accessible by river from the town of Canaima or Kavak. In fact, the word 'Canaima' means 'spirit of evil.' The Pemón people believe the land we are entering now is permanently cursed and inhabited by the devil himself," Captain Sevilla remarked with a straight face, but in a ghastly manner.

The passengers were quiet and pensive. Captain Sevilla reached over to a take sip from his water bottle. Bean considered the coincidence of the mountain's name. *Angel falls from the mountain of the God of evil,* Bean thought for a while. He sat staring out the window, noticing the terrain changing below to a dark green hue. The thick green landscape beneath had some scattered cloud clusters hovering above parts. The brownish-tan water dividing the land was very wide in some areas and was narrowly winding in others. Dozens of flat-top mountains shot straight up from the green earth, creating high cliffs and sudden drop offs.

"So how do you know Isabel?" Bean asked Captain Sevilla, trying to get his mind off the evil environment he'd soon be entering.

The captain looked over at Bean for a second. "We were supposed to get married last year," Captain Sevilla said soberly. "But she had a change of heart."

"What do you mean?" Bean asked.

"Um, it's a little hard to explain. Have you had a girlfriend yet?" Captain Sevilla asked.

"No," Bean answered quickly, but his thoughts went to Adriana.

"Haha, well then it's really hard to explain my young friend." Just then, the plane jolted up and then dropped a few feet. "Sorry everyone, looks like we've hit some turbulence," the captain explained. The plane ride started to get a little choppy as it descended. "Make sure all of your seat belts are fastened."

"But do you still have feelings for her?" Bean pressed Captain Sevilla.

"Yes, I still deeply care for her, Bean," the captain said. After a long pause, Captain Sevilla asked Bean, "Since you are getting rather personal, can I ask you a personal question, too?"

Nothing felt too personal to Bean. "Sure, I don't mind," he replied.

"Why are you going all alone to Kavak?"

"I'm trying to find my dad," Bean answered.

"Why do you think you'll find him there?"

"I'm not sure. But there is an old wise woman who lives outside of Kavak who might help me."

"How do you know this?" the captain asked.

"It's a long story. Maybe I can tell you when we get there."

The captain laughed. "I'm not staying there with you. I need to get back. I'm just doing Isabel a favor. In fact, I don't exactly feel comfortable landing on Kavak's small bumpy air strip either."

"Are the others going to Kavak too?" Bean asked, indicating the other passengers.

"Just one is. The others aren't staying. They just paid for the afternoon plane tour."

"That reminds me, how much do I owe you, Captain Sevilla?" Bean asked.

"Nothing. I told you I had an empty seat. I'm trying to win Isabel back. Just put in a good word for me when you see her again." The captain smiled. "I'm supposed to pick up the other gentleman at nine AM on Sunday morning," he added. "Will this work for you too?"

Bean knew his mother expected him and Hank back home Sunday evening. Bean needed time to find Ramona, but he also didn't think his conversation would be too long with her. "Yeah I think that should be good, but please, no later."

"Attention passengers! Off to your right, you can see the glorious Angel Falls," the captain announced to the crew as he pointed that way. The passengers gasped at the awesome view. The plane's altitude was now at almost eye level with the top of Auyan-tepui. The water from the falls gushed out of the mountain edge and sprayed the rainforest thousands of feet below, like a giant hose watering a garden. It was almost 6pm, and the evening sunlight was dimming fast. Captain Sevilla needed to land soon.

"Crew, prepare for landing," the captain said as the plane descended steadily.

"Bean, I have to say, I'm concerned about a teenage boy wandering the unknown Kamarata valley by himself. I mean, I hate to scare you, but there are a lot of weird things down there," Captain Sevilla said.

Bean was certainly nervous, too. But his drive and determination to find his dad was all the motivation he needed. He responded bravely, "I'll be fine. I have the lady's address."

The landing strip became visible ahead. The runway was red dirt and wasn't the standard length of a typical runway. The land rose quickly with tall green trees, wide rivers, spacious grasslands to either side, and a few palm huts off in the distance.

"Those huts over there is Kavak," the captain showed Bean. "It isn't much. Just a small settlement of Pemón Indians. I hear they are friendly, but odd."

Bean heard what he was saying but was busy bracing himself to absorb the imminent landing. Captain Sevilla slowly glided the plane down while keeping its nose up. The two-propeller plane suddenly lowered to the ground and bounced along until both wheels rolled on the cement-like dirt. The dirt runway was bumpy, and the passengers held on tightly until the plane came to a complete stop. Bean noticed the beads of sweat on Captain Sevilla's face.

"Nice job, man!" Bean commended the captain while others clapped.

"Thanks guys. It's never easy landing on this rough airstrip," Captain Sevilla said, visibly relieved.

He took off his headset, wiped his forehead, and hurried out of the cockpit. He turned to the Venezuelan man behind them and said, "Listo, señor?"

"Sí, gracias por la cola," the man responded. Bean heard this phrase and raspy voice before. Bean timidly turned around to find Toni glaring back at him. Bean was astonished, and his heart sank. While he was pleased to see him, he also felt unsettled like he was in trouble for leaving Toni's side.

"De nada amigo," replied Captain Sevilla. "Déjame agarrar su bolsillo y cosas." The captain opened the side door, pulled out the stairs, and climbed out of the plane.

Not saying a word to Bean, Toni unbuckled his belt and stood. He was dressed in new rugged apparel, fit for the outdoors. Bean followed as they both exited the plane. Bean wasn't sure if he should acknowledge him yet, so as to not confuse Captain Sevilla.

"Aquí están tu bolsillo y cosas," Captain Sevilla said handing Toni a large backpack and some other things wrapped in a tarp material.

"Gracias. Entonces, estará aquí este domingo a las nueve en la mañana?," Toni asked the captain.

"Seguramente, en punto," Captain Sevilla confirmed. Then looking down at Bean and handing him his backpack, he added, "You too, Bean. I will be here at nine AM sharp on Sunday morning."

"Thank you so much, Captain Sevilla," Bean thanked him sincerely. "I will make it up to you somehow, and I will put in a good word," he added with a wink.

"Bueno. Nos vemos amigos. Suerte a ustedes!" Captain Sevilla exclaimed as he shook their hands, and hurriedly lifted the stairs up into the plane. "Oh and try not to look anyone in the eye too long!"

CHAPTER FIFTEEN

Toni walked just behind Bean, away from the dirt runway and toward the cluster of palm-thatched huts. The evening air was about seventy-five degrees, with a light breeze from the east. The air felt damp and very humid to Bean. Hearing the roar of the two propellers motoring the airplane behind them, Bean turned around to see Captain Sevilla take flight. As it gained enough speed, the plane lifted into the air and gradually soared past the dark forest in the west. It climbed even higher and became a faint silhouette against the bright orange and pink sun rays in the west.

"I hope he comes back. How are you my friend?" Toni asked Bean in his low, raspy tone.

A little apprehensive, Bean answered, "I'm good. I was a little nervous to hear about all the freaky wild animals here, and about this place being cursed and all." They continued on toward the huts.

"I don't think there's anything to worry about," Toni replied arrogantly.

"How did you escape the police?" Bean asked after a moment of walking.

"You left me there alone, Bean," Toni said.

"I'm sorry, Toni. But didn't I take out a couple of the cops for you?"

"Yes, you did. That made my escape easier. But not without a good fight," said Toni. "But you were supposed to wait for me until I came for you…"

"Sorry, Toni. I hate waiting for people now," Bean said, recalling the hunting experience with his dad. "That's how I got mixed up in this mess to begin with."

"But gringo, *how* did you get past me?" Toni asked.

Bean knew Toni was committed to never leaving his side and could tell Toni was disappointed in himself that he got away. "I just did what I had to do," Bean answered. "I'm glad you finally put a shirt on though."

Toni rolled his eyes and didn't say anything else as they neared the small village.

Bean noticed a big pasture off to the right and counted six horses grazing peacefully. He also noticed cattle and llamas fenced off in another pasture a little further out. He counted eight palm huts, one larger pavilion, and two square structures with exposed red, cement walls. Suddenly, three men dressed in haggard short sleeve button up shirts, shorts, and hiking boots exited from one of the cement buildings and walked in Bean's direction.

"Hello, gentlemen," the oldest looking one said cheerfully as they got closer. "Welcome to Kavak, our peaceful village. My name is Kele." His strong accent was different from the other Venezuelans Bean had met.

"Hello!" said Bean. "My name is Bean, and this is Toni," signaling to Toni on his left.

"Hi," Toni said. He looked at the men next to Kele as if to size them up.

"This is Moa, and this is Fichu. They are the best guides in Canaima, and my right-hand men," Kele said, introducing the men. Moa had a shaved head, thick eyebrows and an intimidating demeanor. He was about Bean's height, but much thicker and with an athletic build. His eyes were dark, his nose flat, and his mouth wide. Fichu was taller than Moa, but not as tall as Toni. He had long black hair to his shoulders. He too was fit, but slenderer. Both didn't show much personality.

"We were not informed of your coming. Usually our clients arrive in the morning, too. I assume you are here to be guided through our park and see Angel Falls?" he asked.

Before Bean could say anything, Toni said, "Yes. But right now, we are tired and wish to rent a room if you have something available." Bean looked down at his watch to see the time was 6:39pm.

"We are hungry too," Bean added, hearing his stomach growl.

"Very well then," Kele said. "Follow me and we will help get you situated. Unfortunately, there are only a few who speak English in the village. Moa and Fichu speak some English too, but they mainly speak Spanish and Pemón, our native Indian tongue."

The three native Indians led Bean and Toni into their small settlement. As they passed the first few huts, some little children raced in front of them and then around a big tree. Bean noticed one young girl dressed in an orange sundress and with long messy hair standing in a shaded corner alone, not taking notice of him. Some younger women sitting around a table weaving baskets whispered and giggled as Bean and Toni passed by. There was a strong scent in the air, as a few older women tended to a pot of stew and prepared food. Many villagers stopped and curiously observed the new visitors.

"Here is the hut just for clients who spend the night," Kele said directing them to a small hut about ten feet wide by ten feet deep. It had one door opening that came up to Bean's chest. Inside, the ground was bare dirt and there were two cots made of woven bamboo, palm leaves, and hemp. There was a thin brown blanket folded at the end of each cot, too.

"I will get you some water and your supper should be ready shortly," Kele informed Bean and Toni. "After you finish, please join the tribe at the center ring for some music and dancing. It would be our honor to have you as our guests." He smiled and bowed his head as he turned to leave them in their quarters.

Bean unfolded his blanket and threw it neatly over his cot. He set his backpack on the ground next to him and then laid on the cot. He put his hands behind his head, crossed his legs, and inhaled deeply. After enjoying the rest for a minute, he glanced over at Toni. Toni was sitting on his cot, going through his backpack.

"Here, I got these for you," Toni said, handing Bean a new toothbrush, toothpaste, and some deodorant. "You have bad breath and you smell a little too." A rare smirk fixed on Toni's face.

Bean laughed. "Oh man, sweet. You remembered!" He accepted the items from Toni. "I'm gonna brush my teeth so long after dinner."

"I don't think we have time to eat and join in their music," Toni said. "We need to find that old woman soon."

"I need to eat, but yeah, I agree. I need to find her as soon as possible." It was already getting dark, and the directions Bean had for her home were pretty vague. He pulled the directions out again along with Adriana's translation. "Ramona lives in a hidden palm hut, by some cashew trees just outside of Kavak," he read out loud to Toni.

Toni just stared at the ground and listened. "Do we have an idea if she is north or south or west of Kavak?" he asked.

"No, that's all I was given," Bean said. He thought things over for a moment, feeling conflicted. "I'm not so sure you should even come along, Toni. I mean, I don't want to frighten her. She is expecting me, but probably not anyone else." He also wanted to respect Draug's wishes.

"She is *expecting* you?" Toni asked. "How do you know she is expecting you?"

"I can't tell you everything. You'll just have to trust me," Bean responded, a little more guarded.

"I'm gonna help you find her," Toni said firmly. "I won't let you out of my sight again."

Bean heard the hostility in Toni's voice and squirmed some. "You aren't giving me much of a choice. It feels like you're trying to control me, Toni. I don't like it."

Toni sighed, and the hut was silent. "I told you what my purpose is. It is to protect you, Bean."

"Your purpose is to protect me as long as I help you find the platinum kuakilla. But I'm not looking for that. I'm trying to find my dad."

"You are chosen, Bean. My grandfather told me this," Toni said. "And I'm supposed to help you find the kuakilla. I will help you find your father too."

"I already made a promise to someone else who is helping me."

"Who? Have I met him or her?" Toni looked both puzzled and concerned.

"No, you don't know him."

There was another brief silence. "I'm not sure I can even help you, Toni. Yes, you helped me escape the malandros, but I got us the taxi to Ciudad Bolívar. Then you got us in trouble with the police there. I got on the plane and got here to Kavak without your help," Bean said, starting to lose his patience.

"No, I did not get us in trouble with the police. I think that priest called them on us. But don't you see, gringo? You aren't strong. You're not wise. You don't speak Spanish. You got this far because you are *chosen*," Toni reiterated.

"No, I'm not chosen. I'm just determined to find my dad. And some people have offered to help me along the way."

"Those malandros could have killed you," Toni erupted. "Seriously. And they for sure would have taken your backpack. I saved you and your precious backpack."

Bean didn't respond.

"Why did you fight so hard for your backpack? Why do you keep your backpack so close to you at all times? What is in there?" pressed Toni.

Still, Bean sat quiet.

Toni stared at Bean, who was nervous and didn't want to answer. Finally, he looked up at Toni. "Just my stuff... not your business." He stood up, put on his backpack, and started out the door.

"Wait, Bean, I'm sorry," Toni said. Bean stopped. "You're right. You don't owe me anything for helping you escape the malandros last night. But please, let me protect you. If you meet with Ramona, and don't go on to find the platinum kuakilla, I will know I've been wrong."

Bean studied Toni for a few seconds to assess his sincerity. "Okay. You can help me find her, but you can't go with me into Ramona's hut." Toni didn't respond.

"I'm hungry," Bean said as he parted the long dried tweed in the doorway. Toni scrambled to put some items back in his pack and followed Bean out.

~~~ CHAPTER ~~~ SIXTEEN

"Young fellow, here you go," Kele said as he met Bean out in front of his hut and handed him a glass of water. Bean graciously accepted and began to drink. "Where are you from anyway?" Kele asked.

Bean chugged the entire glass of water, wiped his mouth, and handed it back to Kele. Toni walked up next to Bean and waited for Bean's reply. "I come from the United States," Bean answered.

Kele looked Bean up and down, and then in the eye. "You are a very brave boy," he said slowly. Turning over to Toni, Kele asked, "And you, are you from the United States too?"

"No, sir. I come from Caracas. I wanted to show Bean the largest waterfall in the world," Toni answered.

"Well, you've come to the right place, my friends. Moa and Fichu will guide you there and it will be an adventure to remember!" Kele said. "Come, we have some chicken soup for you." Kele motioned them to follow him.

Bean and Toni walked after Kele between the huts and over to an open space in the middle of the structures. The area was dimly lit with surrounding tiki torches and a big fire burning in the center pit. There were four men dressed in red Indian apparel and unique headgear. They were violently beating large drums. A few dozen Indians, both men and women, surrounded them talking, laughing, and enjoying themselves while the drums were pounded on in the background.

As Bean and Toni walked by, some nodded or waved, welcoming them into their festivities. Situated outside of the gathering were two long picnic-like tables in front of some tall palm trees. Kele showed them to their seats where bowls of hot soup, cashew nuts, and arepas awaited them.

"Here, please sit down," Kele said. "We are about to begin our singing." The rhythm of the drums changed to a quicker thumping and some flutists began playing an enchanting, yet foreign melody. Kele set glasses of water down at each place setting. "I will get some more water. If you'd like to dance, come join us." He walked off.

Bean and Toni got comfortable at the table. Bean, remembering the delicious arepas Isabel made earlier that day, quickly reached for an arepa and took a big bite. As he tried to chew the thick arepa, Bean could barely break it down enough to swallow. The flavor was very bland, but Bean's hunger was so intense he forced the food down. He grabbed a handful of cashews and gobbled them up. He then grabbed his spoon to try the soup.

"Hold up, Bean," Toni said as he stirred his own bowl of green broth soup. "I'm not sure what's in it."

"Kele said chicken. I love chicken," Bean said as he put his spoon into the soup bowl. As he stirred the soup, a yellow oval floated to the top. "Oh geez, what's that?"

"I think it's iguana," Toni said, still examining the contents of his own bowl. "And that's an eyeball," he said, pointing to the yellow ball bobbing in Bean's bowl. "They must cook the whole thing at once. It's okay, though. Iguana tastes like chicken. Buen provecho!"

Bean could tell Toni had some sick satisfaction knowing what he was about to eat. Bean lifted up his spoon to his eyes and analyzed the floating yellow oval more closely. "If I ate badger stew, I can eat iguana soup," he told himself. He inserted the spoonful into his mouth. He closed his eyes and swallowed repugnantly. Toni chuckled. Bean was so hungry, he didn't care. He smiled back at Toni and they both began to eat up.

As Bean and Toni ate, they watched the Indians dance and sing along together gleefully to odd songs. Those sitting around the fire would yell chants and others would repeat the chants back. The crowd number had now tripled in size. As Bean watched some children chase around, he was startled to see the same girl in the orange sundress sitting to his far right at the table where he ate. She didn't look over at Bean. Her head was tilted down and her long, black ratty hair covered her face. Bean watched her as she sat very still. He looked back over to the crowd.

"Seleman! Seleman!" the crowd yelled.

Toni perked up. "Did you hear that? Did you hear what they yelled?"

"No," Bean said. "Sounds like a bunch of gibberish to me."

"I know, but that one wasn't."

"Which one?"

"They yelled the name of the evil medicine man from my tribe."

"Really? The one you won't say out loud?"

Toni nodded.

Suddenly, two dark gray images emerged from the group of dancers and headed Bean's direction. Toni didn't seem to notice, content with eating his meal again. The noise and music lightly faded into the background as Bean was captivated with the slowly approaching four-legged creatures.

As they drew near, Bean squint his eyes to get a clearer image. They were big dogs with mangy gray fur. Their ears stood extraordinarily tall and pointed. They stared at Bean with big yellow eyes. Bean watched attentively. With a quick jerk of their necks, the dogs broke their stare and twitched wildly for a few seconds. Bean jumped. He tapped Toni's shoulder, trying to get his attention. The dogs now uncontrollably contorted their bodies in a possessed manner. Bean hit Toni's shoulder again.

"What, gringo?" Toni asked looking at Bean, and then over at the dogs. "The mutts?"

Bean locked eyes with one of the dogs again and its face began to deform and appear human-like. Bean froze. Both dogs seemed to eerily smile at Bean as they stood a few feet in front of the table.

"Do you see this?" Bean frantically asked Toni in a loud whisper. Toni was now alert.

The dogs' twisted smiles turned into evil scowls as they showed their long, fanged teeth. Saliva dripped from their angry mouths. Abruptly, they both stood up on their hind feet and waved front claws violently at Bean and Toni. The growling got louder and more vicious.

"Go on! Get!" Toni stood and yelled at the dogs. But they only got closer.

In a flash, the young girl in the orange dress jumped onto the table top and swung a fiery torch at the dogs. She yelled some strange words at them and they ran off, disappearing back into the crowd of dancers. Then, the girl quietly sat down in front of Bean and Toni and ignored them.

"Sorry, my friends," Kele said with a nervous look as he appeared. "Sometimes they get too close."

"Those things were crazy!" Bean said, terror quavering in his voice.

"Again, my apologies," Kele said emphatically. "How was the soup?" Toni and Bean checked with each other and then both replied that it was good. "Good," Kele said.

"The cashew nuts are really good. Do you guys grow them here?" Bean asked Kele.

"Yes, a lady sells them in town here. You guys should come dance," Kele suggested. Toni and Bean checked with each other again.

"No thanks," they said simultaneously.

"We are enjoying the show from here," Toni said.

"Yeah, it's really quite thrilling," Bean added. "How many people live here in Kavak anyway?"

"In Kavak, maybe a hundred and twenty people. But the Kamarata Valley may have four hundred," Kele answered.

"So, you probably know everyone?" Bean asked.

Kele thought for a moment. "I think so, why?"

"I am looking for..."

"Bean!" Toni interrupted. "Aren't you tired? Let's head back to the hut."

Kele stared curiously at Bean. "You are looking for someone?"

Recognizing his lack of tact and impatience, Bean said, "Um, I just wanted to know where to get more cashew nuts. They are very delicious here."

Kele appeared confused and suspicious. "Let me see. Wait here for a moment." He left Toni and Bean sitting at the table.

Bean looked at Toni. Toni was visibly annoyed.

"Sorry, I was flustered and wanted to get straight to the point." Bean said. "But didn't I recover pretty good?"

Toni sighed. "We need to go back to the hut. We need to make a plan."

The young girl sitting in front of them slowly turned around. Her head was tilted downward and her hair still covered her face. She pointed to Bean's bowl.

Bean glanced at his bowl and asked the girl, "Are you hungry?" Noticing that there were a few more spoonfuls left, Bean gently pushed the bowl in front of the girl. "Here you go."

The girl picked up the bowl and flipped it upside down. She grabbed the spoon and held it up to Bean. Bean watched her gesture, and then looked over at Toni. It didn't faze Toni. Next, the girl reached for the plate of cashews and picked up a small handful. She slowly dropped the cashews one by one back on to the plate.

"Come on, Bean, let's go back to the hut," Toni insisted.

Out of nowhere, Kele appeared with Moa and Fichu on either side of him. Their countenances were less sober than when they first met. This time, Moa spoke first.

"You came all the way here for some cashews?"

"Ha, no sir. We came to explore Salto Ángel," Bean answered.

"Ah okay. We can take you there in the morning. There are some cashew trees on the way," Moa replied.

"You can? There are?" Bean couldn't hide his curiosity. "I mean of course you can. You're the best guides in Canaima!"

Moa glared at Bean as if to read his mind. He turned and consulted with Kele and Fichu in their native Pemón language. Toni stood next to Bean with his arms folded. Bean desperately wanted to find his dad. The drums seemed to beat more wildly in the background, and the excitement of the celebration seemed to climax. Bean looked down at his watch, which said 8:51pm. Together, they all turned back to Bean.

"Moa and Fichu will take you out early tomorrow. The boat ride and hike up to Salto Angel takes about five hours.

Can you guys be ready by five am?" Kele asked Bean and Toni.

"Yes. Please wake us fifteen minutes prior to heading out," Toni replied.

"Yeah that's good," Bean said. "I'm tired. Toni let's head back to the hut."

"Great. It will be a day you'll never forget," Kele said.

They all shook hands and Kele guided them back to their palm hut. As they neared the entry of the hut, they heard a high-pitch moaning right behind them. Bean turned around to see the same young girl in the orange sundress and ratty hair waving the spoon back and forth. She was eerily moaning and chanting some foreign phrases.

"Sorry, don't mind Mumua. She's ill," Kele explained. Then he showed them the entry to their hut.

~~~ CHAPTER ~~~
SEVENTEEN

"Toni, do you think they are suspicious of us?" Bean asked as they settled into their cots to sleep.

"Yes. I am sure we are suspicious visitors to them. We came without notice. You are a boy from the United States. I am from Caracas. We don't match up well," Toni answered. "We need to whisper. These walls are very thin."

"I think we should just ask them about Ramona. That's what I wanted to do before you interrupted me."

"I know. But it didn't seem like the right time."

"But I'm the chosen one, remember? It all just kind of works out for me, right?" Bean asked with some sarcasm.

"Isn't meeting with her extremely important to you? You don't want to mess that up."

"Yeah. She is the whole reason why I'm here."

"Why do you think she is so important to finding your dad?"

"I'm not sure. Draug told me she could help..."

"Who? Who told you?"

"Oh dang. Nevermind," Bean clamped his mouth shut.

"You've said the name before. You said he is a medicine man, right?"

Bean felt defensive and tried to remember all he told Toni. He didn't remember telling Toni about Draug. After a short pause, Bean asked Toni, "When did I mention him before?"

"It was before we entered the cathedral, you said his name. But then Isabel interrupted us. I forgot, but I've been meaning to ask you about this medicine man. I need to know his name."

"Why? I don't wanna say now."

"Gringo, do you even know him? If you made an oath with the wrong medicine man, you could be in serious danger. Everything could go bad. Is he the one you made a pact with?"

"Yes. But I'm not supposed to tell anyone about him," Bean admitted cautiously.

"Why are you so loyal to him?"

"Because he saved my life," Bean replied.

"So did I!"

"And he knows how to find my dad."

"Are you sure? Why would he know such a thing?"

"I'm hoping so. He has powers. He can sense that my dad is alive, but captive somewhere."

"Bean, you are young and naive. This man is evil. He has your father hostage. Once you do what he needs, you think he'll release your dad?"

"Yeah! That's why we made an oath—to help each other," Bean replied, feeling a little unsure of Draug's motives. "I shouldn't tell you anymore."

"Bean, it doesn't seem right," Toni said with concern. "You can trust me. What's his name again?"

"I'm tired."

"This is important Bean. I'm here to help you."

Bean thought for a long while. "Let's get to sleep. Tomorrow, we'll go with them. Hopefully, we'll see some cashew trees that will lead us close to Ramona. If not, we will simply ask them if they know her."

Finally, there was silence. The ruckus and loud drums beating in the background were quieted. To Bean's complete surprise, Toni had fallen fast asleep. There were some villagers laughing faintly. A baby cried in a faraway hut. Eventually, all the distant noises subsided too.

The cool night breezes blew in and through Bean's hut. Utterly exhausted from the day's adventures, Bean still could not sleep. He wondered about his father and what he was going through. He wondered about his mom and sisters. He thought of Kenny and Bo. He wondered if he'd ever see his dad or any of them again. He hoped he could get back to his comfortable life in Utah. He could hardly believe the reality of his strange surroundings and circumstance.

Bean rubbed his heavy eyelids and tried to see what time it was. He could barely see his own hand; the hut was so dark. He pressed the button on his watch to light up the screen to see the time. The tiny light revealed that it was now a few minutes past midnight. "Geez. I need to get some sleep," Bean said quietly.

Clank...clank...clank...

The noise came from outside his hut.

Clank...clank...clank...clank...

What is that? Bean thought.

Clank...CLANK...CLANK...

It was getting louder and steadier.

Clank, clank, CLANK!

Curious, Bean quietly sat up and crawled to the doorway of his hut. He parted the hanging tweed in the doorway, and slowly peeked through the opening. The moonlight illuminated the surroundings to a decent degree of visibility and cast shadows of the other nearby huts.

CLANK!

Startled, Bean pulled his head back into the hut like a turtle's head into its shell.

Clank...clank...clank

The sound was now closer.

He slowly stuck his head back out and peered to his left. Nothing. He turned to the right. He examined the hut's shadow cast by the moonlight. Then to his astonishment, he could make out an even darker shape there. A smaller figure moved.

Clank

Squinting, he recognized the young girl with the ratty hair who scared off the possessed dogs. Mumua wouldn't look at him. She slowly raised her instrument into the moonlight, just outside of the shadow she hid in.

The spoon again! Bean's thoughts raced. *What is she trying to tell me?*

Suddenly, she stood up and slowly walked toward Bean. Although freaked out, Bean didn't move. He was too interested in what she was trying to communicate. As she got closer, her face remained hidden by her long hair. She waved the spoon back and forth.

Bean spoke up. "What? The spoon?"

The girl stopped. She tossed the spoon with a quick jerk of her wrist and it landed in between Bean's hands on the ground. She walked up to Bean and carefully knelt. Bean was frozen. She got on all fours and pointed at Bean, then down to the spoon. She repeated this action three times.

"Hmm. I can't figure this out," Bean thought. "Me, spoon, me, spoon, me, spoon?"

Bean reached for the spoon and put it in front of her. The girl quickly picked up the spoon and tossed it over to the hut next door in frustration. Confused beyond belief, Bean gave up.

"Sorry. I go to sleep." Bean mimed laying his head on his pillow. He carefully tucked his head back in to the hut and crawled back to his cot. He grabbed his backpack for more head support as he lay down. He was perplexed as to what she could possibly be saying.

"Me, spoon...me, spoon...my spoon," he murmured. "My spoon. Do I have a spoon?" It suddenly occurred to Bean as his head rested on his backpack. Draug had inserted that wooden ladle. *Yes, I have a spoon!*

Bean sat up and hastily unzipped his pack but could hardly see anything. He felt around and loudly rummaged through its contents. Toni awoke.

"Gringo, what's going on?" Toni asked in alarm.

Ignoring Toni, Bean walked to the hut doorway to get some light. Then he found it. He pulled out the ladle and started to turn it in his hand. Mumua appeared out of nowhere and snatched it out if his hand. She danced with excitement.

"Wait, give that back!" Bean said in a firm whisper.

Toni watched over Bean's shoulder. "What? What's going on, Bean?"

She shook her head and held the spoon straight up as high as she could as if to examine its shape. Then she motioned for Bean to follow her as she took off into the shadows.

"Oh no. That's Draug's. Geez," Bean said.

"Who? Drog, you say? Is that the medicine man?"

Bean quickly zipped up his backpack. "Come on hurry, Toni. We need to get it back." Bean hastily put on his shoes. Toni beat Bean back to the doorway and stood ready at attention like a soldier awaiting his leader's command. He had his large pack draped over his shoulder. They darted out into the night, in the direction Bean last saw her go.

CHAPTER EIGHTEEN

Their eyes adjusted quickly to the bright moonlit surroundings. The air was less muggy and much cooler than at dinner. After getting a good distance from the huts, they stopped to scan the landscape like Bean did when hunting with his father. He got out his binoculars, but they weren't of much use in the dark. Toni spotted a dark figure about a hundred yards away, scampering awkwardly toward the horse pasture.

"Over there," he signaled to Bean.

"Yes, that's her!" They followed faster.

"Is that the girl from dinner?" Toni asked between breaths as they ran.

"Yes."

"And what did she take from you?"

"She knows something," Bean said, gasping for air.

"What did she take?" Toni insisted as they arrived at an old, wooden fence surrounding the pasture.

Bean was dizzy and out of breath. He bent over placing his hands on his kneecaps. "Toni...do you see her?"

Toni looked over the landscape as much as the moon's lighting would allow.

"I just see horses over on that far side," Toni responded after a few moments.

"She took the ladle," Bean opened up after he caught his breath. "Draug put a wooden ladle in my pack, and she took it. Then she motioned for me to follow her."

"Draug, right? That name isn't the one I was worried about. He still seems like an evil one though," Toni said.

"Maybe, but I am stuck with him until I get my father back."

"You aren't stuck. We have a long journey tomorrow. Shouldn't we go back and get rest?" Toni suggested.

"I think she knows something," Bean said. Just then, a loud moaning was heard off in the dreary distance. "That's her! She's moaning again."

"It came from over there." Toni pointed straight ahead to the other end of the pasture. Bean climbed over the fence and headed out with a brisk pace. Toni sighed and followed.

The two companions traveled approximately two hundred yards into the middle of the pasture. "Gringo, hold up," Toni begged. The ground was riddled with gaping holes and divots the size of horse hooves.

Not wanting to stop, Bean replied, "What now, Toni?"

"Kele said she was mentally ill. She isn't normal."

Bean came to an abrupt halt. He looked at his watch which read 12:43am. "Look, I'm tired too. But my hunch is that she knows something. It's like she was waiting for us... or at least waiting for the ladle." Suddenly, the ground began to rumble and shake. Bean stumbled as he tried to catch his balance. Toni, poised and alert, tried to understand what was occurring around them.

"It's an earthquake, Toni! Get on the ground," Bean yelled as he fell to his knees.

"No, it's a stampede! Horses! Get behind me quick!"

Bean looked back over his shoulder and could make out the rushing of a dozen horses sprinting in their direction, churning up the dirt into a giant cloud of smoke. In the wide open, there was no cover for them. Bean got back to his feet and took refuge behind Toni. He quickly unzipped his backpack and located the whistle.

No, I can't leave Toni again, Bean thought. He grabbed something else and turned it on as fast as he could. "Here, wave this at 'em!" he yelled as he handed Toni a flashlight.

Toni frantically waved the flashlight back and forth toward the fast-approaching herd of horses. Bean hunkered down and covered his head behind Toni with both of his hands. Within seconds the horses changed their course in unison and avoided the waving beam of light. Bean removed his hands slowly from covering his head as the sound and rumbling of the horses faded into a distant corner of the pasture.

"Good thinking, gringo," Toni said, sounding relieved.

"You did it again, Toni. You saved us," Bean said as he got back to his feet and secured his pack over his shoulders. Bean and Toni gazed back at the horses now far off and feeding peacefully again. They got their bearings and were quickly back on course again heading toward Mumua.

"Something spooked those horses," Toni spoke up.

Bean recalled the wild narrative of Captain Sevilla on the flight over and the evil he spoke of in the area. Trying to make light of his anxiety, Bean responded, "You think it was a giant anteater or giant armadillo that scared them?"

Toni cracked a rare smile.

They continued their pursuit. With their adrenaline still pumping, they walked faster than before and finally made it to the other side of the pasture. The treeline was thick in front of them making it hard for them to have much depth perception.

"Eeeeek! Eeeeek!" The moaning was loud and shrill. It was off to the left, seemingly not too deep in the trees.

Bean and Toni hurried after her shrilling cry, not able to see what lay in their path. The crying went away, but they forged ahead. They made it through the thick forest and found themselves in some dense brush and softer ground. The once clear, starry sky now seemed to dull as an eerie, thick darkness blanketed the area. Chilling breezes whizzed past them.

"Gringo, get the flashlight again," Toni said.

Bean fumbled through his pack. He came across his knife and stuffed it in the pocket of his pants. He felt around and grabbed the whistle too. He put it in the other pocket. Finally, he found the flashlight. That's when he and Toni both heard some scrambling in the shrubs to their left about twenty-five feet. Standing extra still, Bean gently raised the flashlight and pointed it in the direction of the noise. Its beam of light cut through the darkness and cast a circular spotlight into the midst.

Like an actor parting a curtain on stage, a wild and ferocious dog crept out between the tall bushes. Its golden eyes glowed with anger. Its wrinkled, gray muzzle revealed sharp fangs and dripped with drool. Its mangy gray hair was unable to conceal the muscular contours of its shoulders and frame. And then its larger twin appeared beside it. It looked even more savage and vicious, with the intent to kill.

Toni instantly unsheathed a large blade and welcomed the fight. The large dog leaped high at Toni. Toni knocked it down with a wave of his forearm. The smaller one targeted Bean. Toni kicked the big dog in the side. Bean had a second to move. With Toni's back exposed, the first dog struck again, jumping on his back.

Bean stepped to the right, threw down his pack, and pulled out his knife. Terrified, he dropped the flashlight and reached for the whistle. But the dog was too quick and lunged at Bean's leg. Its jaw locked on to Bean's ankle like a metal bear trap. Strong and powerful, the rabid-like dog yanked Bean to the ground.

Off to the side, he could see that Toni had all he could handle. Toni's attacker was skilled and scrappy. Each time Toni shook it to reach Bean, the dog only grew more ferocious. Its claws were long and sharp, like four knives slashing at once. Toni had to give it all his attention or he'd lose.

The wild canine attacker pinned down Bean's shoulders and leaned on top of him. The dog's face began to contort and foamed at the mouth. With a mean, human-like grin, the dog spoke in a demonic tone.

"Your bloodline ends here."

Bean's fear turned to anger. He struggled back and forth, trying to shake the dog off him, but it was abnormally strong. The dog laughed loud and obnoxious like a hyena, raising its head up and down. Bean clenched his knife tightly. With all his might, Bean swiftly swiped upward, stabbing his enemy. The knife sank deep into the dog's sternum and then its laugh turned into a violent gag. His eyes glazed over and rolled back into his head. Bean watched in horror. The animal fell lifeless on top of Bean. Bean fidgeted and maneuvered himself out from under the bleeding carcass.

Feeling braver and bolder, Bean punched and pulled at the other dog wrestling with Toni. The dog jumped backward and became aware of its defeated teammate. The surviving dog glared at Bean as if it had underestimated the strength of its victims. In a flash, it retreated into the dark shrubbery where it came from.

Wounded and visibly fatigued, Toni got his balance and brushed himself off. He had a dozen cuts and scratches. He was bloody, and his clothes were torn in many places. But he had no deep or serious lacerations.

"Toni, are you okay?" Bean asked.

Toni nodded. "Yes, but that thing was tough. Wrestled like a human but with animal strength." He caught his breath. "Sorry I couldn't handle yours too." Right after he spoke, Toni discovered the dog lying limp on the ground behind Bean. He stared back at Bean in awe.

"Is...it dead?"

"Yes."

Impressed, Toni kept his eyes on Bean. Bean felt uncomfortable but could sense Toni's respect for him was growing deeper. Breaking the awkwardness, Bean picked up the flashlight. He felt around and confirmed the whistle was still in his pocket. He was proud he didn't have to use it. Then a sharp, jolting pain struck Bean in his ankle and he dropped to the dirt.

"Bean! What is it?" Toni gasped.

Panting against the pain, Bean raised his head enough to see blood and raw, torn flesh around his lower leg.

Toni knelt beside his partner. "Lay down on your back. Let me help you," he said, taking the flashlight out of Bean's hand. He began to take off his shirt to wrap the wound.

"No! Keep your shirt on!" Bean exclaimed.

"Gringo, not time to joke."

"Grab the red cloth out of my bag. Wrap my ankle with that instead," Bean said in anguish.

"Oh, right." Toni flashed the light inside Bean's backpack and rummaged around until he found the red cloth. He started to wrap up Bean's ankle tightly to stop any bleeding and give it some support.

"Geez man, take it easy." Bean whined and cringed as Toni finished up. The pain was unspeakable.

"EEEEKK! EEEEKK!" The moaning shriek of Mumua rang out right above their heads, startling Toni and Bean. She stood over Toni's shoulder. He leaped forward and spun around, poised for another wrestling match. Mumua's black hair dangled in her face as she shook anxiously in her orange dress and bare feet. She still clutched the wooden spoon.

Bean, now in between Mumua and Toni, tried to sit up. Sensing Toni's defenses still were on high alert, Bean spoke up.

"Toni, it's okay. She means no harm."

Toni watched her every move. After a short pause, Mumua slowly knelt down and patted Bean's ankle, acknowledging his wound. Then shaking the spoon to her left, she screeched and made more odd noises. She seemed to point the way they should go. Toni was confused by her weird body language and gestures.

"Help me up, man. I think she is saying we're close," Bean said.

Mumua vanished again, leaving them behind. Toni bent over and lifted Bean up from his back, grabbing him under the arms. As Bean got his balance, Toni reached down and jerked the dagger out of the dog's chest. He wiped it off on a dry part of the dog's fur and then put it back in Bean's pack. He secured the backpack onto Bean, threw Bean's left arm over his shoulder, and helped Bean carry on after Mumua.

"I think I know who spooked the horses...and it wasn't her," Bean joked.

CHAPTER NINETEEN

The remaining trek through wetlands, up big hills, and down through tall grasses was approximately two miles long. It felt extra long and arduous to Bean and Toni who were in great pain and near exhaustion. Mumua would come in and out of view as she led them through the foreign terrain. Any odd sound of an animal or bird startled Bean, now feeling unable to defend himself. Toni staunchly aided Bean with each step despite his own suffering.

"Did you see the evil in their eyes?" Toni asked Bean, referring to the vicious dogs.

Remembering the big dog on top of him, Bean responded, "Yeah." And then he added, "It spoke to me."

"What do you mean?"

"It did. It said: 'Your blood line ends here' or something."

Toni stopped walking. "I think they were skin-walkers. Humans who, through a séance or witch's spell, can turn into an animal."

"Really? Like they were the same ones back at the village bonfire earlier tonight?"

"Quite possibly."

"They were haunting and hunting us," Bean said. "Not sure why."

"Yes. Maybe protecting something."

They continued on. Bean's mind went back to the blazing bonfire where the people chanted odd melodies and from where the possessed dogs emerged. He recalled Draug's séance and drawing blood from his forearm. He looked down at his left arm to see the small scar inside his elbow. Bean thought of what Canaima and the area was named for, having the *spirit of evil*. He remembered what Captain Sevilla said on the flight over about the mountain Auyan-tepui being the "mountain of the God of evil." The eeriness was freaking him out. He desperately wanted to wake up from this nightmare, but not without his dad.

Abruptly, Toni nudged Bean. "Look, over there!"

A small human figure had just crossed a rickety bridge, heading toward a small square orange light, that could hardly be seen from atop the hill they were standing on. The two could barely track her.

"Let's go, we can't lose her," Toni said.

With Toni's assistance, the two hurried down the slope and made their way through some tall grasses. Parting the grass, they came to a small opening that led to an old wooden bridge. They could see a light coming from a hut like structure about fifty yards away. The silhouette of Mumua stood in front of the lit doorway. Bean froze.

"Could that be Ramona's hut?" he whispered.

They could hear the rushing of water. "It must be, gringo. Let's go," Toni said with some impatience.

They advanced to the bridge, almost completely out of energy.

"Whoa," said Bean as he glanced over the edge of the bank. He hated heights. It was probably a steep thirty-foot drop into a raging river. The river was fifty feet wide. The two wearied companions examined the dilapidated bridge in front of them. It was very narrow, with planks only two feet wide, with about a foot separating each from the next. It had some broken planks too. The rope-like handrails appeared worn, weak and weathered. It didn't seem very sturdy, so they decided to go one at a time.

"You go first, Toni," Bean insisted.

After assessing the situation, Toni removed the backpack from Bean's shoulder and somehow added it to his equipment. He grabbed both sides of the rope rails and stepped onto the first plank of the wobbly bridge. After all his weight was on the bridge, he looked more confident, though Bean continued to watch in distress.

Toni looked back at Bean. "Use the hand rails as crutches for support. Then you only need to put your right foot down,"

Bean nodded, acknowledging his advice. Toni turned around and proceeded cautiously to the other side. Bean was impressed with how quick Toni got across.

Bean limped to the edge of the bridge and grabbed both rope rails. He identified the first plank to land on. He looked over at Toni across the bridge, now a shadowy image against a gray background. Then he glanced beyond Toni to the lit doorway of Ramona's dwelling. "I am so close. I've come so far. I'm gonna find you, dad," Bean said to himself. Bean made the first hoist. I did it! I've got this. Very carefully, he did it again.

Bean was just over halfway across the bridge when it trembled a little. The rope handrail in his right hand was vibrating. Not understanding what was happening, he tightened his grip and secured his stance. He shimmied forward another two planks and secured himself again. The shaking became more violent, moving the bridge up and down. He could hardly hang on.

"Toni, what's going on?" Bean yelled.

Toni looked past Bean. His whole body stiffened, and he cupped his hands to yell, "Come on, Gringo, hurry!"

Still unaware of the threat, Bean made another attempt, catapulting himself forward three planks. Getting his grip and balance, he did it again. But he had to rest his fatigued muscles, still with the bridge shaking. His ankle was hurting bad. That's when he looked up at Toni again.

Toni had unloaded the packs from his shoulders and unveiled a bow. He took a few steps to his right, trying to get the best angle for the shot. He bent one knee down and pulled an arrow from the quiver. He nocked the arrow, drew it back, then held himself stable on the other knee. Toni was aiming at something behind Bean. Curious, Bean turned halfway around to see Toni's target.

The skin-walker had followed them. The possessed dog was angrily gnawing and clawing at the rope rail on the other end. The worn rope was down to its last few weaves. Bean had to hurry, or he'd be drowning in the raging river beneath him. He turned back around with new energy and determination. As Bean hoisted himself forward another two planks, he heard the whiz of an arrow zip past him to the left. After a short pause, the bridge began to tremble again.

Dang, he must've missed! Bean concluded.

Bean had six more planks to go until he reached the other side. He glanced over at Toni as he was nocking another arrow. To his alarm, Mumua stood directly behind Toni, holding a large rock high above her head with both hands.

"Watch out!" Bean hollered. Toni turned, but too late. Mumua struck Toni hard and squarely on the back of the head with the rock. Toni collapsed and fell forward over his knees, limp and motionless.

"No! Toni!" Bean glanced back at the dog trying to cut the bridge's rope. It was clawing with much less force and vigor. Bean could see the shaft of an arrow lodged in its hind leg. Toni didn't miss, but Bean knew the integrity of the rope couldn't last much longer. He had to hurry.

Bean advanced another two planks.

Snap!

The rope handrail snapped and ripped past Bean's head. Like a giant slingshot, the right side of the flimsy bridge flung up and back down, ripping planks out and twisting the loose rope around the left side. Bean clung on for his life until the bridge settled and unraveled itself. He didn't dare move yet.

The skin-walker laughed maniacally. Bean slowly lifted his head to see the possessed mutt enjoying the peril it put Bean in. It began to claw at the other side of the rope rail. With his weight and more pressure on that side of the bridge, Bean knew it wouldn't be long until it snapped too, and he'd fall into the river below.

Bean held on tight, ignoring the pain, knowing his hands were turning raw. He wanted to blow the whistle. He could be rescued. But he didn't want to see Draug. And he certainly didn't want to set back the progress he had made, after being so close to Ramona's hut. Bean decided to move forward one plank.

"Just three more planks and I will be across," he gasped. "...And Toni needs me." He advanced another plank. He anticipated the weak bridge collapsing. As the bridge shook, he carefully lowered himself down to the planks, lying on his stomach. He began to army crawl, moving up one plank. "Just one more and I'm there."

Snap!

The left hand rail now busted and again flung the bridge up and down, twisting the bridge around itself. Bean hung on only because he got entangled in the snarled planks and rope. His right foot got caught between another plank. He was now upside down, with the river rushing beneath him.

"Your bloodline ends here!" the skin-walker roared.

Bean heard the familiar taunt. He wasn't fazed. He knew he had a mission to fulfill, and conquering this obstacle was just part of the path. He started to unlatch his foot and let his body swing down, intending to walk up the side of the riverbank. Just as he did, the dog pounced on the first plank, trying to throw Bean off. Bean's legs swung down and crashed into the dirt wall. But still, he hung on.

With all his strength, he pulled himself up, using his right foot as a support against the dirt bank wall. He fought through the sway of the bridge, and now clung on to the rope anchored into the ground on the other side. With one leg, he pushed himself off the last plank and onto the other side of the river. Bean crossed the bridge.

"Toni!" he cried out, not taking much time to consider what he just overcame. On his hands and knees, he crawled as fast as he could over to where Toni was. But Toni's body was gone. "Toni! Mumua!"

No reply. Bean spun around, trying to figure out where Toni had gone. There was no sign of Mumua either, but their packs, gear, and other things were there. Then he saw the skin-walker on the other side of the riverbank, pacing back and forth. They made eye contact.

"He's dead you fool! And soon you'll be too!" it taunted.

Bean didn't respond. Instead, he grabbed the bow and nocked an arrow. Bean and his dad only bow hunted twice, but they practiced every summer, and Bean was a decent shot. He raised the bow and tried to aim it at his enemy. But the skin-walker had vanished into the dark.

Succumbing to utter exhaustion, Bean dropped to the ground. After a brief moment, he gained some air back in his lungs, but desperately needed water. He needed medical attention too. He grabbed their equipment and slowly lugged it to the base of a nearby tree, thirty feet from the hut's entry. Bean looked down at his wrist and read the time. It was 2:22am.

The light was still on inside the hut and now he could see smoke coiling in the air above it. The hut sat at the base of a big, dome-like hill, like the entry to a gigantic igloo. Bean noticed a few large trees around the hut. He reached up and grabbed its fruit. *The cashew trees,* Bean thought. *Am I really here?*

Almost totally numb from all the pain, lack of energy, danger, and dehydration, Bean hobbled toward the lit doorway like a zombie. When he got to about ten feet from the door, a figure appeared from the inside. As it began to take shape, Bean could tell it was a taller woman with extra-long, wavy hair. Bean stopped.

"Bean the Whistler, is that you?" the woman asked in the softest of tones.

Bean's dry mouth and physical condition made it hard to speak. "Yes..." He gulped and responded, "Ramona? Are you Ramona?"

"Yes, that is the correct code word. I've been expecting you, Bean. Please come forth," the woman said warmly.

Bean hopped forward. The woman stepped backward into the hut. Bean followed and limped inside. The lighting was so bright, Bean was blinded. "Wha...where's Toni?"

"Please, sit down," the woman said as she handed him a cup of water. "You must be thirsty."

Still unable to make out anything around him because of the strong illumination, he felt around and stumbled into a reclined chair of bamboo. He took a huge sip of water. Then another and finished the cup. He shut his eyes and inhaled deeply.

"Bean, can I heal you?" she asked as she gently placed a blanket over Bean. Bean nodded affirmatively, still with his eyes closed. His young battered body had been through more than he ever expected. Feeling the healing had already begun, he surrendered to the stranger. Soon Bean fell into a deep sleep.

CHAPTER TWENTY

"Bean, Bean," his hostess whispered closely in his ear. Bean moved and turned onto his side. "It's time, Bean." Bean cracked open an eyelid. She waited patiently for Bean to fully awake from the trance-like slumber he was in. Bean rubbed his eyes with both hands like a young child from a nap, and then sat up. The woman watched as he gradually came to.

Bean still wasn't totally coherent. He turned his head to the right, then slowly back to the left to observe his new surroundings. The empty space and the high-pitched ceiling gave the hut a wide-open feel. The lighting wasn't as bright as it was when he entered earlier. A small fire burned in a raised, stone altar at the center of the room.

"How do you feel?" the woman asked.

Bean was well rested. He had no idea how long he had been asleep. It seemed like he had slept in like he used to do on Sunday mornings back home. He stroked his arms and legs, then checked the time on his wristwatch. It read

5:48am. His recollection of the previous night's events came into focus. He noticed his shoes were off.

He remembered the dogs. He moved his left ankle. There was no pain or any kind of tenderness. He pulled up his pants leg to find a wide, jagged M-shaped scar stretched across his ankle and lower leg, but it was fully healed. Grateful, he looked up and was stunned to see the angelic being now in front of him.

Struggling to utter the words, Bean finally answered, "Good. I mean, great actually. I feel great."

The woman in a long yellow-and-black spotted leopard print gown smiled at him. Bean rubbed his eyes again. Although well aged, the woman's beauty and majestic aura was mesmerizing. Her hair was long, wavy, and shimmered with a golden hue. Her green eyes glistened as the light from the fire reflected off them. Her cheekbones were high and defined her trim, pale face. Her lips were full. She stood about Bean's height.

As if sensing her effect on the young man, she answered Bean's next question before he could even ask it. "I am Anomar. I am not an angel, but rather a witch."

"A witch?" Bean asked.

She closed her catlike eyes, grinned, and nodded. "You have no need to fear me. I am indebted to you."

"Indebted to...me?" Bean asked with a dozen questions racing through his mind. "What did I do for you?"

"You risked your life and came all this way to bring me the wooden ladle. For this, I will repay you greatly."

"The ladle?" Bean tried hard to put it all together. "The ladle...was special?"

Anomar answered, "Yes, the ladle is very powerful, and I am its rightful heiress. Anything I stir and brew with it while chanting the correct spell shall come to pass. I can now fulfill my calling as the Queen of Hutoriane."

Really? That wooden spoon? Bean thought. *Why did Draug even have it?* He spoke up, "What about Mumua? And where is Toni?"

"You followed *me* here. I was Mumua. I've been under a curse for generations," she said. "The people of Kavak know Mumua as the dumb orphan who lost her grandmother, and never knew her mother."

Satisfied with that answer, but now defensive and concerned for Toni, Bean asked,

"Where is Toni? What did you do to him?"

"He is in a deep sleep, resting, healing, and recharging like you were."

Bean was getting upset and stood up. He was about to look around for him when Anomar gently put her hand with claw-like fingernails on his right shoulder and asked, "Who is Toni?"

"Uh..." Bean wasn't sure how to respond.

"Draug didn't mention you'd have a companion."

"I met him on the way here. He has protected me and helped me get here. He's my friend," Bean said, surprising himself with the truth of his words.

Anomar stared off into the burning fire over Bean's shoulder. "Bean, we don't have much time. They are coming for you."

"Who? More dogs?"

"Kele and the cazadors, or hunters," she said.

"Why are they coming for *me* and how do they know where I am?"

"Fichu informed them. You killed Moa last night."

Bean was beside himself. "But it was a dog, not a human."

"It was Moa. I can explain that later. Quick, grab the scroll." Anomar handed Bean his backpack.

Bean pulled out the leather scroll. "Open it and lay it out here," she said pointing to a small wooden table. "I don't understand," Bean said nervously as he carefully unraveled the scroll. "Draug sent me here to give you a wooden ladle..."

"And in turn, I will interpret the map and help you finish your mission," Anomar said as she waved the spoon over the map's surface. She closed her eyes, and then waved back over the map in the opposite direction with her left hand.

The map seemed to glow again to Bean. Having seen it three times, he reviewed out loud what he saw. Bean pointed to the left corner of the map and said, "This circle-X symbol represents Hutoriane and its four dimensions, right? And this big picture in the middle of the scroll is...well I'm not sure, but some kind of map? And the Indian writing over here to the far right...do you know what it says?"

Anomar watched with some amusement as Bean stumbled through his explanation of the leather scroll. "The language here to the right is ancient. It is not Pemón, but rather Muellaman. Still, I can read and understand it, because my grandparents were Muellaman."

Bean was anxious to know what the writing said. But the word "Muellaman" sounded very familiar to him. He remembered some of the history Toni gave him back in Ciudad Bolívar, at the street café. "Muellama? Where is the Muellama tribe from?" he asked.

"The tribe originates deep in the Andes Mountains, in what is now the country of Ecuador." Anomar's answer confirmed Bean's hunch.

"So how did you end up here in Canaima?" Bean asked.

"It's a long tale. But a few of my ancestors were told to leave the tribe and take with them a very sacred item called the platinum sphere. They were led here by the sphere, and buried it there," Anomar gravely explained as she pointed to a tree-like image on the map. "This is where you are headed."

Bean's jaw dropped, and eyes widened. "How far is it from here? Is my dad there?"

"It's about ten miles from here through rivers, caves, forests, and up the mountain. Only you will know where it is precisely," Anomar said as Bean listened intently. "It is located in the center of the heart of Hutoriane," she added as she outlined a heart-shaped area with her long index finger. "Also known as Auyan-tepui, or 'house of the devil' as the locals call it."

Bean gulped. "Devil's house? Is my dad there?"

"No, Bean. Your dad is not there," Anomar answered impatiently. "Your mission is to obtain the platinum sphere and get it to Draug," she explained. "Then Draug will help you get your dad."

Overwhelmed with anxiety, Bean slumped down onto the bunk next to the map. *Oh my gosh, I am supposed to get the kuakilla or platinum sphere*, Bean thought. Never in his life did he feel so conflicted. He desperately wanted to find his father. Yet, he knew Toni desperately wanted the platinum sphere for his own purpose. He could sense the two causes would intersect in the near future and knew it wouldn't end well.

"Bean, what's the matter?" Anomar asked noticing Bean's distress.

"What does it say? The ancient writing?" Bean demanded.

Anomar read over the writing on the map, sliding her finger over each phrase. "When the angel ascends, the demons shall rise. If the angel falls, the demons will reign," she said slowly.

Bean repeated what she said out loud twice, trying to commit the phrase to memory. He heard it similarly from Draug and from Toni. "Well, what does it mean?" he asked.

"I'm not completely sure. Only you will know the full meaning as it unfolds to you," Anomar said. "Lie down again and take my right hand," she directed Bean. "I will show you the course you should traverse to obtain the platinum sphere."

Bean lay down and trusted her. Anomar set the wooden spoon on the table. She put her left hand on the big image in the center of the scroll. "Close your eyes. I will show you in your mind." Then she closed her eyes too and began to hum.

In an instant, Bean couldn't move. Just like when Draug performed his ceremony, Bean was totally alert and aware but could not move a muscle. However, this time he could feel. Anomar squeezed his hand tightly. Suddenly, an electric current ran up his arm, through his entire body, up his spine, and into his brain. It wasn't a shocking sensation, but rather warm and tingly. It was as if Anomar was downloading the data from the map into her being and then transmitting it straight to Bean's mind.

Eyes closed, Bean felt like he was watching his own action movie in fast forward. Bean saw flashes of himself in a canoe floating up a black river. He was spelunking through caves and mysterious dark passages. He was trudging through a thick rain forest and then up a steep mountain side, all the while avoiding unknown conflicts seemingly at every turn. All of a sudden, the movie stopped and Anomar fell to her knees drained from the transmission. Her hand loosened its grip and dropped to her side. Bean's muscles soon regained their strength and responsiveness.

"Anomar! Are you okay?" Bean asked with concern as he sat up. "What's wrong?"

"Bean, the ending, isn't good," Anomar reluctantly replied.

"What happens?" he asked.

"I can't say." She started to regain her strength.

"Do I die?"

"I don't know. The ending got blurry and then went... cold...and black," she said grimly.

Bean sat still in thought. "I miss my dad. He's counting on me."

"Bean! I hear the dogs! They are close!" Anomar's warning scared Bean, disrupting his pensive pause. "You need to get moving! And I do too."

Bean looked up in terror. "Okay. Okay. This is what I came for. My shoes! Where are my shoes? And Toni! Where is Toni?"

Anomar rolled her big green eyes in annoyance. "The discussion we've had is very private, Bean. Do not divulge it to anyone, especially Toni."

"I won't," Bean promised as he tied his hiking boots. He knew he couldn't tell Toni anyway.

"Toni is waiting for you through that back door." She motioned over at a dark brown, wooden door shaped like a giant football. "He has all your other things."

"Oh good," Bean said with some relief. He was glad Toni was okay and knew he would need his help.

"Here, take these," Anomar said while handing him three flasks of odd pink liquid. "Drink them when you get tired or hungry or think you can't go on. They are pure energy."

"I love energy drinks!" Bean said lightheartedly, trying to ignore his mounting anxiety. "Anything else?"

Anomar paused and then took a step closer to Bean. She stared at Bean and he could see his reflection in her eyes like small mirrors.

"Bean, you are the Whistler of Hutoriane." Bean was listening but could now hear dogs barking and men yelling in the not-too-distant background. "The whistle in your pocket responds to only you. That is how you summoned Draug. But there is more to learn with the whistle."

"More...as in what?" he asked.

"More melodies and more powers," she answered. "Learn it masterfully."

"Okay, I will try," Bean said. The incessant barking and yelling were now upon them.

"If you succeed in getting the sacred platinum sphere to Draug, you will be the most beloved entity in all of Hutoriane." She gently kissed him on the forehead. "And you will be reunited with your father."

Bean smiled with newfound hope and courage. He picked up his backpack and dashed for the back door excited to see Toni.

～～ CHAPTER ～～ TWENTY-ONE

Bean cranked open the door, stepped through its threshold, and then slammed the door behind him. There he stood in a pitch black, hollowed-out tunnel. The air was muggy. Water trickled somewhere.

"Toni? Psst! Toni!" Bean took a few cautious steps forward. He couldn't see anything in front of him. He extended both arms and felt the earthy walls on either side of him. "Toni!" He took another step. "Toni!" He slipped as the ground sloped beneath him.

Bean yelled as he rapidly slid down, twisting and winding like he did on water slide rides back home. Seconds later, Bean dropped into a shallow pool of water and rolled over and over until he came to stop.

"Ha, gringo!" Toni laughed uncharacteristically. "Nice landing! Muy bien!"

Bean got to his feet, regained his balance from the dizziness, and wiped his eyes. Toni stood next to a canoe close by on the side of a wide, slow-moving river. In the early morning light, he appeared more muscular than ever.

"Hey man!" Bean walked over and started to put his arm around Toni.

"Whoa, whoa, boy," Toni said, awkwardly backing out of Bean's hug. "Good to see you, but no hugging please."

"Okay, man," Bean chuckled. "I'm glad to see you're okay. I thought you might be dead! You took quite a hit to the head."

Toni glared at Bean. "Nah, chico, you think I'm gonna go that easy? I have a mission to complete."

Bean immediately felt uneasy as he was reminded that they shared the same mission. "That's right. To protect me, right?"

"Of course, gringo. Now let's get going," Toni said.

"Yeah, let's get going.... but to where though, Toni?" Bean asked, testing Toni further.

"Amigo, you know, don't you?" Toni asked.

Bean stood still for a minute. He looked around as if to completely soak in the environment. The forest was thick on both sides of the river, and some trees were enormously tall. The air was damp. Birds chirped close by along with an occasional cry of other creatures. The smell was fishy, similar to the pond by his house back home. Anomar assured him that with the course he took, each step of the way would be unfolded to him. He glanced down at the canoe.

"Let's take the canoe upstream, that way," Bean said with some authority. He started to remember Anomar's mental transmission of the map.

"Makes sense to me," Toni agreed.

They loaded their things and pushed the wooden dugout canoe into a calmer part of the river. They each grabbed a paddle.

"You first this time," Toni said.

Bean carefully got in while Toni pushed the canoe a little more out into water up to his waist. Then he climbed in too and they were off.

Both Bean and Toni enjoyed the indescribable serenity canoeing down the river in a foreign tropical land. It was a surreal paradise, something Bean only saw in movies. The different sounds of animals awakening to the new day could be heard on both sides of the river. The two kept a steady rhythm in their oar strokes, alternating sides of the canoe while each maintained opposing positions.

Toni broke the silence. "So, do you know what happened to me?"

Sitting in front, Bean didn't have to make eye contact with Toni but did have to speak up. "I saw Mumua hit you over the head with a large rock. Do you remember that?"

"No. I just remember you were having trouble crossing the bridge."

"That's all I know," Bean said. "Did you meet anyone?"

"Yeah. An exotic-looking, older woman woke me up, healed my wounds, and gave me water. I wasn't totally awake when she shoved me through the door this morning."

"Oh really?"

"Yes."

"And you fell down the waterslide tunnel too?"

"Yes."

Bean laughed. "Like she flushed you down a big toilet?"

"I guess."

"And you fell into a shallow pool of water?"

"Yes."

"That's too funny. I guess that woke you up pretty good?"

"Yes."

"Dang, I wish I saw that." Bean laughed harder. "You knew what it felt like first!"

"Yeah, and then she threw our things down too. Was it Ramona?" Toni asked.

Bean stopped laughing. He carefully thought about how to respond. "Probably."

"You met with her then? How was it?"

"It went okay."

"Did she give you more information about the mission?"

"Yeah, but I told you before that it was private."

"No, you just didn't want me there during your meeting."

"Same thing, man."

"Bean, I need to know."

"Know what?"

"If you're the chosen one...to lead me to the kuakilla."

Bean didn't know what to do. He was an honest young man. He also didn't want to have conflict with Toni, not because he was a fierce fighter. Rather, he regarded Toni as a friend. He wasn't sure how Toni would respond.

"Gringo..."

"I don't know if I'm the chosen one," Bean answered with some impatience. "What does that even mean?" Bean remembered Draug calling him the chosen one too. The phrase annoyed him. He just wanted his normal life back.

"The esfera platina...the platinum sphere...the platinum moon...the kuakilla!" Toni raised his voice. "Did she mention it?"

"I can't say!" Bean matched his intensity.

The tension in the canoe rose, higher than ever between the two. Suddenly, two big splashes came on the right of their boat. Something large had entered the river. The swells from the splash quickly rippled outward and toward the canoe.

"Hang on,"Toni cried. "The canoe can tip over!"

Bean pulled his paddle in and held tightly to each side of the canoe. The two watched as the swells widened the closer they came. Balancing their weight, Bean and Toni sat nervously in the center of the canoe.

"Holy cow! Do you see that, man?" Bean yelled as a gigantic, dark creature surfaced to the top of the water and skimmed along parallel to the canoe twenty feet away.

"Yes. Hang on tight. Keep steady."

Another large seal-like animal surfaced and swam in sync behind its companion. The once smooth river around them swayed the canoe up and down. Bean and Toni found the rhythm with the swells and actually enjoyed the ride.

They watched as the creatures swiftly swam by. One disappeared and then resurfaced, wrestling with some object. They eventually made their way to the other side of the river. One after the other climbed onto the river bank.

"I think they're otters," said Toni.

"Huge otters," Bean added in amazement.

The second one had a long, slimy snake or eel in its mouth. The leader turned around and tag-teamed the wiggly reptile, pouncing on its other end. Bean watched as the giant otters enjoyed their breakfast.

With their attention still on the giant otters, Bean and Toni put their oar back in the muddy water and resumed their pace. Although one otter made the catch, both otters reaped the benefits of their teamwork. Bean was enlightened by his observation.

Turning toward Toni, Bean said in a calmer tone, "Yes, she spoke of the platinum sphere. But I still don't know much about it."

Toni's stiff posture eased, and his uptight face softened. Bean could sense this news added confirmation to Toni's purpose, not just coming from the lore of his grandfather. Bean faced the front again.

A few seconds later, Toni spoke up. "I'm not sure how it works either. My grandfather told me some, but it was mostly mythical to him."

"You think it's important enough to risk your life for?"

"That's what I was taught and raised for. My people sacrificed all they had to get me here. Yes, it is my destiny and obligation to obtain the kuakilla."

"And then what?"

Toni was quiet again. "Restore my people to their rightful inheritance."

"Inheritance," Bean repeated. "What is that? You need the kuakilla to do that?" Toni didn't respond. "Well for me, I just want my dad back. He's my best friend."

"Your father...did Ramona talk about him?"

"No."

"You thought she would, right?"

"Yeah, but I was wrong."

Toni sounded concerned. "Did that Draug guy tell you she would?"

"Not exactly. I was just hoping so. They need me to complete the mission and then he'll help me get my dad back."

"And your mission then is to obtain the kuakilla or platinum sphere too?" Toni asked.

"I think so," Bean responded casually. Oddly enough, he was glad Toni now knew. He didn't have to hide it anymore, even though he was nervous how it would all unfold. He was still confident Toni needed him more than he needed Toni though. The canoe went quiet again for a long while.

CHAPTER TWENTY-TWO

The dawn produced a bright orange sky which lit up the top of the lush green jungle treeline. Rising thousands of feet above and behind the jungle was the steep rock background of Auyan-tepui. Bean and Toni traveled in a northwest direction, the meandering river carried them closer and closer to the base of the mountain.

Bean stopped rowing to rest and soak in the majestic beauty of the natural wonders all around him. He tilted his head back on his shoulders and tried to find the top of the towering mountain they'd soon be ascending. But the misty clouds hugging the mountainside were too thick to see through.

"Wow, this place is magnificent," Bean remarked. "I'd love to show my family." Toni stopped rowing too. They both sat still as their canoe glided forward.

"Toni, do you have any brothers or sisters?"

"I have a younger sister who stayed in Ecuador with my uncle's family," Toni said. "And had an older brother who got sick and passed away when we were young."

"Aw, sad. Do you talk much with your sister?"

"No." After a brief pause, Toni asked, "Do you have a brother or sister?"

"Yeah, two younger sisters. I miss them. I mean, we were supposed to be gone a few days anyway, but if they only knew what has happened to me and where I've been and all..."

"What do you mean? They knew you were leaving them?"

"Well, yeah. My dad and I were gone for the hunt," Bean said. "Every year my dad and I go deer hunting. This time, I lost him...or actually, he lost me. But they aren't expecting us back until tomorrow night."

Toni sat quietly in thought. "I think I would like to hunt."

"You totally would! When we get out of this mess, you need to come visit me in Utah. Then we'll go hunting."

"I'd like that, but I have too much work to do for my people," Toni said.

"What kind of work? I mean, you don't talk to your own sister, so why do you care for all the others?" Bean asked. Toni didn't respond for a while.

"You were hunting, then lost your dad...so how did you meet Draug?" Toni asked after a few minutes.

Now Bean didn't respond. He didn't want to give any more information. The sounds of the jungle were none that either was used to. They would paddle a few strokes, and then coast, allowing the river to carry them along. They didn't talk for about twenty minutes. The silence grew uncomfortable for Bean. Suddenly, they could hear the familiar sound of dogs barking in the distant background behind them.

Alarmed, Bean sat up. "Did I mention that Kele is after us with his men?"

"Kele? No, how do you know?" Toni asked.

"Anomar told me. And I could hear yelling and dogs barking outside the hut right before I left through the back door."

"Are you serious? And who is Anomar?"

"Yeah. Anomar must have hid her secret passage from them, or else they'd be right on our tail."

"Who is Anomar? You never tell me enough!" Toni said impatiently.

"Sorry, man. I think she is the same person as Ramona and Mumua."

Toni shook his head and sighed. "I am so confused. But yes, that must be Kele and his men. They can't be too far behind us. Why are they pursuing us?"

Bean felt uneasy for leaving out this big detail too. "I guess Fichu and Moa were the dogs that attacked us last night. Anomar called them skin-walkers. I killed Moa, so that's probably why."

"Wow," Toni said with more confusion. "But they wanted to kill us first. So, I don't understand. And skin-walkers? My grandfather spoke of skin-walkers in ancient times."

They paddled with more urgency. Bean noticed the canoe was moving faster in the river's current. "Uh, Toni, the river is speeding up," Bean said nervously.

"This isn't good. We need to paddle hard to the left. I see a big fallen tree over there," Toni said with his usual poise. "Let's try and get lodged into it to stop us."

The two paddled forcefully, but the river's current intensified. The river doubled in width about three hundred yards up ahead, and the horizon seemed to drop off. They advanced quickly. With the river widening, they made minimal progress to the left side and knew they wouldn't get there in time. Closing fast, they could see beyond the falls. The river seemed to bend to the left with the illusion of trees on top of the horizon now, directly in front of them.

"Bean, we are going over. I don't think it's a huge drop," Toni said.

Bean was terrified. "Okay," he answered with eyes wide and bracing himself. He felt for the whistle in the right pocket of his pants. It was there if he needed it.

"Secure your things at your feet and beneath your seat."

"Okay."

"Keep the canoe as straight as possible," Toni directed. "Steady, steady." They were now fifty feet from their doom. Bean couldn't speak. "Pull your paddle in and put it across your lap. Evenly!"

Bean obeyed in time. Before they knew it, their canoe took flight over the falls. Bean screamed. In one fell swoop, both guys were tossed from the canoe and crashed into the water. Luckily, the drop was only ten feet high. The raging water spun them around like clothes in a washing machine. Bean was spit out and popped up to the surface. With a mouthful of water, trying to catch his breath, he gagged and coughed. Treading to stay afloat, he frantically looked around for Toni.

"Toni!" Bean called out. There was no response. With his pursuers in mind, Bean was nervous to call out too loud and often. Toni was nowhere to be seen. But to Bean's surprise, he saw the canoe only twenty-five feet away from him floating upright. *The backpack. Oh no!* He swam hard toward the canoe. The experience reminded him of scout camp and trying to swim in all his clothes for the swimming merit badge.

Reaching the side of the canoe, Bean called out for Toni again. Still no sign of him. He hoisted himself up with both hands high enough to look inside the canoe. There was the backpack, stuck under his front seat but soaked and sitting in about five inches of water at the bottom of the canoe. He also saw another package somehow secured to Toni's backseat. Everything else was gone. He lowered himself back into the water.

The water from the falls pooled creating a calm lagoon in the middle of the jungle. A portion of the river continued to the right and then curved back to the left toward the mountain. It also thinned out to approximately sixty feet wide. The river's current slowed down as Bean and the canoe floated along quietly.

Bean hated the idea of what creatures might be in the river with him, whether it was a hungry crocodile or angry piranhas or water snakes. But he knew he shouldn't get back in the canoe without a paddle. He didn't want to go aimlessly down the river without the ability to steer. Clinging to one side of the canoe, he could only see part of the river—the side away from the rocky mountain wall. The dark brown river made it hard to identify anything with a similar color.

Just as he was about to try and maneuver to the other side of the canoe to search for the paddles, Bean heard the dogs barking again. This time they were much closer. He stopped and held on, trying not to move a muscle or make a sound. He knew the canoe would be visible to any onlooker. *I'm a sitting duck. I need to get out of the river, with my backpack. But I don't want the backpack getting wetter, and how am I even gonna swim with it?*

"Por allá, una canoa!" a man's voice cried out clearly.

Dang, they see the canoe. I'm a dead man. He examined the river bank to his right, the only side he could see. He couldn't spot the group yet. *They're probably on the other side, close to the mountain.* Bean decided to pull the whole canoe with him and make a push for the river bank on the right.

More yells, dogs barking, and commotion echoed across the river. He'd chosen the correct side. But pulling the canoe with his left arm while kicking his feet and stroking the water with his right arm was extremely difficult. He was running out of energy fast and couldn't tell if he made any progress. Then, out of nowhere, Toni's face slowly rose out the river.

"Pssst," Toni shocked Bean as he busily pulled the canoe. "Let go of the canoe."

"Toni!" Bean exclaimed in a loud whisper, relieved to see him. "I can't. My backpack is still inside it and you have something too."

Toni latched on to the canoe and joined Bean in pulling it to the side. They had about twenty feet more. Although they remained hidden from view, Bean was certain their enemies had noticed the canoe bobbing and making its way in the opposite direction toward the riverbank. The men started yelling again.

Boom...boom...boom! Three shots fired.

Two bullets struck chunks off the wooden canoe.

"They're shooting at us!" Bean cried, panicked. "We need to hurry."

Every thirty seconds, three of four shots went off. Some bullets hit the canoe, some the water around them, and some whizzed overhead. Now about ten feet away from the bush-filled riverbank, Bean's feet could touch the mushy river bottom.

"I'm gonna tilt the canoe over so you can grab your pack," Toni said.

"Okay," Bean nodded at Toni to go ahead.

Toni reached up and pulled the canoe on its side, enough for Bean to reach in but high enough to keep the water from rushing in. Bean yanked his backpack out and put his arms through the straps. Next, Bean held the canoe down at the same angle for Toni. But the knot holding the bow and quiver to the seat was wet and too difficult for Toni to untie. Bean reached into his pocket and passed Toni his knife. Toni began cutting the knot when three more shots rang out.

Wood sprayed, and Bean felt a sharp pain in his chest just below his shoulder and collarbone. He let out a short cry. The strap on his backpack snapped and Bean lost control of his right arm, letting go of the canoe.

"Bean!" Toni yelled as he finally cut his bow loose. The canoe bounced back over and wobbled on the roiling water. "Hang on." Toni put the bow over his right shoulder. "I'm gonna get you out of here!"

"Toni, it hurts. I'm bleeding pretty bad." Bean whimpered as he covered the wound with his hand.

"I have you," said Toni. He helped Bean trudge through the shallow water, trying to stay low and behind the canoe.

Two vicious dogs were swimming closer. Toni affixed Bean between some low hanging branches, and then pushed the canoe out away from their wooded refuge on the side of the river. Hidden behind some huge fern leaves, Toni ripped out his bow and quiver. With expert precision, he shot each dog in the forehead, and each sank like sand bags.

Kele's men were quiet on the other side of the river. Toni and Bean were still undetected by them. Bean was propped up over a log and stared over the moving water in shock. He saw Toni unzip his backpack and find the red healing cloth. He tightly wrapped it under Bean's armpit and over his shoulder diagonally, covering the bullet wound.

More shots were fired. Toni looked back and located one shooter across the river mounted over a downed tree. He nocked an arrow, arched the bow for some loft, aimed, and then let the arrow fly. The arrow struck the shooter knocking him to the ground. Some men rushed over to aid him and that was Toni's window to move Bean inland.

Toni threw his things up on the side into the bushes. Swiftly, he got behind Bean and lifted him up out of the water, Bean assisting a little with his legs. Toni carried Bean about thirty feet into the damp jungle floor. They were well out of view from their enemies, concealing themselves under some very thick, dark green forest undergrowth. They'd be safe for a few minutes.

CHAPTER TWENTY-THREE

"I can't move my arm," Bean said, severely weakened from the loss of blood.

"Lay down. I need to get the bullet out of you," Toni said.

As he lay on the ground, the trees above Bean appeared to spin around like a merry-go-round. He could hardly think straight, but he remembered feeling the same dizziness at a doctor's office once when getting a shot. They gave him juice then. "Juice," Bean said in a shaky voice. "I need juice."

"Juice? What do you mean? We don't have juice," Toni said.

"Anomar...gave me some juice. In my pack," Bean could hardly speak.

Toni ripped open Bean's backpack and fished around until he drew out a corked plastic test tube with pink liquid inside. "This?" Toni said as he held it in front of Bean's face.

Bean nodded, "Yeah."

Toni plucked off the corked top, then put the clear bottle up to Bean's lips. Carefully, he poured all of it into his mouth. Bean closed his eyes and swallowed the pink fluid. He recharged as Toni assessed their surroundings and tried to listen for any sound or movement of their assailants.

Toni army crawled over to retrieve his bow and quiver a dozen feet away. Bean watched as Toni parted some large fern leaves and peaked through to get a visual across the river. From Toni's calm posturing, it seemed to Bean that the men had disappeared.

Tracking Toni, Bean saw him turn to the right and follow the river's curve around to the left until he disappeared into the dense forest. With Toni out of sight, Bean felt uneasy and sat up. He observed that the river reappeared a ways down leading back toward the mountain. In the distance, he recognized an enormous black cave at the base of the mountain wall.

To Bean's surprise, he felt a surge in energy. He decided to get moving. He found Toni and snuck up behind him. "That's the spot," Bean whispered in Toni's ear as he pointed to the black cave.

Toni flinched and jumped. "Gringo, que cosa!"

"Sorry, amigo."

"Wow, that pink juice really worked!" Toni said.

"I guess. I feel energized. But I still can't move my arm," Bean said, holding his right arm and the backpack hanging over his left shoulder.

"It's quiet, but Kele and his men are over there somewhere," Toni said.

"Yeah. I recognize that black cave. That is the entrance to Auyan-tepui."

"Let's stay on this side and carefully work our way down there then," said Toni.

The two companions turned and walked parallel to the river, staying concealed behind the thick green brush. Bean was in a lot of pain though with each step. The red cloth was drenched in his blood and he wasn't sure how long his energy would last. He thought of how Draug healed him a few days ago and how Anomar healed him last night. He knew he'd fail the mission and let everyone down in his current condition. He needed to get help soon.

Above them, saki monkeys played and called to each other in the tall trees. Fascinated with the wildlife, Bean stopped walking and tried to spot them. Out of the corner of his eye, he saw something swing across the sky. He located it on a high, bare tree branch. Looking down at Bean, the monkey had a bright white face. It held a long vine with its right toes, and some food in its hands. The monkey hollered over to one of its friends in another tree. Bean spotted that one too. Then, something curious happened. It tossed the vine back in the direction to his friend in the other tree. Nature inspired Bean again.

"Pssst, Toni!" Bean whispered. Toni turned around, checking in all directions.

"I have a plan to cross the river," Bean said. He signaled upward and Toni quickly spotted the monkeys. "Watch them. They throw the vine back and forth to each other." Then Bean pointed to some long, dangling vines by the riverside a few feet away from him and Toni.

"Okay, I get it," Toni responded, sounding unimpressed.

That was the first half of Bean's wily plan. Bean couldn't share the second part. Toni and Bean settled down between two short palm trees whose branches and leaves fanned down in front creating a natural blind hiding post. Bean checked his watch and the time read 7:16am.

"Wow, we've already been gone over an hour," he remarked to Toni. "The guys said it takes approximately seven hours to get to Salto Ángel."

"It's going to take longer than that with them in our way. We need to keep pace though."

Bean knew he was right. And Bean didn't want to spend any evening hours in the "house of the devil." "Do you know what the locals call this place?" Bean asked Toni.

"They call it the *House of the Devil,* right?"

"Does that bother you at all?"

"No."

Bean rolled his eyes. He wasn't sure how much Toni pretended to be fearless, or if he was actually fearless. "You ready to cross over then?"

"I think so. But if the men are over there, we'll have some problems. We may have to split up. We need a meeting point."

Bean agreed, especially with his own plan in mind. "So where is a good place to meet up?" They scanned the environment and then up the rugged mountainside. A few hundred feet up the mountain wall was a shelf of land with a cluster of bushes and trees that was familiar to Bean. The wide ledge wrapped around to an opening of some kind before the wall went straight up again. "Up there, amigo." He pointed.

Toni sighed. "Neither of us knows how to get up there."

"If we get separated, listen for my whistle then," Bean said, feeling the sharp sensation under his collarbone. He needed to hurry. "I'll blow it three times every so often."

"Kele and his men will hear you though," Toni said looking anxious.

"Do you have a better plan?"

"Yeah, let's not get split up."

Toni and Bean stealthily advanced to the water's edge and found a long, strong vine that they determined would cross the forty-foot-wide river. Each secured their things.

"You go first this time," Bean said.

Toni thought for a second, and then nodded. "Okay."

"But don't yell like Tarzan." Bean joked.

Toni gave Bean a rare smile. He took hold of the vine and backed up as far as it would allow. In a flash, Toni sprinted through an opening in the bushes and vaulted himself over the edge with all his might. The riverside they stood on was a bit higher than the side they were jumping to. This leverage allowed Toni to swing over the river and clear the other side with relative ease. He let go of the vine and plunged into a thicket of green plants.

Bean watched nervously. After a few seconds, Toni popped up again and Bean quietly celebrated raising and shaking his left fist to Toni. Toni gave Bean thumbs up. Toni then wound up with the vine in hand and tossed it back over to Bean. Bean was able to catch it on the first attempt, but Toni peered back at Bean with confusion and concern. Bean knew what he wanted to ask if he could do so out loud. Toni reached over and patted his right shoulder as if to ask, *how are you going to hang on with only one arm?*

Bean signaled back, waving his left hand and disregarding Toni's concern as if to say, *No problem. I got this.* With the vine in his left hand, Bean walked back about twenty feet, disappearing from Toni's sight. He pinned the vine under his left armpit and reached for his whistle. More than ever, Bean valued Toni's protection. He dreaded a visit to Draug's lair, but he knew he desperately needed healing. He also had many questions for the old medicine man.

Bean hoped Toni would be fine. His biggest reservation was not backtracking and having to reset the huge progress he made with the mission. But, he had an idea to solve this concern. Bean raised the whistle to his mouth and blew. As he expected, no sound came out the first attempt. Next, he blew two, three, and four more times. A blurry portal opened up to his left. Holding the vine firmly, Bean leaped into the portal.

~~~ CHAPTER ~~~
TWENTY-FOUR

Bean plopped to the hard ground of Draug's musty, black lair, still holding the vine. "Draug?" Bean called out. "Draug?"

"What are you doing, Bean? The portal won't close!" Draug said struggling.

"I have a connection to where I was, so I don't lose my progress," Bean explained. "I've worked very, very hard to get where I'm at."

"Then decide if you want to stay here or get back to the mission! Hurry though!" Draug demanded.

"But can you get me even close?"

"Decide, Bean!"

The twinge in the upper right part of Bean's chest was unbearable. His right arm was extremely cold. He was worried he'd never be able to move it again. With that, Bean tossed the vine back through the portal opening and it zapped shut.

Two torches lit up across the room. Draug sat between them at the stone table. With one hand holding his elk staff and the other arm resting on the table's surface, he shook his head back and forth.

"If I could see, I'd be happy to see you, young lad," Draug spoke up.

Bean pushed off the ground with only his left arm. He could feel the juice was wearing off and he was weakening again. "Draug, I've been shot."

Unaffected by Bean's emotion and dire situation, Draug dryly responded, "I'd say let's have a look at it, but I can't see."

"Draug, seriously. Enough with the blind jokes. I need your help! That's why I'm here."

"That's *why* you are here?" Draug didn't give Bean time to respond. "Come, set your backpack down, and lay on the altar."

"I'm shot in the chest. I think we need to hurry and remove the bullet."

"In that case, remove your shirt," Draug said as he left the room for a moment.

Bean set down his wet pack. He struggled to remove the red cloth wrapped around him. He peeled it off and somehow managed to get his shirt off too, despite the anguish. Bean gingerly got onto the rock table top.

"You met Ramona then?" Draug asked as he re-entered the room, carrying a case full of odd instruments.

Bean nodded. "I think so. She called herself Anomar, though. She said 'Ramona' was the correct password."

"Very good. I must've got her name backward."

Bean rolled his eyes.

"I need to know everything she told you," Draug said.

"Okay, but I can't feel my arm. And my chest is killing me."

"Close your eyes. You will be alright," Draug said in complete confidence as he prepared for the operation. Draug lifted a wet cloth out of the pot and wrung it out directly over Bean's wound. The liquid poured into Bean's wound and fizzed like soda.

"Geez, that stings!" Bean cried out. "And it smells...what is that stuff?"

"Try to be still Bean. It's a powerful cleansing potion called whiskey. I need to clean out the wound."

Bean groaned in grief. He opened his eyes just in time to see Draug grab a knife with a long thin blade and lower it into the wound. Bean writhed in panic.

"No, wait! What are you doing? You can't even see, remember?"

"Close your eyes, Bean. No need to watch. I feel the bullet. It didn't go in very far."

"It went through the canoe, and then hit the strap of my backpack before it hit me. That's probably why."

"A canoe? Why were you in a canoe?" Draug asked trying to distract Bean from the surgical procedure.

"Um, I was headed to Auyan-tepui to get the platinum sphere, but Kele and his men were chasing us."

"The platinum sphere? And who is Kele? And how did they know you were looking for that?"

"They don't, I don't think. They are mad because I killed one of their men."

"*You killed* one of their men?" Draug sounded very curious.

"Well, kind of. There was this dog attacking me and..." Bean shrieked as fiery pain lanced through his chest.

Draug held the bullet over Bean's face and in his scratchy voice said, "Extracted."

"Phew. Still hurts, Draug."

"The hard part is done. Now for the healing," Draug said calmly. "Go on. The dog was attacking you..."

Bean slurred as he spoke, "I...stabbed...it." Then Bean fainted from the pain.

Bean's dreaming mind began to replay parts of the movie Anomar passed to him earlier that morning. He somehow made it past the river and through the caves, and now saw himself on a super high ridge overlooking the vast, lush jungle below. The giant rock he stood on was one of hundreds stacked along the edge of the steep mountainside.

About a half mile in the distance was another majestic tepui, with a flat plateau like top. Three separate waterfalls burst out of the mountainside, through the middle and from the very top level. Like surround sound, he could hear the roar of crashing water nearby him too.

"Angel Falls!" Bean said. Still locked in the dream, he hiked up through the tall trees, trying to get closer to the water he could hear now even closer. He found a narrow passageway between two high rock crevasses. Upon reaching the opening at the other side, he heard some men talking. He crept up behind the wide trunk of a tree and peeked around into the open area where they stood.

It was Kele and Fichu with three other men. Kele was waving his arms and hands as if he was giving instructions to the others. One had his hands tied up behind his back, his head hung down. Kele hollered in the man's ear and then smacked the bound man on the back of the head. The poor man whipped around off balance and fell to the ground. Bean now recognized their prisoner.

"Toni!" Bean yelled, this time waking himself up. He blinked a few times before his eyes remained open. "Where...am I?"

"Still with me," Draug said with a wide frown, standing beside Bean at the head of the table.

"Draug! I need to go back now," Bean said as he collected himself.

"First, we need to discuss the mission," Draug replied. "It seems you have jeopardized the outcome."

"I don't know what you mean."

"You have advanced far, Bean. You have gone further than any of the others. But I can't have you go any further until I know you will be completely loyal to me."

"Others? What others? And I am loyal."

"Who is Toni then?"

"Toni? I... I met him in Caracas. He has protected me. He saved me and has helped me much of the way."

"Why does he want to protect you? Are you so naive to think he just wants to be your friend?"

"Ha, no. He isn't exactly a nice guy. But I'd say we're friends. We've been through a lot together."

"Bean, you were told not to mention me or your mission to anyone."

"I didn't really. His grandpa told him to look for me, that I was chosen and to protect me. He thinks I'm gonna help him. He knew about the platinum sphere before I did."

"Bean!"

"What?"

"That is precisely the reason not to tell!"

"I didn't mean for it to happen. I mean, are you so naive to think that a blonde, teenager knowing only a few words in Spanish could march down to Venezuela and not be suspicious to anyone?"

Draug was quiet. He chose his words carefully. "That is fair. But no, I knew what you were up against. Not the details nor the exact path, but I knew your loyalty would be challenged. That is part of your test."

"*My* loyalty? You mean my life has been challenged! Everyone and everything are trying to kill me...except Toni!"

"Not yet, he isn't. Until he gets what he came for," Draug mumbled. "You need to settle your temper. Your body needs to heal."

Bean closed his and took some deep breaths. "Draug, you might be right. But this has been very, very hard. I just want my dad back."

"I understand. But getting the platinum sphere is *your mission* only. Do you still not understand the magnitude of the quest? Your quest?"

Bean closed his eyes. "Not really. I mean, I know it's a big deal to you and to Toni and to Anomar...but I don't know *why*."

"Exactly, it's very important to Anomar too. You delivered the wooden ladle to her. I've been waiting almost an entire century to get that to her. What all did she tell you in exchange?"

"A lot. She said with the wooden ladle, she could now be the queen or something...of Hutoriane. She even called herself a witch. And then the map..."

"Queen? Interesting. Go on. The map?"

"Um, she explained some things to me and translated the ancient Indian writing...."

"Good. And...?"

Bean raised his right arm and scratched his head. "I think I have it memorized. It says something like 'when the angel ascends, the demons shall rise.' ...and...'when the angel falls, the demons shall reign.' Something like that."

"Hmmm. 'When the angel ascends...the demons shall rise.' 'When the angel falls, the demons shall reign?'" Draug repeated carefully. "It seems incomplete. Do you remember any more?"

"No. I memorized what she told me."

"Let's look at the map, shall we?"

Bean sat up and slid off the table. He picked up his backpack and set it on the table. It wasn't totally dry yet. He unzipped it and pulled out the wet leather scroll.

"Your arm seems to be feeling better?"

Having moved it without any pain, Bean now noticed he also had a good range of motion. "Wow, yeah. Thank you."

"The wound still needs a little while longer to fully heal. Keep it wrapped up."

"Okay," Bean said as he unrolled the map. He didn't need to pin down the edges this time as the dense wetness weighed it down. "What are you looking for?"

"Remember I can't actually see the map. But for you... what do you see?"

The map didn't seem to glow like it had before. The emblem, lines, wording, and images of the map were smeared in places from all the water drenching the backpack. Bean cringed. "Draug, the map got wet," Bean said timidly.

"What's wrong with it? Is it ruined?"

"The images are a little blurry and the wording runs together in spots."

Draug was quiet again. Bean knew he was upset. "But Anomar showed me the way," Bean said, breaking the silence.

"What do you mean?"

"She put her hand on the map and her other hand on my forehead and, like, downloaded the map to my brain. I mean, I saw my journey and the way to go to find the platinum sphere in fast forward."

"Excellent," Draug responded with some cheer. "That means you, Bean, are the *living* map. Only you know the way. But what about the translation? Are there more lines?"

"I can't tell. Maybe. It's smeared and kind of runs together," Bean said looking closer at the ancient writing.

Draug sighed. "Well, you must know a good portion of it. If Anomar didn't translate all of it, I will boil her head in a soup pot."

"You said there were *others* though. Who were the others?" Bean asked.

Draug cleared his throat. "There have been others who have tried to obtain the platinum sphere. Throughout the centuries, there have been many who have searched for it, but to no avail."

"Who? How did they know about it and learn of its importance?" Bean asked.

"Lore. Other healers from other tribes throughout other places in Hutoriane. They tell their sons and grandsons about it."

"Healers? As in medicine men?" Bean asked, listening intently.

"Yes. You see, Bean, a healer is many things," Draug said. "In fact, there exists an elite Council of Healers who control all of Hutoriane. These are powerful master healers from the many tribes, families and clans all throughout the history of Hutoriane. Occasionally, a healer rises to more greatness and joins this brotherhood of master healers."

"Are you a part of this brotherhood of healers?" Bean asked.

"Once upon a time I was. I am not part of the Council now. But I am a healer. There is much to teach you," Draug answered growing impatient.

"Go on then," Bean said.

"We don't have the time."

"But I need to know, don't I? It's *my* mission."

"It is well known among the Council the magnitude and all-encompassing power of the platinum sphere. Many have sought to find it and gain this power. They also want to prevent it from getting into the wrong hands. He who possesses the platinum sphere shall rightfully preside among the Council of Healers and therefore, rule all of Hutoriane."

"And you want this power?" Bean asked innocently. "You want to rule all of Hutoriane?"

"Boy, do you still not understand?" Draug asked. "This is all for the inheritance of my people. *You* are my people."

Bean was quiet. "I guess I do now. But Anomar healed me too," said Bean. "Is she a healer?"

"Our powers and motives are different."

"So where do you get your power from?"

"From he who *actually* rules Hutoriane."

"Oh, you mean God?"

"The master," Draug answered in a grim tone.

Bean got the chills and felt uneasy. "But he can't be good. I mean, you live in a dark cave...and you did some weird evil séance to me?"

"It all serves a good purpose in the end."

"And Anomar calls herself a witch. All this doesn't seem like the good God I've learned about," Bean said.

"Bean, you are young. There is much more to learn of beings, good and bad. Some beings appear good but are the blackest of evil. Some appear evil and aren't that bad. Others have good intentions, but don't have the will to uphold them. Few, very few, actually desire good and choose good. To each, there is a motive and a purpose that requires a deeper understanding."

"What kind of being are *you* then?"

"Fulfill your calling, and you will get your father back," Draug said ignoring the question.

Bean sat still. He recalled the phrase his father told him: *Is following me more important than doing the right thing?* Bean wasn't sure anymore. It struck him that Toni could be in trouble too. He spoke up, "Toni! I need to help Toni!"

Draug slammed his staff to the ground and shrieked. "No! You will not help Toni! He is your enemy. Don't you see? He wants the same thing."

Bean staggered back and fell to the rock floor. He stared up with wide eyes at Draug standing angrily over him. Bean was stunned and too frightened to speak.

Draug collected himself. "You must see Toni for what he wants. He wants the platinum sphere and so do you. You have made an oath with me to get it. You chose this. I will help you get your father. I made an oath to do this."

Bean was scared. He understood the implications of the mission, and how desperately Draug needed him to succeed. Slowly, Bean muttered, "You *need* me. I am the chosen one to help you. You said I am the living map. And Anomar said that the whistle has even more powers that will *only* work for me."

Draug stood frozen like a mannequin in his elk skin raiment and with the silver chain dangling from his neck. "I don't *need* you boy. I don't need anything. Hutoriane needs you," Draug uttered. "Go on back to your simple life. The ladder in the other room is the exit."

"Yes, you do. I am your last and only hope."

"For what?"

"For you to...have more power...*all the power*...and run Hutoriane," Bean guessed.

"Nonsense. I understand you feel conflicted, because who I am is so strange to your reality. But remember, I told you when we made our oath, my purpose is to restore *our* people to their proper inheritance."

Bean was taken aback. This was what Toni said his purpose was too. And their common purpose was too large, unfathomable, and complicated for Bean to fully comprehend. But for some reason, it sunk in a little more this time. "You're right. It is nonsense. All of it. None of it matters to me," Bean said. Sad and tired, he just wanted the nightmare to be over.

"Do you want to see your father again?" Draug asked tersely.

"Yes! That's the only thing that matters to me!"

"Then keep that as your only focus. Go get the platinum sphere and bring it to me," Draug commanded.

Bean's emotion quickly turned from sadness to anger. He was pumped up like he felt before a football game. His determination to find his dad was greater than any confusion he was feeling. The mission was once again simple to him.

"I'll finish this. Drop me past the river, beyond the jungle, through the caves, and onto Auyan-tepui. I don't have the time or energy to start somewhere less than this."

"You said Auyan-tepui? I know the place well. Not a problem. But first, take your binoculars. You will need them. They are under the table."

Thrilled, Bean rushed over to the table and collected his binoculars. He put his head through the straps, and then he threw his pack over his shoulders. Like a soldier off to battle, Bean declared, "I am ready. Send me."

Draug raised his staff, lifted his left hand, and chanted, "I am the Guard of Hutoriane, gatekeeper of the portals. House of the Devil, open your door!" The two portals opened in a flash before Bean. Bean dashed forward and jumped into the blurry orange door to the right.

CHAPTER TWENTY-FIVE

The portal spit Bean out and dropped him a few feet higher than the last couple times he exited, as if Draug was punishing Bean with a small lesson. Bean believed that easily enough when his stomach jittered as he fell and hit the rock surface.

Bean found himself just inside the opening of a narrow cave. Facing the bright daylight, Bean walked a few feet out. His eyes grew larger and his heart beat faster as he soaked in his dreadful predicament. Bean stood on the edge of a thousand-foot-high cliff, straight down. Not able to take any more steps, he slowly turned his head and shoulders to get his bearings. Two red macaws flew by directly in front of him. Terrified of heights, Bean carefully backed against the rock ledge to his left and froze.

There wasn't much space to the left, and none to the right of the cave. He could see for miles where low scattered clouds didn't obstruct the view. Bean counted three more tepuis off in the remote distance. The light breeze blew the misty air against his cheeks. He could taste the fresh oxygen he was inhaling. The dark green jungle below stretched infinitely in every direction.

"Geez, Draug, I swear you do this on purpose," Bean said. "I thought you wanted me to succeed." Bean turned around again gazing into the black cave. "I'm not going in there," he said to himself. "I need light and sun." Now facing the wall to the left, he got on his tippy-toes. Above him was a larger platform of rocks and small bushes with yellow flowers. He needed to climb the shallow five-foot wall and get to safer ground.

Bean carefully tossed his pack up to the platform above him to the left. Bean set the binoculars up there too. "Let's see if Bean can scale a rock wall and not fall," he said sarcastically.

He found his first step, secured his footing, and hopped up. There wasn't anything to grab onto, other than the thin grooves in the rock ground. He dug in and wedged his fingers inside these. Bean's heart raced; upward and forward was the only acceptable direction to avoid falling a thousand feet to his doom.

"One...two..." he hesitated. "Screw you, Draug.... and three!" Bean grunted loudly as he clambered up and swung his left leg over the top. Almost there, Bean clawed at the rock surface and pulled himself up away from the edge. He stood above the cave opening on the rock landing, breathing fast like he had just chased down a quarterback in one of his football games.

Bean was gathering his things when he heard a faint, high-pitched whistling. He instinctively felt for the outline of his own whistle in his pants pocket. It was there. He heard the whistling again, and then one more time. To his dismay, the noise seemed to come from back by the ledge. Begrudgingly, he grabbed his binoculars and carefully crawled back to the edge. Overlooking the drop off, he used the binoculars to scan the mountain wall up and down. Startled, he heard the whistling again down to the right, three times in a row, like the last time. He determined it was human whistling. Bean tried to identify where the noise came from.

The tepui on which Bean perched jogged out to his right allowing him to see down the rock wall quite a ways. About four hundred feet below him lay a shelf of green vegetation. He traced the mountainside all the way down to the bottom and discovered a muddy river winding in the forest. Bean figured that was the same river where he and Toni were canoeing earlier. This confirmed that he indeed was somewhere on Auyan-tepui. "Good job, Draug," Bean mumbled. "You got me further than where I was."

His eyes went back to the green shelf, which looked more familiar. *No way!* Bean thought. *Could that be the same shelf of land Toni and I talked about meeting at down below?* Then he heard the whistling again. *Could that be Toni whistling for me?* He heard it two more times. *It must be. I said I'd blow my whistle three times, just like that. He must be calling to me.*

Bean watched the shelf through his binoculars, determined to locate Toni. Toni whistled again.

"Geez," Bean whispered. "He's making me feel guilty." Bean felt conflicted. He knew Toni had come all this way and had greatly supported him. Toni whistled twice more in ten-second intervals. Bean's conscience was getting the best of him. *He deserves a response. I'll blow my whistle three times to let him know I'm okay, but I won't wait for him. I'll get moving.*

Bean took out his whistle and turned it over a few times in his hands. He noticed its distinct markings again. On the back side, he recognized the circle-X emblem of Hutoriane and the odd figures in each cross section. On the front were the three holes spaced evenly apart. Bean wanted to be careful not to summon Draug. He decided to cover the top hole and blow three times in ten second intervals, matching Toni's call.

With his index finger over the top hole, Bean put the orange wooden whistle to his lips and blew. To his surprise, a light tinkering of chimes sounded. He waited ten seconds, and then blew it again, exactly the same way with the same resulting tone. After ten seconds, he blew it a third time. The same tone sounded but was immediately followed by a strong gust of wind. The wind swirled around Bean and twisted upward like a small tornado. It pushed and pulled and rolled him over and over.

Abruptly, the funnel disappeared, and Bean lay dizzy on the rock ground, ten feet from the edge of the cliff. *Whoah... what was that? Good thing it didn't push me in the other direction, or I'd be falling over that cliff.* He got on his knees and brushed himself off.

"You must be the Whistler, I presume?" a mysterious female voice shocked Bean.

Bean popped up to his feet in a squatting position. He pivoted in a circle and was alarmed to see dozens of exotic birds of all kinds landing around him. There were toucans, parrots, macaws, yellow birds, orange, blue ones in countless shapes and variations. He gulped and cleared his throat. "What's this? Who...who's there?"

"I am the spirit Ria," the voice answered.

"Uh, okay," Bean responded nervously.

"Did you mean to call on me?" she asked.

"No, sorry, it was an accident," Bean said. "And, I don't see who is speaking." He continued to look around and over his shoulder.

"You cannot see me. You can only hear me and see my acts," explained the voice.

"But *who* are you and *where* are you?"

"Where there is air, I am. I can direct and affect the Outer realm of Hutoriane. Any creature that flies adheres to my command. The storms that stir and rage listen to me. Even sound obeys my word."

"Oh, okay, so you are here, but I can't see you?" Bean asked standing motionless and trying to grasp all that Ria was saying.

"Yes, Whistler. In what way can I help you?" Ria asked politely.

"I'm not sure," Bean said, as if in a stupor.

"What are you endeavoring to accomplish?"

"I am trying to find something. But I want to tell someone something first. And then hopefully I can get something to someone else, so I can find my dad before the end of tomorrow," mumbled Bean, realizing he hardly made any sense to her.

"Where is this someone you'd like to communicate something to?" Ria asked, surprising Bean.

"I think he is on a ledge about four hundred feet down the mountainside from here. I want to tell him I'm okay and... good luck," said Bean. "I'd yell to him, but there are others close by who want to kill me."

"Write down your message and the birds will deliver it to that someone."

Bean was baffled and astonished this was happening. "Let me see."

Bean rummaged through his backpack. The only thing he could think of was the leather scroll. Bean considered giving Toni the map. *The scroll? I don't really need it anymore since I have it burned into my head. I know the way in my mind and the translation, and it's all smeared anyway.* He hesitated. *But it belongs to Draug. Maybe he will need it. I better not.*

Then he remembered the paper and pen he stored in a clear baggie in the front pocket of his backpack. He pulled it out and hurriedly wrote a message:

Dear Toni, I am above you on Auyan-tepui. Sorry I had to disappear again. Thanks for all your help, but I need to go on alone now. We share the same purpose in getting the platinum sphere, and I don't know how that would work out. I consider you a friend. Good luck to you and may the best man win! —Bean

"All finished," Bean spoke up loudly, hoping Ria could hear him.

A large toucan hopped and wobbled over to Bean. It seized the note from Bean's grip with its long, rainbow-colored beak. Then it flapped its black wings up and flew out over the edge. Bean watched in amazement. He cautiously returned to the ledge with the binoculars in both hands, and tracked the toucan soaring gracefully down in a spiral flight pattern. It hovered over the shelf of land where Toni was hiding. Bean lost track of it as it vanished between the trees below. Still and patiently, he watched.

"Mission complete. Anything else, Whistler?" Ria reported back.

Seriously? So, Toni really is down there somewhere? Bean thought. "I don't think so. I guess I don't understand how you work. You just help me if I call you?"

"I will decline your request if it interferes with the wellbeing of Outer Hutoriane. I will decline your request if it is something you can do alone. Be judicious with my services and do not take advantage of them," Ria admonished. "But you as the Whistler of Hutoriane have the right to call on me whenever you have an appropriate need."

"Oh, okay," Bean responded. He hoped Toni would understand. And then he got to thinking of Hutoriane and the Outer realm.

"Whistler?"

"Yes, sorry," Bean replied. "I am just trying to understand all this. The Outer, the Inner, Under, and...um..."

"The Natural realm. That is the realm in which you live and operate Bean."

"So, the Earth really is more than the natural world I see and know?"

"Much more. The Inner world is subterranean. The crust of the Earth is eighteen miles thick. This realm is enormous. There are numerous Inner villages filled with Inner beings. They use thousands of miles of tunnels and caves to travel through. They don't have much need for light."

"Can they not live in the Natural realm?" Bean thought of Draug.

"Not long. They will age and die quicker. Some appear in the Natural realm as a skin-walker."

"Like as an animal? Are they human?"

"Yes, at first. Most commit to trolling permanently in the Inner realm for a longer life."

Bean thought of Draug.

He continued, "And the Underworld? Who lives there?"

"The spirits of bad beings who once lived in the Natural realm in the flesh reside there. The Underworld is the opposite of all things creative, productive, positive and good. Its overall influence plays an important role for the proper balance, progress, and function of Hutoriane."

"Okay," Bean said, still feeling unclear. "And *where is* the Under realm?"

"Right here. The Natural world is what you see and experience physically. The Underworld is the negative spiritual realm."

Bean was confused, and Ria must've sensed it. She added, "Like your shirt. Worn correctly, it is the Natural realm, and inside-out or reversed it is the Under realm."

Bean understood a little better, but time pressed on his mind. "I'm really glad to meet you, Ria, but I need to get going."

"Whistler be very careful. Right now, all of Hutoriane is out of balance. The rulers of the Inner and Under realms are at war and threatening the very existence of the planet."

"I will."

"Whistler, your soul is pure. You are a good being. This mountain is not friendly. Don't let it change you. Stay out of the dark. That is where your enemies have their power. And they are very strong."

Bean nodded, unsure how to respond. "Thank you for all this information."

"Godspeed, my young friend. Maybe I will need your assistance someday somewhere with someone or something," she said in jest.

Bean smiled, catching the humor of his new invisible friend. "Of course I'll help you!"

He watched as all the birds took flight, leaving him alone again on the rocky platform. "That was cool... and odd," he said to himself. Uncertain of what would surprise him or attack him on his journey up the mountain, Bean set off.

CHAPTER TWENTY-SIX

Traversing the large rocks, jumping over rock fissures and the deep crevasses between them, while weaving in and out of the strange plant outcroppings, Bean was determined to complete his mission. He was going to reunite with his dad and nothing would stop him.

After overcoming the rugged boulders, Bean ascended a wide valley of tall grasses and the top of a giant root system. The long, yellow, snake-like roots sprung up from the dirt and entangled themselves, and then buried into the ground again. The area appeared like the large plate of spaghetti without any sauce his mom would make. He recalled this part from Anomar's connection to his mind. Bean was confident he was on the right track.

Bean climb onto a slippery root and then jump off again, making his progress slow. Sometimes a root even seemed to move subtly and widen, like it was inhaling. Other moments, the ground rumbled. An occasional burst of air would release from different areas out of the earth, startling Bean each time. He felt like the mountain was waking up, agitated that he was there.

Next, Bean entered a forest far different and drier from the jungle floor a few thousand feet below at the base of Auyan-tepui. The tall trees were unlike any he had ever seen before and varied in every shade of green. Bean could hear an occasional call of a bird or the scurrying of a small animal. There were also loud moans and cries in the distance that weren't from any animal he recognized, and certainly not human. His thoughts went back to when his father, Uncle Kenny, and Bo all left him alone on the mountain in Utah a few days prior. Except this time, he wasn't anxious from feeling alone. The unnatural noises were getting to him.

Winding his way through the unusual trees and plants, Bean picked up the pace. To get his mind off the strange environment, he tried to review the course of events from the last few days. *Kenny probably took Bo back to camp, but my dad? Where could dad seriously have gone? He knows that mountain too well to get lost. And he knew how nervous I'd be sitting alone too long. Nothing could capture my dad or keep him from returning to me. Maybe he fell and got injured?*

Bean stopped and assessed his position. His watch said 11:12am. He sensed he was moving in the right direction, but he didn't feel like he had made much progress after hiking an hour through the forest. Rays of sunlight broke through the gaps of the branches high above him. He thought he saw a bright clearing a hundred yards in front of him. Bean decided to head there.

And Draug...he's a troll! Maybe Toni is right. Maybe he's the one who did something to my dad. Bean continued to analyze. *What are the chances that all this isn't even real? It's all so bizarre. A mountain lion was chasing me. Then I was rescued by an old mad man. He sent me to South America where I met an assassin, skin-walkers, a witch, and now some kind of spirit that controls air? All in the hopes of finding my dad. No one back home will believe me.*

The air around Bean was getting foggy and dense. What he thought was a clearing was actually a white, misty area that diminished his visibility. Suddenly, a loud cracking and crashing of branches sounded off to his right. Bean stopped walking and held still to listen. He waited, but the cracking sounds had halted too.

Now only able to see a few feet in front of him, Bean cautiously advanced. He heard it again. This time the crunching of branches came louder and much closer. *Geez, what is that?* Bean wondered, sweating in fright. Again, he waited quietly, but so did whatever was following him. Nervously, he picked up his pace and trotted along feeling his way between tree trunks and bushes. The fog-shrouded environment kept Bean from recognizing anything, but the fog itself. He kept moving.

Crack!

Boom!

The noise was just ten feet away from him. An enormous tree came crashing down in front of him. It slammed to the forest floor, creating a tremor under Bean's feet. Bean halted and stopped breathing.

Crack!

Another tree, this time to his left, thundered down in front of him at an angle. It crashed on top of the other tree, creating a giant X on the ground. All fell silent, except for the loud beating of Bean's heart.

Ten feet directly in front of Bean, a large black figure with a crooked human shape rose in the air on the other side of the crossed section of downed trees. Bean stood frozen. Against the foggy background, Bean could tell the being had no physical form. Three more images appeared. The dark spirits began to laugh and moan. Bean was too frightened to move. He blinked, and suddenly he was surrounded by dozens of oddly shaped spirits making shrill cries. Bean began to shake in terror. He closed his eyes, feeling utterly doomed.

"No angel shall ascend this mountain freely," roared a guttural, demonic voice.

Bean slowly opened his eyes. The black demons were floating up and down, some fading into the fog while others appeared.

"No angel shall ascend this mountain freely," it repeated louder. Bean couldn't tell which if any of the spirits addressed him. It felt as though the message was communicated to his mind from the spirits collectively.

"I... I don't... I don't understand," Bean stuttered.

A ring of fire lit up on the ground, encircling Bean and the downed trees. A massive golden serpent slithered over the downed trees toward Bean. About fifteen feet long, it crawled behind Bean, over Bean's feet and then coiled itself three feet in front of him. Slowly, the snake raised its head. Bean watched in horror as its huge, cone-shaped head was now at his eye level. Glaring at Bean, the snake's eyes were a deep purple. Its sharp red tongue hissed outward and then retracted inside its mouth, leaving a residue of green saliva dripping from the corners.

The demons chanted again, "No angel shall ascend—"

"The mountain freely!" Bean angrily interrupted. "I heard you the first two times! What do you want? I don't have any money!"

"The whistle in your possession does not belong to you," muttered the evil voice.

"Yes, it's mine," Bean answered firmly. The occurrence was surreal, but the initial shock was wearing off. Bean's fear was suppressed by his newfound courage. He didn't feel frozen anymore. Discreetly, he wiggled his fingers.

The snake in front of Bean widened its mouth, revealing sharp fangs, and continued to viciously hiss; it seemed to be waiting for a command like a dog does with its master.

"The demons are rising," the evil voice warned Bean.

The ring of fire went out. The dense fog began to thin as sunlight pierced the trees, drying the misty air. The black spirits began to wail and swirled around hysterically. To Bean's surprise, the demons disappeared one by one as the warm sunlight gradually displaced the fog. Finally, the lanky serpent spun its head back over the downed trees and Bean saw the rest of it unravel and slide into the dark forest floor.

"This place really is the devil's house," Bean said to himself as the threat vanished. He heard a softer voice, "Stay out of the dark."

Bean looked around. "Ria? Are you there?"

There was no response. But Bean realized Ria was right about the dark. He knew the further he carried on, the more danger he would face. With his environment now well lit, Bean took a few steps forward and stood over the huge wooden X lying on the ground. There was a charred circle in the ground around him. And imprinted into the earth in each of the four cross sections was a curious symbol. "The Emblem of Hutoriane?" Bean recognized it.

He reached for the whistle in his pocket. He pulled it out and twisted it over in his palm. He compared each symbol in the circle-X with the much larger version on the ground. The symbol in the top quarter section looked like the sun or a six-pointed star. The marking imprinted in the right quadrant looked like a lolly-pop on its side. The one in the bottom part where Bean stood upon looked like a wave or the letter M in cursive. And lastly, the symbol in the left quadrant had four small triangles.

What is all this about? What do all these mean? Bean gathered his things and fled the scene.

CHAPTER TWENTY-SEVEN

After another forty-five minutes of arduous hiking, he arrived at a small lagoon surrounded with more flowers, orchids, bromeliads, and bright colors than he'd ever seen in one place. It was a paradisiacal setting of lush vegetation. The fall sun was at its zenith overhead. Bean traced the source of the lagoon to a tall and narrow waterfall emptying into a crystal-clear stream. Bean was extremely thirsty. He knew moving water was safer to drink than still water. He went to rest by the stream, with the noisy waterfall in the background.

Bean set down his things, bent over, and cupped his hands in the water to get a drink. Never had water tasted so rich and fresh. As Bean continued to drink from the stream, he noticed the scar inside his left elbow—the one Draug made when he drew Bean's blood. "Geez, that guy," Bean talked to himself. "He freaking drank my blood. I guess this scar will remind me of that creepy moment forever."

Bean then observed his reflection in the flowing water. His face was splotchy with dirt and sweat. His hair looked like a wild bird's nest. *Wow, I'm a filthy mess,* he thought. The heat of the day and hours of hiking had dampened his shirt from all the sweating. Bean took off his shirt and hung it on a tree limb to dry in the sun. Carefully, he undid the red cloth around his shoulder and hung it too next to his shirt.

He examined the gunshot wound. "That is crazy," he said, impressed on how it had fully healed. Bean pressed two fingers along his skin and felt the outline of the wound's scar. Bean wanted to see it in the stream's reflection, so he knelt back down and leaned over the water. Bean was surprised to see the scar was distinctly shaped like a star.

That actually looks kind of cool, he thought, feeling its outline again. *Don't know if my mom will like it though.* He glanced back at the scar on his left arm. The scars looked eerily familiar and triggered a surge of panic.

Bean quickly pulled out the whistle and turned it over. "Oh no..."

He compared the Emblem of Hutoriane on the whistle, specifically the star in the top cross section and the lollipop symbol with the scars on his young body. They matched up too well. A terrorizing thought occurred to him. In slow motion, Bean pulled up his left pant leg and then pushed down his sock to uncover the scar shaped like a cursive M. Sure enough, Bean found a similar shape in the lower quadrant of the circle-X.

"What is all this? What's happening to me?" Bean cried out.

Bean anxiously checked his right leg, torso, and around his body for any scar resembling the odd markings in the last cross section. He didn't find one. "This is either a crazy coincidence, or someone or something is messing with me," he said, gazing down at his marked-up body.

"We are gonna mess with you," said a mean voice behind Bean.

Caught off guard, Bean turned to find Kele, Fichu, and another rugged man standing right behind him. Kele pointed a handgun at Bean's face. Fichu had a machete in his right hand. The other man held an old rifle with a wooden stock low at his waist. With the noisy waterfall in the background, Bean didn't hear the three sneak up so close. He couldn't do anything but put both arms up in the air and surrender to the native hostiles.

"I'm sorry, but I don't know why you guys are after me," Bean said, trying not to shake.

Fichu limped over to Bean and raised his machete to Bean's neck. Growling, he gritted his teeth and said, "Mataste a mi hermano anoche!"

"What? Brother? Last night? I don't understand," Bean said.

"You killed his brother last night," Kele explained.

"No, I didn't kill anyone. Just a dog. Two dogs attacked me and Toni. I defended myself," Bean said frightened and struggling to get the words out. He pretended not to know the dog was actually Moa as a skin-walker. He was hoping not to even bring up Anomar.

"Mentiroso!" Fichu yelled and grabbed the back of Bean's bushy head.

"Fichu! Espérate! " commanded Kele. "Boy, you better tell me what happened last night. And why you left the hut in the middle of the night."

Bean gulped and then spoke up, "Mumua...took something from me. And I went after her...tried to find her. Then these vicious dogs attacked us. I just stabbed the one on top of me that was gonna kill me. Honestly, I never saw Moa."

Kele stared at Bean and then looked at Fichu. "Fichu, were you and Moa out wandering last night?"

Fichu breathed heavily over Bean. The blade of his machete pressed against Bean's neck. Fichu turned back to Kele and spoke in Spanish. Kele argued back in the same language. After a few exchanges, the two men seemed to come to an understanding. The other man pulled out some rope from one of their packs and tied Bean's hands roughly behind his back while Fichu held Bean still with the knife.

Kele stared at Bean while the man tied him up, looking him up and down. "Boy, you have a lot to tell us," Kele said. "This area is our land. This is our mountain. Whatever you came here for, you must tell us why. And tell us who sent you."

The rope was now tied tightly around Bean's wrists and up his forearms. Bean wasn't sure how to respond and certainly didn't want to tell them all he knew. "Kele, you know this land is cursed, right?"

"That is how we like it," Kele said.

Bean quickly adjusted his approach. "Okay, I mean...I think I can help your people."

"Hurry, boy! Tell me why we shouldn't kill you right now!" Kele yelled.

"Sorry! There is a treasure hidden up by Salto Ángel. And only I know where it is."

"A treasure?" Kele's interest was piqued. "What kind of treasure? How do you know?"

"Yes, a treasure. Not of gold, but even more valuable. Of platinum." Bean sensed he was gaining some leverage with Kele. "Look in my backpack. You'll see the ancient treasure map."

Kele spoke in the Pemón language to the other man and motioned to grab Bean's backpack. The rugged man ripped open Bean's backpack and flipped it upside down, emptying the contents onto the ground. The scroll fumbled out. Kele picked it up and unrolled it.

After trying to read and analyze it, Kele said, "This map is hard to understand. But it leads to a treasure here on Auyan-tepui?"

Bean nodded.

"You've come all this way and know where it is?"

"It's up higher on the mountain. On the top, by Salto Ángel."

"Mentiroso!" Fichu said in anger.

"Cállate!" Kele said. Then he looked at Bean. "Where did you get the map? And who sent you?"

"In a cave in the mountains of Utah, where I live. And I met Toni when I came here. He liked treasure hunts too. I showed him the map and he said he recognized the area. He told me it was of Salto Ángel here in Venezuela." The others listened intently, and Bean couldn't believe he had their interest.

"Interesting. And Toni, your companion, where is he?"

"I don't know. We got split up after you guys chased us the first time down by the river."

"He for sure is a dead man. He killed one of our men. I am personally going to kill him," promised Kele.

Fichu let down the knife and walked over to Kele. They spoke in their language for a few moments. Bean was quiet and nervous again.

Finally, Kele said, "The legend in Kavak among our people is that there is a treasure hidden up here somewhere. This is why I believe you."

"Oh really? It's cool you guys heard of it too," Bean said, trying to get on their side.

"We will summit the mountain and go after the treasure for two reasons. First, Toni will look for you and we will kill him. Second, for the treasure. If there is no treasure, Fichu will kill you. If there is, we take it all and you get to live."

Bean peered at the ground. He was glad there was a legend of the treasure among the Pemón people. In a way, it validated the mission he was on; and now more experienced in his dealings, he knew he had value to them.

"I'll need my things. And I need my hands free for hiking," Bean responded with more confidence.

"Fine. But we will take your knife and keep the map," Kele said. "Do you have any other weapon?" He signaled for the others to search Bean.

They pulled out the whistle and threw it on the ground by the other things from his backpack. As they pulled out his knife from the other pocket, Bean replied, "Just a knife."

Fichu spoke fiercely, holding Bean's own knife to his face, "I kill you...with same knife...you killed Moa."

Bean didn't respond. Fichu nearly cut Bean as he sliced the ties loose. Bean grabbed his shirt off the tree limb and put it on. He intentionally left the red cloth hanging, knowing Toni would recognize it if he came that way. He picked up the whistle and put it back in his pocket. Lastly, Bean hurriedly replaced the other items from the ground into his backpack.

"This way," Kele said, leading the group and their young hostage.

CHAPTER TWENTY-EIGHT

In a weird way, Bean was glad to be the prisoner of Kele and his men. Their regular job was to guide tourists up Auyan-tepui and summit Angel Falls. They knew any forbidden paths, dangerous pitfalls, and traps to avoid. The group hiked for over an hour, traveling through peculiar tropical settings and different terrains. Bean would have occasional recollections from what Anomar showed him earlier that confirmed they headed in the right direction. But more than guiding him, Bean was grateful to have company through the evil environment.

They arrived at a second terrace of rugged terrain with oddly eroded rocks and rifts. Looming behind the rocks was a steep vertical escarpment, which shot straight up into the thin clouds above. Sounds of cascading water were close by and the damp, misty air also attested to a nearby waterfall. Although refreshing, Bean was exhausted and thirsty. The others would drink from their canteens along the way. But Bean had none. He needed water.

"Él Libertador! We've arrived at the entrance to the summit of Salto Ángel," Kele announced. "The mist you are breathing in is from Angel Falls," he continued. "It is just around that bend, and that giant rock wall." He pointed off to the right. "We are going to take a more difficult path up boulders and take a shortcut through the bend."

Bean was thrilled to be so close but also confused. "Where do we go from here?" Bean looked down at his watch, which read 2:27pm.

"Quédate quieto!" Fichu raised a hand like he was going to slap Bean. Bean stepped backward, flinching.

"Now we begin to boulder. Using these knotted ropes, we will climb the large rocks and then make our way through the narrow cleft up at the top," Kele explained. "Tighten up your gear."

Bean didn't like heights. He began to tighten the straps on his backpack when he remembered the other two flasks of fluid. They were in the front pocket and hadn't fallen out for his captors to notice earlier. Discreetly, he unzipped the front pocket. To his delight, he grabbed one of the plastic bottles of pink liquid and bit off the cork. Bean downed the drink in one gulp.

"Let's go, gringo!" Fichu yelled.

The word *gringo* reminded Bean of Toni. He tossed the flask, zipped up his pack, and secured it tightly over his shoulders. Bean ran over to the others where two were already climbing up the boulders using the knotted ropes. Bean grabbed a rope and began his climb over the first boulder. Fichu followed last.

It didn't take long for the pink energy drink to kick in. Bean found it easy to climb the large, slick boulders. Bean figured each one was the size of his dad's pickup truck, Trusty Rusty. Kele and the others would rest after getting over one or two boulders, but Bean kept moving along. Fichu was especially slow dealing with his injured leg. It was about three hundred feet of sloping mountainside they endeavored to climb.

"Slow down boy!" Kele warned Bean as he pointed the handgun in his direction. Bean was a full six boulders above the other three men.

"Okay, sorry," Bean answered. He stopped, but not to rest. He perched on a huge rock and observed the vast sea of dark green below. He watched the three struggling to climb beneath him.

I wonder where Toni is right now, Bean thought. *I hope he's okay, and not too mad at me.* He thought of when he got shot earlier and how Toni aided him. He remembered how weak and desperate he felt until he drank the pink liquid. He figured his energy must have been completely depleted, since he'd had such little strength then, just enough to move around for a short while. This time he felt incredible and invincible. *Should I make a run for it while I'm so energized? Or do I need the map?*

He decided to climb again. Bean only had a few more boulders to go before he made it to the high flank with the narrow cleft. As he pulled himself up along the knotted ropes, his mind went back to the dark demons he encountered in the misty forest. He mumbled under his breath,"What did they say again...'no angel shall ascend...the mountain freely' or something? What does that mean? Wait, were they referring to *me* as an angel? I am ascending the mountain."

"I am going to shoot you if you don't stop!" Kele yelled. Bean froze holding onto the ragged rope as he was now closer to the top and a good distance above the other men. "Wait for us!"

"I won't go anywhere. I'll wait for you at the top," Bean yelled back.

Bean made it to the top of the boulders and saw that the ledge pathway was only two or three feet wide. The tall rock wall shot straight up for as high as Bean could see. Bean located the narrow cleft in the wall about thirty feet to the right, along the skinny edge. The cliff drop off in front of the narrow cleft was thousands of feet down. Bean couldn't see the bottom through the clouds, nor did he look straight down for long.

Bean could barely see Fichu stumbling far below him. He estimated that Kele and the other man were probably five minutes out before they arrived. He thought of Toni again. He felt bad for leaving him and could really use his help now. Bean pulled out his whistle. *If I whistle three times, maybe Toni will hear me. But then again, Kele is hoping I will bring Toni in so he can kill him.*

"Boy, you better stay where you are!" Kele hollered again, a little closer now and out of breath. Bean could not see any of the men.

"I will!" Bean shouted.

Bean knew this was his chance to call for help, being the only free moment he had in the last two hours. "I'm gonna do it," Bean said, despite his angst. He didn't want to call Draug or Ria. He just wanted to let Toni know where he was. Bean decided to blow the whistle, but this time he would cover the second hole.

Bean licked his lips and put the whistle up to them. With his right middle finger, he covered the second hole slit in the pipe. He blew. A loud and low tuba sound rang out. *Dang. I hope Toni can hear it.* After ten seconds, he blew the whistle again and the same tone came out. *I should at least keep ten seconds between each time.* Bean blew it a third time resulting in the same low noise. Suddenly, the blue sky went gray and the vibrant color all around Bean went dull.

Kele clambered over the last boulder. "What's that noise?"

Shoot! Bean fought down panic. He didn't want to have to surrender the whistle.

"And where are you? I told you to wait, boy!" Kele said, visibly furious.

Bean stood just ten feet away from Kele, in what he thought was plain sight. "Right here, like I said I'd be!"

Kele looked in every direction, including where Bean stood. "I'm gonna let Fichu give you a good beating! No time for games!"

Bean stood still. *Can he not see me? Can he even hear me?* Bean looked down at his hands and then felt his body. *I can see me.*

"You have three seconds to come out wherever you are hiding," Kele demanded, now standing up on the ledge only a few feet to Bean's right. Kele turned sharply toward Bean and walked hastily that way.

"Easy man, I'm right here," Bean said, keeping his ground.

Kele kept walking at Bean. There wasn't much room on the ledge. Bean flattened himself against the mountain wall and readied for impact. Kele scowled as he passed right by Bean. "That kid is gonna die," Kele said only about a foot from where Bean stood. He pivoted to return to where the other two men were catching their breath from the climb.

"He's gone. Dumb kid ran off," Kele said.

"We should've taken care of him down below," Fichu grumbled. "He seemed full of it anyway."

Bean continued to listen and watch in amazement. But he wanted to be certain they couldn't hear him, so he took a risk. "Guys, I'm right here!" Bean yelled at the top of his lungs. The men didn't turn around. "Holy cow, they don't hear me." Anomar told him the whistle had more powers but going invisible and muted wasn't anything Bean imagined. The men headed toward the high narrow crack between the sheer vertical flanks of the mountain wall. Bean followed.

He picked up his feet and tried to get closer to hear what they were saying. But the men only spoke in their native language. Bean still wanted to keep pace with them in case he didn't recognize an area. They got to the cleft, which was about three feet wide. Little light seemed to shine down inside it. The men entered one by one.

"Boy, you better wait! I promise, we won't hurt you," Kele said, voice echoing ahead.

Bean couldn't help but giggle, enjoying his sneakiness. He picked up a small rock to throw at the men and taunt them. He tossed one at Kele's back, but the rock went right through him. This made Bean suddenly nervous about his new condition.

CHAPTER TWENTY-NINE

After he took a few more steps, a rock hit Bean's backpack from behind. Bean slowly turned around to find a dark red creature standing about four feet tall. It stared at him with big yellow eyes, floppy ears, and one sharp tooth poked out from its bottom lip. Bean was too scared to move. He rubbed his eyes. Then another creature resembling the first appeared, clinging to the wall. Pulse pounding, Bean turned and ran for his life.

The freaky goblin creatures scrambled after Bean. Bean came up to Kele and the others with the creatures approaching fast. The gap was too tight. Bean tried to sneak by the other three but oddly enough, he moved right through them as if they weren't there. Bean didn't stop to think about it.

A smaller goblin dropped onto Bean's shoulders from above. In total terror, Bean punched upward as he ran, trying to shake it off. But the goblin held on tightly to Bean's hair with both claws. Bean could see more light as he neared the other end of the cleft. But he didn't make it.

A different goblin jumped at his feet, causing him to stumble and fall with the smaller one still on his back. Two others mounted Bean and wrestled him. With four goblins now on top of Bean, he could hardly maneuver in the tight space.

Bean thrashed against their vicious assault, feeling severely claustrophobic. He cried out, "What do you want? Get off me!"

The red goblins held him down on his back as he twitched and jerked. Studying their prey up close, they tilted their tiny heads side to side in a curious manner. Bean could tell something was holding them back from completely devouring him. Seemingly frustrated, they all wailed in a high pitch squeal. Then one grumbled in a squeaky voice, "You... came from the Natural world?"

Bean thought he had met a horrific and gory death, and so was caught off guard that the monster calmly spoke to him. Bean tried to gain some composure and collect his thoughts as the four goblins drooled over him.

"Wha... what did you say?" Bean asked, chest heaving.

"You are from the Natural world?" it asked again.

Bean understood this time. He recalled his conversations with Draug and more recently with Ria about the dimensions of Hutoriane. Bean replied, "Yes. I do. Why... what is *this* place?"

"This is not the Natural realm. This is the Underworld," it answered. "And you are trespassing."

Just then, Kele and his men passed right through them on the ground. Bean watched and was confused. "I'm sorry. The Underworld? But I see the Natural world?"

"Why are you here?" the goblin piped up in anger.

"It was an accident. I just blew my whistle and then..."

"You are an intruder in the devil's kingdom. You cannot proceed without proper payment," the goblin leader explained.

Bean gulped. "Wha... what kind of payment?"

"Your body. We want to eat you," the goblin said candidly. Bean squirmed, trying to get an arm free. "But for some reason we can't eat you. You...are too pure. You are not evil enough."

Bean cleared his throat. "So, how do I pay you?"

"Any living animal will do from the natural world."

Bean settled down for a moment. "How do I do that when they are in the Natural world?"

"You passed through to this realm with your clothes and backpack. You just need to hold onto one."

"I don't understand. I mean, this is my first time coming here. How do I go back?"

"You go back the same way you got in," the goblin said impatiently.

Bean quickly thought, *Just blow the whistle three times with my finger on the middle hole?* He responded out loud to the goblins, "Okay. And what if..."

"You don't return as promised with a living animal?" the goblin insightfully completed Bean's question.

Bean slowly nodded.

"Then we have permission to haunt you and hunt you down in the Natural realm and bring you to the Underworld."

Struck with fear, Bean replied, "Okay. I'll do it. Please get off me." Bean said under his breath, "I'm getting used to making deals with devils." He stood up and brushed himself off. "Wait, but I still don't understand."

The goblins gave Bean an ugly look. One spoke, "What?"

"If I was a bad human, you would've eaten me. And that would've been my payment, but then I wouldn't be able to trespass because I'd be dead."

The goblins rolled their eyes and sighed. "That's just it. No one from the Natural world trespasses in the Underworld and lives. But since we can't eat you, bring us something we can eat."

"Okay. Can I follow those guys for a few minutes while I'm still in the Underworld?"

"We've waited hundreds of years to eat something alive and fresh from the Natural world. We can wait a little longer," it replied. "But I warn you, there will be others who won't be as patient. You better not venture too far off. And always come prepared with payment."

Bean understood clearly. "Thank you. I will return with a squirrel or something."

Bean walked away from the goblins and made it to the end of the narrow passage. The dull colors and overcast environment made more sense to him now. He was invisible to the Natural world because he wasn't actually there anymore. He could see, observe, and even hear things as they were occurring in the Natural world; but he was physically in the bleak Underworld and was starting to learn the order of things in that realm. Being invisible quite literally came with a price.

He stepped out of the passage into a grassy opening with some tall trees blocking his view of anything beyond. Bean remained alert to the threat of supernatural beings. Creeping out into the open, he looked over his shoulder while trying to find any sign of Kele and his men. He advanced into the trees and could hear the crashing of the deafening waterfall close by. That's when he saw them. He snuck up closer.

"There is no place for him to go," Kele said. "The only way to move forward to the falls is through the narrow cleft. Let's wait here and then take him out."

Bean was surprised to hear so clearly. *They must be talking about Toni. It's my fault if he gets ambushed. I need to warn him.* But just as Bean turned around, Toni stuck his head out of the narrow passage behind him. *No! I'm too late!* Bean sprinted through the grass over to Toni.

"Go back, man! Go back!" Bean yelled, but Toni couldn't hear him. Bean entered the narrow cleft. He hovered over Toni as he knelt and drew his bow. Bean noticed the red cloth dangling, tucked in the top of Toni's pants. "Don't go out there, Toni. They'll kill you!"

Toni concealed himself noiselessly just inside the shadows of the passage walls, aiming his bow outward. Knowing where Kele and his men were standing, Bean keenly watched for any movement in that direction. Surprising Bean, Toni whispered, "I don't see Bean. I hope my gringo amigo is okay." Bean was pleased to hear Toni regarded him as a friend. Now even more determined, he wanted to help Toni but had no weapons for his own defense.

"Don't be a coward, Bean. He's here because of you," Bean told himself. The goblins began to laugh in the background. Bean glanced back at the four red goblins, their huge grins revealing sharp teeth.

"Crap, I need to get back to the Natural world." Bean pulled out his whistle and put his finger over the middle slit. He blew it once. Suddenly, Toni let an arrow fly. With eyes wide open and the whistle on his wet lips, Bean saw the arrow strike one of Kele's men square in the chest. The man dropped.

Kele quickly responded and fired two shots into the cleft. Toni stumbled while trying to dodge the bullets. He backed up and removed another arrow from his quiver. Bean blew the whistle again. Toni turned around and ran in the other direction toward the ledge and boulders below. Kele pursued fast after Toni. Now standing next to Bean, Kele fired two more shots into the dark passageway. Toni had no place to hide and was headed toward a dead end. Kele advanced guardedly into the dark passage.

Bean turned around toward the exit and saw Fichu crawling in the tall grass. Bean stepped out of the cleft and stood to the right of the rock aisle. Fichu got to his feet and made it to the entrance of the narrow passage. Bean waited until Fichu stepped inside the passage. Finally, Bean blew whistle a third time. Instantly, he reappeared into the Natural realm.

Subduing his fears, Bean tip-toed back to the cleft's exit and peeked into the dark passageway. He couldn't see anything but could hear Fichu walking. He desperately wanted to save Toni but didn't have a plan. With his adrenaline pumping and the opportunity slipping away, Bean hollered into the dark cleft, "Fichu! Come fight like a man!" Bean could not believe the words that left his mouth.

Bean scampered backward through the tall grass and hunkered down behind a tree, waiting for the imminent confrontation. Within seconds, Fichu scampered out of the passage with his long machete in hand. Fichu stopped a few feet from the entrance and tried to spot Bean.

Bean had a stroke of brilliance. He quickly got out his whistle, plugged the middle slit, and blew. Fichu rushed toward the direction of the noise. Bean ran behind some other trees to Fichu's right and blew the whistle again. Although limping, Fichu was hot on Bean's trail and closing in fast.

"You die now!" Fichu yelled as he hobbled after Bean.

Bean had circled back around close to the narrow passage and stopped running. Frantic, Bean knew how Fichu wanted him dead. Bean held onto the whistle and braced for impact. Fichu caught Bean with one hand and tried to head butt Bean. Luckily, Bean moved his head in time. Bean clenched onto Fichu's arm and put the whistle to his mouth.

Fichu intentionally dropped the machete and threw Bean off him. They danced in circles and then Fichu slapped Bean across the face as if to toy with him. Fichu faked with another slap of his left hand and delivered a jarring punch to Bean's chest with his right fist. Bean flew backward, dropping the whistle in the dirt. Bean was dazed and didn't see where it landed. Fichu continued his assault grabbing Bean's hair and getting up close to his face.

"Dumb gringo! I kill you with no weapon," Fichu taunted. He slammed Bean's head down to his right knee and Bean fell to the ground dazed.

"You killed Moa. Now I..."

Bean kicked and swept Fichu's injured leg. Fichu stumbled and lost his balance. Bean scrambled and found the whistle. Fichu pounced on top of him again punching him in the mouth. Bean turned to his side, tried to block Fichu's blows, and blew the whistle while tightly gripping Fichu's arm. In an instant, they were wrestling in the Underworld.

Rolling around and trying to survive Fichu's relentless strikes, Bean cried out, "Here's...your...payment!"

The red goblins arrived just in time to save Bean. They turned into raging savages and jumped onto Fichu, attacking him from every angle. Bean somehow maneuvered out from under all the bodies. He got to his feet and backed away in horror. He watched as Fichu was devoured alive by the squad of evil goblins. Bean escaped the gory scene to go help Toni through the passageway.

CHAPTER THIRTY

Still in the Underworld, Bean's adrenaline carried him through the narrow passageway, back toward where he first entered. His head throbbed and had a bloody face, but he didn't feel any pain yet. He wiped some blood from the corner of his mouth. He had taken a good beating but was thankful to not have sustained any serious injury for once.

As he approached the other entrance, two human silhouettes appeared in the tall and narrow threshold against the sky's light gray background. The one in front hung his head down and limped along as the one in back forcefully nudged the hostage forward. In suspense, Bean paused and waited for the men to walk by him.

"Cállate! No hablas más!" one yelled to the other in a familiar voice.

Kele would've shot Toni. He wouldn't keep him as a prisoner, would he? Bean wondered.

The men got closer to Bean. The man in front blocked the view of the man in back. Bean held still as they approached him. *Could it be?* Bean now recognized Kele in front. *Oh sweet! Nice job, Toni!* Kele passed first, hobbling along with a bloodied nose and a cut over his eye. His hands were bound behind him with some cord. Toni didn't appear to have any bruises at all, but it wasn't bright to see well either. Typical of Toni, his face was emotionless as he passed Bean, holding Kele's own gun at his back. Bean was in awe and thrilled Toni was not only safe, but in control.

"Now you are my personal guide," Toni told Kele.

Bean followed them out the passageway, when they halted. "Come out Fichu! Kele needs your help!" Toni yelled. They waited, but the only sound was the thundering of the waterfall behind the trees in front of them.

Bean wiggled through the gory mess of Fichu's clothes and bloody remnants on the ground in the Underworld to get a better view. Toni spotted something on the ground in front of them. He bent over and picked it up. Toni waved a long machete in front of Kele's face.

"This isn't yours," said Toni. "And it isn't that guy's over there either," he said, pointing into the trees where he had shot one of the men dead with his bow. Toni observed the disrupted grasses directly at their feet and the scuffed mounds of dirt in the ground where he picked up the machete. "Either Fichu is setting me up, or something happened to him, because something violent happened right here."

Kele broke his silence. "He probably found the boy and killed him!"

Toni knocked Kele forward and remained on high alert as he escorted Kele into the trees.

Bean followed. He felt uneasy about how long and far he could go without being assaulted again in the Underworld. He wasn't sure if he should reveal himself yet to Toni though. *Toni is okay without me. He has a guide who will take him to Angel Falls.* Bean began to hear some anomalous, alarming noises not far away. *I gotta get back to the Natural world. I will keep a safe distance behind them.*

Bean blew the whistle three times while covering the second hole. He reappeared in a flash behind a crooked tree. He watched as Toni and Kele walked a little further through the grove. Suddenly, a thought occurred to Bean. *Which one of these guys had my knife? And more importantly...the map?*

Squatting down, Bean rushed over to find the man Toni killed with the bow. Bean discovered the body between two bushes and bent over backward on the ground. Bean saw the arrow lodged in his sternum. "Nice shot, Toni. But now I have to move this gross body to find my knife," Bean whispered to himself. He examined the area and then found his knife tucked in the side of the man's pants. Bean slid the knife out carefully. *Now for the map. Kele must have it in his pack.*

Like a cat creeping up on some playful mice, Bean snuck up quietly behind Toni and Kele, trying to maintain about fifty feet of separation. He stopped and checked his watch. *Just after four pm. This has taken longer than I thought. I need to hurry. I need to have enough daylight to locate the platinum sphere.*

The boisterous roar of cascading water close by lured him along. Toni and Kele finally left the trees and disappeared from Bean's sight. A few minutes later, Bean came to the edge of the tree line too, still staying a good distance behind the others. He spotted them again to the left, but he was immediately captivated by the exquisite panoramic view in every direction.

Standing not far from the rim of the cliff, Bean finally beheld the spectacular Angel Falls. Bean's vantage point gave him a panoramic view of the northeastern side of Auyantepui. He gazed at the flow of water bursting from the top of the mountain and falling straight down for thousands of feet into a dark green, bowl-like canyon below. The water created thin clouds of mist and fog below. Mesmerized, Bean took a few minutes watching how the falls formed a river below, meandering and splintering in many directions through the vast jungle. "I don't recall *this* magnificent sight," Bean said referring to the vision Anomar gave him from the map. "Maybe this is when she stopped."

Bean was ecstatic to be standing so close to the mountain's flat, green top. He assumed the platinum sphere was close and a reunion with his dad would be shortly thereafter. The only way to get up to the falls was a thin gravel ledge along the vertical mountainside that steeply ascended toward the waterfall, and then back above again the same distance. He figured the switchback was about five hundred yards each way. The incline looked terrifying. There was also minimal vegetation on the path. Bean saw some small trees outcropping and occasional bushes along the ledge path. He knew that if he followed any closer distance behind Toni and Kele, he would have no cover and they'd certainly discover him.

Toni and Kele were now well ahead of Bean traversing the steep mountainside. Bean began this last leg of the summit and warily followed them. After ten minutes of hiking, he saw Toni and Kele had stopped to rest. Bean tried to get out of their sight by hiding behind a protruding rock in the mountain wall. The two were arguing about something, but Bean couldn't hear anything with the waterfall raging in the background. Suddenly, Toni had Kele kneeling on the ground with the hand gun pointed at his head. Toni bent over and pulled something out of Kele's backpack. Toni stepped away and unraveled it.

Bean's stomach turned. *Oh no, he's looking at the map.* At the same time, Bean noticed two large birds circling high above them in the air. With his attention back to Toni, he worried, *Toni is Muellaman.... what if he can actually read the map?* Bean was nervous at the thought of Toni as a potential threat. He wasn't sure what to do. Out of nowhere, the giant birds swooped down at Kele and Toni, and Toni shooed them away. "Vultures!" Bean said in a loud whisper. Quickly, Toni rolled up the map and the two moved on.

The vultures soared high overhead again. Bean watched them between steps, but almost lost his footing. To Bean's right waited a gruesome death, falling thousands of feet down. His heart pounding out of his chest, Bean decided to ignore the birds and carefully focus on each step. He was halfway to the turn when Toni and Kele approached the switchback point. *I need to find cover fast. When they turn around, they're gonna see me.* There was nothing to hide behind, though. Bean decided to make himself skinny against the mountainside. He put his stomach to the rock wall and held onto some grooves with both hands. Bean watched Toni and Kele as they rounded the turn and started up the second leg of the switchback above him.

Thank goodness they didn't see me. From the corner of his eye, Bean saw a black object fly right by him. The second vulture snagged Bean's backpack with its sharp talons and carried him off the cliff. Before Bean knew it, he was suspended in the air high above the earth beneath. His stomach sank. His heart raced. And Bean couldn't do anything but hope the giant bird didn't drop him.

Bean gradually descended in the vulture's grasp, too heavy for the bird to carry him. "Help! Help!" Bean cried. He thought of Ria but couldn't get the whistle. Toni and Kele looked up, observing Bean's helpless plight. Suddenly, the other bird swooped in and dug its talons into the flesh of Bean's right leg.

Bean screamed in pain. The birds carried Bean straight up into the sky, above the flat green table top of Auyan-tepui. Through tears of agony, Bean observed the strange world below, swept up in a miasma of wonder and terror. Everything was out of his control. Bean prayed for a miracle.

CHAPTER THIRTY-ONE

The vultures gave Bean a wild and unforgettable aerial tour of Auyan-tepui. Scared beyond belief and in pain, Bean couldn't find any joy in the experience though. They flew him back over the mountain's edge, right over Angel Falls, and dropped sharply with the water. The waterfall seemed to never end as Bean descended lower and lower into the canyon.

Bean's right calf cramped in anguish as the vulture's talons clutched harder. The birds were now so low, they hovered just over the treetops of the rainforest. Bean had never felt more apprehension and uneasiness than on this surreal ride. They dove again right through the crowded trees and winding branches. Simultaneously, they let go of Bean.

Above a mossy pond somewhere in the middle of the jungle, Bean fell straight down. He hollered as he anticipated a dreadful impact. Bean had no time to prepare other than trying to keep his feet under him as he plunged into the brown water.

Splash!

Bean hit the water hard. Submerged, Bean paddled in a frenzy, trying to find his way back to the surface. After what felt like an eternity, he emerged from beneath the murky water.

"Oh...my...gosh...oh my!" Bean said between breaths, grateful to have survived the entire ordeal. The last four minutes of his life was the scariest and most exhilarating he'd ever had. Now in the middle of a scummy pond, it was unnerving for Bean to swim over to any side for safety. There was a stinging sensation in his lower right leg and his backpack made it hard to swim too.

Bean fought his way through the water. To his alarm, he noticed movement over at the water's edge. Trying to float in place, he stared in the same direction for a few seconds. Then he saw it, camouflaged and tucked between the bushes. Its massive spotted head with huge yellow eyes, a wide black nose, and gaping mouth with long sharp teeth gave it away. "A jaguar? No. No way," Bean said in denial. It hissed ferociously at Bean and its giant paws spread out, ready to attack.

I'm gonna die for real this time, Bean thought. He hurried and changed directions. He didn't want to ditch his backpack, but he was already tired and terribly slow with it on. It occurred to him, *the pink juice. I have one more bottle.* Shaking nervously, he opened the front pocket while trying to stay afloat by kicking his legs. Bean downed the last bottle of energy drink. He started to swim again with fresh determination.

Bean looked back for the jaguar. To his dismay, he watched just as the jaguar leaped into the water. *Holy crap, its gonna eat me!* It was now life or death, and he couldn't let the backpack slow him down any longer. Bean regretfully ditched his beloved backpack, letting it sink into the murky water.

The juice kicked in. Bean couldn't believe how fast he swam. The large cat closed in on him faster though. As Bean rushed, he remembered how Captain Sevilla described the way a jaguar killed its prey, biting through the skull. Terrified, Bean literally swam for his life.

He finally came into shallow water and hopped along. Bean reached into his pants pocket and pulled out the whistle. Bean needed Draug. He blew the whistle. The cat was now thirty feet away. He got up to the water's edge and blew it again.

"No, stop!" Bean heard a woman yelling but didn't stop. He tottered into the brush.

"Bean!" came the same voice again. Bean stopped and slowly turned around.

Just five feet from him stood Anomar in all her beauty, wearing her feline spotted robe. "Bean, it's me. It's okay, really," she assured him, holding her hand out.

Bean panted, not understanding what was happening. "Anomar? Where... where did you come from?"

"I've been looking for you, Bean. You're in serious danger."

Still panicky and breathing heavily, Bean looked around, but the jaguar was nowhere to be found. Putting it together, he stared back into Anomar's big yellow eyes. "Anomar... you're a skin-walker too?"

Anomar paused. "I can explain. I can't just parade through the middle of the jungle as a beautiful witch, can I?" She snickered at herself. "I'd get harassed and maybe eaten."

"Right. Okay... but..." Bean looked down at the steady bleeding of his right lower leg.

"You're bleeding! And exhausted. Let me help you." She advanced toward him.

"No, wait!" Bean yelled, thrusting his left palm up.

"Bean, you can trust me. We had a nice visit earlier this morning, remember?"

Bean nodded but was still unsure about her. In an emotional trance, he stared at her and then over her shoulder. He could see Angel Falls high up in the distant background, pouring down into the treetops. "I was so close," Bean said. "I was almost there," he lamented, holding back the tears. "Did *you* send the vultures after me?"

"Again, let me explain," she responded. "Toni would have killed you. I had to save you."

Right then, the clouds gathered above the forest and the area darkened to a dreary gray. Painful whining cries were heard in the foggy vicinity. And then a towering tree crashed behind Bean.

"Bean, they're coming for you!"

"Who is? Why? What should I do?"

Anomar rushed over to Bean, who was physically and emotionally spent. She opened up her jaguar-skin cape and wrapped her arms around him. Another tall tree fell diagonally over the first one.

Anomar chanted, "Father of lies, hear our cries!" In a strange tongue, she cried out, "Eeeeerf aleuzenev morf noisserppo! I command a transport home!" Anomar and Bean vanished into thin air just as a swarm of angry demons appeared.

Bean found himself on the same reclined cot where he woke earlier that morning. Anomar once again stood next to him, administering aid to the deep cuts in his right calf muscle. "Hold still, this may sting a little," she said as she poured a mysterious tan liquid over Bean's wound.

"Let me guess, whiskey?" Bean asked.

"Ha, not quite. It's my own healing potion," she said.

Anomar cleaned four triangle-shaped holes the size of guitar picks on the side of his lower right leg. "Anomar, what's going on?" Bean asked as she wrapped his wound.

"Have a drink of water," she said, handing him a tall mug. "I'm sorry you're in pain and had to go through so much. But there is more to tell you."

"But why *now*? I was so close. I'm losing daylight. I need to go. I might not make it now," Bean complained.

"I understand. But listen. Toni was going to see you...and kill you," she said.

"No, not Toni." Bean refused to believe her.

"Yes, Bean. And in order to get the ladle, I too made an oath," she said. "I waited years for that ladle, so that I might be my normal self again. And now, I might lose it."

"Why?"

"Because I was supposed to tell you everything on the map. There's more to the translation."

"What do you mean?" Bean asked.

"As I transmitted the map into your mind, do you remember I stopped?"

"Yeah. You were frightened by something."

"Yes, and now I will tell you why. I need to make it right with you...and Draug."

Bean didn't totally understand. And he felt like he was quickly losing time. "Look, I don't care. I just need to find the platinum sphere before Toni does. He has the map too."

Anomar's yellow eyes grew large. "Toni? Has the map? I thought Kele and his men did."

"You did? Well, they did after they captured me..." Bean stopped himself. He was confused how she knew, but was also in a hurry. "Toni has the map now and he's holding Kele hostage," Bean told her.

"He has the map?" Anomar said sounding nervous. "Bean, that Toni is a very dangerous human. You're right, we need to stop him."

"I'm not scared of Toni. I am just scared he'll beat me to the platinum sphere and I won't save my dad. So, I need to get out of here. Please hurry and tell me. What else does the translation say?"

Anomar hesitated, and then explained, "There are powerful entities that want to destroy you and me and Draug. I thought that if I told you enough, then Draug would be satisfied and not harm you. But then, I saw I would lose the ladle if I didn't tell you everything."

"You did?" Bean said surprised. "What happens?"

"The markings on your body, have you noticed them?" Anomar asked.

"Actually yeah, when I was getting a drink from the stream."

"And what did you find?"

"That they strangely matched the symbols in the Emblem of Hutoriane."

"Exactly."

"Except for…" Bean's heart sank. He peered down at his right leg and at the wrapped bandage covering his new wounds. With a worried face, he looked up at Anomar.

"It's complete. You are fully marked and prepared now," Anomar said with slightly crazed eyes.

"Prepared for what?"

"To rightfully obtain the platinum sphere. And for the sacrifice," Anomar said, mollifying her excitement.

"I don't get it. So, I needed the scars before I could get the platinum sphere?"

"Yes. And there's more. I didn't want to tell you earlier. But Draug intends to have you killed. Kele works for him. That is why I stopped the transmission. No angel shall ascend the devil's mountain freely, unless the proper sacrifice is made. You are the angel, Bean."

Bean recognized the phrase but remained very confused. "Are you serious? But he and I made a promise to each other."

"It is true. And you cannot fall, or the demons will reign."

Bean sat quietly trying to discern everything she was saying.

"Bean, the message in the ancient Indian writing. It said a properly marked sacrifice must be made to gain total use of the platinum sphere. The only way Draug can gain all the power of the platinum sphere is if he makes a marked human sacrifice in the Natural world. But he can't survive in the Natural world. You are the one to be sacrificed on the top of Auyan-tepui. Your blood shall spill into the Churun River, drop with the waterfall and disperse throughout all of the waters of Hutoriane."

Bean was beside himself. *No way,* he thought. He wasn't sure what to believe. He didn't fully trust Anomar, knowing she purposely left this part out of the translation.

"Sacrifice *me*?" he asked. "But I'm helping him. That doesn't make any sense."

"Haven't you seen that when someone gets a little power, they only want more?" Anomar asked.

"Not really."

"Whoever possesses the platinum sphere will control all of Hutoriane. If Draug gets it, you will die and the demons will reign."

"I don't know what to believe anymore."

"It's true. When he does, he will finally be recognized by the Council of Healers," Anomar said. Bean remembered Draug referring to the Council of Healers too. "Draug intends to have you sacrificed, Bean."

Bean remembered lying on Draug's altar. "He really wants to kill me after all I've done? Drain all my blood into a river?" Bean was baffled, frustrated, and saddened. He didn't want to believe Anomar. "Is this why you plucked me off the mountain? To tell me Draug wants to kill me? You're freaking me out. I need to get out of here." He turned around and started toward the hut's doorway.

"No, I sent the vultures to save you from Toni and Draug! You must listen to me! And now fully marked, you are ready to obtain the sphere," Anomar said sternly. Bean turned back. He sensed she was getting desperate and her anger was getting the best of her. But he listened. "I will protect you. I will help you."

"You'll help me? You'll save me from Draug... and Toni?" Bean felt betrayed and confused. Bean was worried his entire journey was all for nothing. But he felt urgent to go save his dad. In a panic, Bean fled to the doorway.

"I won't let you fall, Bean!" she yelled as he darted out.

CHAPTER THIRTY-TWO

Bean ran out of the hut. Right away, he noticed the cashew trees surrounding the hut's entrance. He didn't have time to waste. Bean sprinted over to the broken wooden bridge where Fichu tried to shake him. He stopped. Bean gazed back at the cashew trees and studied them. They were in a perfect circle. The hut's doorway was at the edge of them, backing up to a steep hill. Now in the daylight, he saw the setting differently.

Slowly, he walked back to one of the trees. The branches of each tree extended out widely. *The cashew trees*, Bean thought. The pathway leading to the hut's entrance was made of river rock and was about two feet wide. Another pathway of flattened river rock crisscrossed the other one diagonally, making a giant X on the ground. Bean walked to the end of the pathway, and noticed the ground was in a large circular pattern. He kicked back the overgrowth with his feet. Underneath the tall grasses was a circle of river rock.

"Bean?" Anomar's voice disrupted his observations as she stood in the hut's doorway. "What do you see?"

Bean ignored her. He pulled out his whistle and gently turned it over in his hand. He compared the Emblem of Hutoriane with the life-sized circle-X made by the river rock pathways on the ground. Gray cloud clusters began to form a hundred feet above. A drizzle of rain came along with them.

Intrigued, Bean entered the lower cross section and discovered some concealed rocks in the middle of that same section. He hastily kicked back the earth, the moss, and more of the grassy overgrowth. He finally made out the shape of a cursive M. With his heart pounding and nerves jittering, he thought for a moment, *Could it be right here?* He didn't need to uncover the other markings. He was in a hurry. Intuitively, Bean walked to the center of the emblem on the ground, where the river rock pathways intersected. He knelt down and loosened one of the rocks with his bare hands.

"Good, Bean, you're connecting." Anomar stood over him.

"I need a shovel or something to dig with," Bean said.

"Would you like my help?"

"Yes. Please. Do you have something?" Bean asked, trying to extract another rock.

It was raining more. Bean had removed a few rocks by the time Anomar returned with a shovel. He stood up and stared at Anomar in amazement for producing the perfect tool so fast.

"What? Surprised? I told you I'm a witch. With the ladle, there's nothing I can't do," Anomar said proudly.

Bean vigorously went to work. Anomar stood over Bean, holding her cape above him to keep the rain off as he dug like a dog seeking a bone. Bean wildly followed his premonition. *I'm close, Dad,* he thought as he kept at it relentlessly. Bean hesitated for a moment. *If the platinum sphere is here, what is my next move?*

Looking over his shoulders, Anomar asked, "Why did you stop? Go on, Bean!"

"Just...tired," he answered as he determined his next move. If Anomar was telling the truth, Bean didn't want to call on Draug and deliver the platinum sphere, only to die. If she was wrong, he wanted to be able to escape. Freakishly loud moaning and wailing was heard beyond the trees.

"They're coming, Bean! You have to hurry!"

The rain came down hard. Bean had already dug about two and a half feet deep. He jabbed the shovel back in the hole as hard as he could and hefted out another big mound of earth. He did it again and again, when suddenly, the shovel hit something solid.

Clack!

"What was that?" Anomar asked excitedly.

Too focused on the task at hand, Bean ignored her question. He carefully removed some more dirt around the object. He couldn't see much with her cape overshadowing the dig site. "Can you step back for a second? I can't see what I'm doing," Bean asked, slightly annoyed.

Thunder shook the sky. The dark storm clouds raged above. The moaning in the background was louder and more frequent. Anomar wasn't giving Bean much space to work. Despite all the pressure, Bean plugged away, digging around the object in the ground. Now he could see it was a dark brown, rectangular shape at the top. The water from the rain poured into the hole. Bean pulled out his knife and leaned down into the hole to carefully clear out the mud immediately around the wooden chest.

Strong winds began to blow the rain sideways. Bean could hardly see what he was working on but could feel that he had removed enough mud to now shift the wooden box. He nudged it forward and back, trying to loosen it from centuries of settling in the earth. Finally, he reached both hands down on either side of the box and lifted. With sheer determination and grit, he maneuvered and hefted the wooden box up to the surface.

"Good devil, you did it, Whistler!" Anomar celebrated.

Bean didn't say a word. Breathing heavily, he saw that there were two latches on both sides locking down the top of the chest. With his knife, he carefully unlatched and cut each of the four rope cinches on all sides.

Lightning struck. Suddenly, all the cashew trees were ablaze creating an enormous ring of fire. Dozens of demonic spirits burst onto the scene, swarming around the giant circle of river rock.

"Hurry, Bean!" Anomar yelled over the chaos.

With a few jerks, Bean popped off the wooden lid. Inside, was an odd package wrapped in a ratty orange blanket with a white zig-zag design. He grabbed the package and hugged it tightly. Bean poked his head outside Anomar's cloak and froze in fright at the hellish sight.

The evil beings had now infiltrated the circle and were stridently chanting the phrase, "No angel shall ascend the mountain freely!" The earth trembled. Bean and Anomar warily looked on as something just beneath the topsoil rumbled and circled around them, spiraling closer and closer.

Anomar draped her cape around Bean, enveloping his body. Once again, she called as loud as she could, "Father of lies, hear our cries!" At the same moment, a huge golden serpent burst through the ground, up into the air, and twisted around as she continued, "Eeeeeerf aleuzenev morf noisserppo! I command a transport atop Auyan-tepui!"

In a flash, Bean and Anomar disappeared just as the snake struck.

~~~ CHAPTER ~~~
THIRTY-THREE

Anomar magically appeared with Bean out of thin air, covering him next to a wide river. They were in the same huddled position as they were when they escaped the serpent. There was no storm. Bean held the wrapped package tightly in his left arm, and a knife in his right hand. Bean turned his wrist and read the time. It was 5:52pm.

Bean readily became aware of no mountain rock walls in the background or any thicket of trees. Except for scattered clusters of bushes, the grassy flat terrain allowed for great visibility in all directions. They faced the river as the bright pink-orange sun set behind them. Bean traced the river to his left and could see it dropped off about five hundred yards in the distance. The green terrain stretched to suddenly meet the rainbow-colored sky in almost every direction. Anomar had successfully transported them onto the top of Auyan-tepui.

"Wow, good work," Bean said in relief as Anomar released him from her arms and they separated.

Anomar responded morosely, "Yes, that was close. But it won't be long until they arrive here too."

"I need to unwrap this before I get it to Draug. I'm nervous. What if it's not here?" Bean knelt in the tall grass and set down his knife.

Anomar looked on and her countenance began to change. Bean carefully unwound the blanket from the object inside. As he finished, Anomar stood back over his shoulder, growing impatient. It was all happening so fast. Bean couldn't believe the moment had arrived. He laid the old orange blanket on the ground and turned over the last fold. Unveiled was a small woven purse with a strap and an overlapping flap. "It looks like an ancient satchel," Bean commented. Anomar was oddly silent.

Bean inhaled deeply and gulped as he lifted the woven flap. He parted the opening and reached inside. He could feel a round shape the size of a baseball. Guardedly, he pulled out the dense and weighty sphere. Just as Toni's grandfather described, the ball was tightly wrapped and woven with hemp-like material. Bean wanted to see the actual platinum artifact, but decided it was Draug's to unravel. He didn't want to tamper anymore with the sphere, so he gently put it back in the woven satchel.

"Bean, it's time!" Anomar said sternly, startling Bean. She grabbed him under the armpit and stood him up with unexpected strength.

"What? To call Draug?" Bean asked.

"For the sacrifice and to pay the demons. You will never be able to keep this without the proper sacrifice," she said.

Bean was frightened and confused. He bent back over to pick up the blanket and wrap up the satchel when Anomar yanked him back and demanded, "No, leave it!"

Bean looked back at her and the pupils of her large yellow eyes were long and very narrow.

"But, Anomar..." Bean could hardly put his thoughts into words. "W-what's going on?" Bean stuttered as he tried to put the satchel over his shoulder.

Anomar ripped the satchel out of Bean's hand. "I will hold the sphere while the sacrifice is being performed," she said angrily.

"No! That's not yours!" Bean answered, raising his voice. He reached for the satchel. But with a quick twist of his wrist, Anomar had Bean's arm pinned behind his back. He was no match for her strength.

"Walk closer to the water," she growled. "You fool. Did you really think I worked with Draug for all those years only to gain the power of the ladle?"

"I... don't know," Bean answered, disorientated.

"When I transmitted the story of the map to you, the passage, the markings, and the sacrifice were all made clear to me. I saw myself and where I could interject my will. That's why I stopped. I just needed you to ascend the mountain and receive all the markings before I revealed to you where the sphere was and what the translation meant."

Bean couldn't believe what he was hearing. Anomar had just saved him from the giant serpent. She had healed Bean twice and translated the map for him. Bean never felt she was a threat to his mission. The ladle apparently wasn't enough power for her. His mind went blank. Her strength and wit were too much for Bean.

Wrenching him forward, she marched Bean toward the riverbank.

They got to the river's edge. The water rushed past a few feet beneath them. "Kneel to the gods of Auyan-tepui!" Anomar yelled as she forced Bean to his knees facing the river, his back to her.

Bean could hardly bend his knees, as his body had tightened up from the shock. Without warning, Anomar lowered Bean's own knife in front of his eyes and down to his throat as he stared across the river. "But, but Anomar... why?"

"Because I am the rightful ruler of Hutoriane, and possessor of the platinum sphere!" she answered. "And you're a thief! You stole the sphere even from my own home!"

Bean's heart pounded, and his blood coursed faster. He could see the dark clouds approaching from the southeast. "Maybe Draug knew this all along," he said to himself as he began to doubt the entire mission. He felt the whistle from the outside of his pocket.

"Hurry and remove your shirt!" Anomar directed as she let go of his arm, still holding him at knife point. Bean removed his shirt. Immediately, she grabbed the back of his neck and firmly held him in position over the river. Bean couldn't move an inch; her strength was so powerful. She raised the knife above Bean's head. Bean's chin started to quiver, and tears welled.

Anomar began the ritual. "Father of lies, hear our cries! The angel has ascended, and the demons have risen! Upon this magnificent altar, accept this marked sacrifice! Behold, the angel falls!"

Thunk!

At that sick sound, Anomar went silent. Her grip on the back of Bean's neck loosened and the knife fell in front of Bean. Bean quickly turned to see an arrow had penetrated Anomar's throat. Anomar staggered a few steps to the right and dropped the satchel. Then she tumbled forward off the edge of the embankment and rolled down into the rushing waters. Stunned, Bean turned back around trying to locate her assassin.

"Gringo!" Toni yelled out across the river, standing up behind a small bush.

Bean could hardly catch his breath. "Toni! Toni!" he hollered back, grateful to have been saved. "You saved me again!"

Toni walked to the river's edge, and yelled out, "You beat me to it, gringo!"

Bean laughed and hastily picked up the satchel. He held the platinum sphere high in the air, "No way. Together. You and me! We both did it!"

Suddenly, three gunshots rang out.

Bean watched as Toni's body jolted and jerked. The gunshots thrust Toni forward and he too fell into the river. Twenty yards behind where Toni stood, Bean spotted Kele standing still with a pistol in hand. Kele had emptied the gun's magazine into his friend.

"Toni! No!" Bean cried out. He hurriedly secured the satchel over his shoulder. Bean raced down the river bank as the flow of water carried Toni's body along. "I'm gonna get you, man!"

After gaining a good distance ahead of Toni, Bean leaped into the river. Although he could stand, the river was more powerful than Bean expected. As he hopped forward, the river pushed him out. Bean tried to hold his ground and resist the current, hoping to intercept Toni's floating body. As Toni got closer, Bean could see it was all Toni could do to keep his head above water. Timing it perfectly, Bean trudged to the right position and captured Toni in the current.

"Toni, can you hear me?" Bean said, holding Toni's head up. The dark clouds now overshadowed the terrain.

"Gringo..." Toni mumbled as the red bloodied water swirled around his body. "He must've found the gun."

"I'm sorry I left you, Toni," Bean said. "I'm here now. I got you. I'm gonna help you."

"Where is your shirt, gringo?" Toni joked. "You trying... to be... like me?"

Bean smiled and sniffed at the same time. "Yeah. Of course." Toni closed his eyes. "No, Toni, stay with me," Bean said, starting to cry.

"Amigo… I read… the map," Toni spoke slowly. "Let me go. I am marked. I am the sacrifice."

"No way, the platinum sphere is ours together," Bean said tearfully.

"Take care of my people, gringo. You… are… my friend," Toni uttered his last words.

"You're *my* friend!" Bean sobbed. "You are my friend!" Bean held onto Toni.

The storm clouds were gathering and thundering. The demons were coming. The river was raging. And Bean needed to find refuge quick. Reluctantly, he released Toni's body back into the fast-moving current.

Bean tried to make his way to the edge while watching Toni drift further away. With each step, the river pushed him back and Bean noticed the water was up to his chest. The river was rushing, gaining more and more momentum. He took another step forward and this time didn't find any footing. The river's current was too strong and swept Bean along before he could do anything to stop.

The falls were only a couple hundred yards in front of him. *I need to summon Draug,* he thought totally trapped in the river's flow. He reached in his pocket and pulled out the wooden whistle. He studied it again as he floated along at a faster pace. "You got me into this mess," he said spitefully. "Get me out of it."

Dark clouds clamored above him. Rain began to pour. Even over the rushing water, Bean could hear the wailing of demons. They seemed to be laughing and cheering. Bean calmly blew the whistle. No sound came out. He blew it again and a flute tone rang out. Bean blew it a third time and a low trombone noise sounded. All the ruckus and chaos were muted to Bean as he watched Toni's body go over the edge. His heart sank.

Bean blew the whistle the last time. As expected, no sound was heard. But a gust of wind blew at his back and carried Bean faster toward the drop of the legendary Angel Falls. Bean didn't see any sign of Draug. In desperation, Bean cried out, "Draug!"

He went over the edge. Bean stared straight down thousands of feet below, falling as if in slow motion. When out of nowhere, Draug snatched him with his elk staff and yanked him into a dark cave dwelling.

With all his might, Draug left the portal window open to show Bean the sight. "Bean, behold my boy!"

Bean barely collected himself, awed that he had survived. He gazed back through the portal's window and watched as the raging water gushed out in front of them. For a moment, they stood behind the curtain of the magnificent Angel Falls. The portal vanished.

CHAPTER THIRTY-FOUR

Draug escorted Bean over to the other room in the black lair. He helped Bean take off the woven satchel from over his shoulder. Bean lay down on the straw bed where he first slept, and Draug set the satchel down next to Bean. Draug put a blanket over Bean as he shivered on the bed. He wiped a dry rag over Bean's face. Bean's body was drained of energy but wasn't injured.

"Well done, Bean," Draug whispered. "You fulfilled your mission."

"Did you... look at *it* yet?" Bean asked in a muffled voice.

"I can't see anything," Draug said. "But may I handle it?"

Bean was surprised Draug asked, after waiting all these years for it. "Of course, it's yours."

Draug chuckled. He felt around for the satchel and then opened it. He gently lifted it up and down as if to feel the weight of it. "You still don't understand, Bean."

"What? What don't I understand?" Bean asked. "Aren't you more powerful now?"

"Yes, I am more powerful because of *you*," Draug said vaguely. Draug carefully slit the hemp rope surrounding the platinum sphere. He pulled it out and turned it over and over. He lit up the torch on the wall next to Bean's bed. "Here, look at its markings. Do you see them?"

"Wow, yeah. I see each section. It is the literal Emblem of Hutoriane," Bean said in amazement.

"You earned this, Bean," Draug said proudly.

Bean didn't get what Draug really meant. "Yeah, almost died a few times too. Wait. Where's my dad, Draug?" His breaths came short and shallow. He swayed close to falling asleep.

"He will be with you soon enough," Draug said. "Rest a little while. Your reunion is near."

Bean was asleep.

A few hours later, Bean awoke in a sweat and sat up fast. "Am I dreaming?" Bean asked himself. The room was completely black, and it took him a second to remember where he was. "Draug?" he called out. "Draug?"

The torches on the wall lit up around Bean. Bean saw the ladder going up through a hole in the earth ceiling.

"Your father awaits you," Draug spoke up. "But can I have a few words with you first?"

Bean was still a little discombobulated and was anxious to see his dad. "Sure."

"The scars on your body resemble the symbols in each quarter section of the Emblem of Hutoriane," Draug began. "Have you noticed?"

Bean remembered getting a drink at the stream somewhere on his ascent of Auyan-tepui. He recalled his conversations with Anomar too. "Yes," Bean said while remembering his last healing. "Wait a minute," Bean said as he pulled up his right pant leg and put it in the torchlight. There was the final marking. The vulture's talons had scarred his right calf, leaving four small triangles in the shape of a kite.

"You have been anointed to rule Hutoriane, Bean," Draug said.

"What do you mean? Aren't *you* going to do that?" Bean replied.

"No, Bean. The mission was your apprenticeship. The entire ordeal, the successful completion and fulfillment of your oath with me, has earned you the right." Draug stepped forward with no elk staff, but with the platinum sphere in one hand and the platinum necklace he once wore in the other.

"Huh? No, not me," Bean said, confused.

"Our family shall rule Hutoriane," Draug said. "Beginning with you. You have restored me. And you will restore our people to their rightful inheritance."

Bean was overwhelmed. "No, no, Draug. You do it. I just want my dad. I want to go home."

"I will do it *through you*. You are my purpose. I am far too old. You are young. Through you, goodness will reign over Hutoriane."

"Please, I just want to get back to my normal, simple life."

"That can never be. Your body is marked, and the sacrifice has been accepted. You have been rightfully anointed."

"No, Draug, No!" Bean raised his voice.

Draug stopped pressing. "I am the Guard of Hutoriane. I shall guard these things with all I have. But I can't for long, Bean. The demons have risen. And there is one more powerful than I. It shall not be long until their master finds me and the sphere. Soon they will be swarming here and influencing the hearts of men in this area to do evil, like they did in Venezuela. All of Hutoriane is in chaos and disarray without a righteous ruler."

"Seems like no one should ever have *all* the power."

"You are probably right."

Bean rubbed his eyes. "Will this nightmare ever end?"

"Bean, there's more to know. Anomar needed *you* to remove the platinum sphere because you are good and pure."

Bean sat still and pondered his experience over the past few days. "Why did she turn on me? She said you or Toni wanted to kill me."

"Nonsense. The power of the ladle wasn't enough for her. She intended to sacrifice you once you removed the platinum sphere. But first, she needed you to be properly marked, so she sent you up the mountain."

"Why didn't you stop her?"

"I didn't know her intentions. I just knew we needed to get the ladle to Ramona so that the map could be translated to you. But once I sensed your trouble, I was ready when you called."

"She knew all along where the sphere was?"

"Probably. But she'd never be able to remove it herself with all her evil and greed. She had been marked years before but lost her innocence and desires for good. That's when she was cursed."

Bean began to understand better. "Toni was marked too. Was he an acceptable sacrifice?"

"To remove the platinum sphere, one needed to be good and *chosen*. But for a sufficient sacrifice, one just needed to be properly marked."

"Ah, okay." Bean contemplated.

"Bean, goodness is the most powerful attribute. This is *your* power. It took me over a hundred years to learn this.

You were exposed to all kinds of evil and threats, but you overcame it all because of your righteous determination and goodness. Don't you see? You kept evil from obtaining the platinum sphere."

"I think I see."

"With the platinum sphere, you must keep evil from destroying Hutoriane."

"I need to see my dad," Bean directed.

"Go then! Your father is waiting!" A wall cracked open in the room. Bean jumped back. Crumbs of earth sprinkled over the slight threshold. Rays of daylight burst inside, making a triangle on the rock floor.

Bean walked over to the opening, and then looked back at Draug. "Thank you, Draug. I can't promise I'm gonna carry the whistle with me all the time."

Draug nodded. "Go, my boy."

Bean left Draug and departed the cave. The crack shut instantly behind him.

CHAPTER THIRTY-FIVE

The morning mountain air was damp, and its smell was nostalgic for Bean. He was elated to be back in the Uintas. The grass was wet too. Only absent a few days, Bean missed the familiar cool autumn temperature of the mountains. The sun hadn't fully risen, but there was enough light in the ravine to see where he was going. Bean looked at his watch and saw it was 10:12am. He immediately gathered that his watch was still a few hours ahead. In just a few steps, Bean found his gun laying in the same place he dropped it a few days previous.

As he continued walking, he remembered the mountain lion chasing him. "Did Draug cause that?" he wondered.

"Bean! Son!" Bean heard the familiar voice of his father. "Up here, Bean!" Standing at the top of the ravine, Bean saw his dad waving both of his hands.

"Dad! Dad!" Bean hollered back. Adrenaline pumped through his veins. As fast as his legs allowed, Bean climbed the hill, weaving in and out of the native scrub oak trees and sagebrush.

Hank headed part way down the hill and met Bean with open arms. Bean and Hank hugged and squeezed each other. Bean pulled back after a minute and looked into his dad's eyes. He examined each contour and wrinkle in his dad's forehead. He even rubbed and tugged at his dad's beard.

"Dad, I never thought I'd see you again," Bean said happily, starting to cry.

"Bean, I've missed you too, bud. Are you hurt? Everything okay?" Hank said with overwhelming emotion. They embraced again tightly.

With his arm around Bean, they walked up to the original spot where Bean was told to stay. Bean saw their things were still there. "Dad, we have a lot to talk about, but... you, you promised to not leave me alone for long."

"I am so sorry, Bean. The trees, the terrain, everything seemed to change before my eyes. I became delusional and even hysterical. I'm ashamed to admit it, but I got lost," Hank said. Bean knew Draug had some kind of effect on Hank's experience. "But after almost twenty-four hours of hiking alone, somehow I made it back here. And then I found your note." Hank grabbed the note out of his pocket and showed Bean the note.

"'Please stay here until I return,'" Bean read the last line out loud. "You've been *right here* the whole time?" he asked in awe.

Hank nodded. "I would've waited the rest of my life too. I love you, son." The two hugged again.

"I love you too, dad. That's what kept me going," Bean said.

"I want to hear all about it. Come on, we can still get home on time. And let's get this jacket on you, bud," Hank said, putting his arm around Bean.

"Yeah I'm a bit cold," Bean agreed. "What about Kenny and Bo?"

"Oh, you didn't talk to them again?"

"No, why?"

"Because I found this other note when I awoke one morning saying that Bo was feeling sick, so Kenny took him home."

"But did you ever see Kenny after we split up that first morning?"

"No, just the note."

"Weird. So, he never knew we were all lost, and he didn't wake you?"

"I guess not."

Hank and Bean picked up the few items that remained. They began the three-mile hike back to camp. Although there was a lot to recount, the trek back was mostly quiet. Their love for each other didn't need any more words, just each other's company. Hank hummed the song "Stand by Me" and Bean just smiled.

Bean began to review the wild journey he experienced over the last few days. He figured Captain Sevilla would be waiting at the airstrip for him in Kavak around the same time. He decided he would email Adriana when he got cell service. His thoughts eventually stayed on Toni. He didn't want Toni's sacrifice to go in vain. Bean wasn't sure how to honor him but was determined to do so in some way.

Along the game trail they were following, Hank looked up and spotted a huge bull elk eating on the side of a ridge. "Check that guy out, Bean," Hank said. "I bet it's the same one we saw on the way in."

"Yeah, I see him," Bean answered. The royal elk turned its head and seemed to watch them with abnormal interest. *Draug? Is that you?* Bean wondered as he felt the outline of the wooden whistle over his pocket.

EPILOGUE

Draug knew Seleman would find him soon. After overcoming the strongest of urges to don the platinum sphere, Draug placed it into a thick wooden box along with the platinum necklace. He deposited it deep into the earthen wall inside his domain. With his mind, Draug lifted a two-ton rock and fit it perfectly into the wall enclosing the wooden box. "That should keep me away for a day or two," he joked.

Draug slowly entered another room in his lair, adjacent to the main room with the rock altar. The room was pitch black. Draug lit the torch on the wall behind him. He set up a flint scalpel over the flame to heat it up. Next, he walked over to a rustic medicine chest and gathered some other special instruments, liquid, and a couple red rags. Lastly, he made his way over to a straw bed where a muscular, yet limp human body lay face down.

He cleared his throat. "I knew your great grandfather's grandfather. The Muellaman order may be the most powerful of healers, but it is not the most noble." Draug set down his things and prepared for the operation.

Toni couldn't respond. The room was completely silent, except for Draug fumbling around with different tools, unable to decide with which to start. "However, you've proven yourself to be a very loyal and lethal guardian for my grandson," Draug said as he examined and wiped the three wounds in Toni's shoulder and lower back. "You earned the boy's trust."

Draug sloppily dumped some whiskey into each wound. He grabbed the flint scalpel and carefully inserted it into the one beneath Toni's shoulder blade and excavated the bad tissue. "This won't hurt much, since you are ninety percent dead," Draug said, snickering.

"Most impressive to me, you saved Bean's life. A few times at that. These acts have kept things possible for me to carry out my plan too. For this, I thank you and want you to live."

As the Guard of Hutoriane, Draug had exceptional powers in addition to those of the healing orders. His bloodline was peculiar. But with only half his power available, Draug wasn't sure he could bring Toni back at all. In his own curious ways and unconventional methods, Draug would give it his best attempt.

He raised his wrist over Toni's torso and then slit it with the scalpel just enough for a steady drip of blood to drop down into Toni's wounds. With each open wound, he donated precisely twenty-five drops of blood. Quickly, Draug wrapped his wrist up with a red cloth, but left Toni's wounds open.

Draug considered three different bottles. One label said *squirrel blood*. Another said *eagle blood*. "Not these two," he said. "Ah, this one." He reached for a corked green glass bottle of fluid. "Do they even have these where you live?" He uncorked the bottle and poured the liquid into each wound and down Toni's throat. "This here is the blood of a wolverine. I am going to get it into your system and then chant with all the energy of my soul to bring you back to life as a skin-walker. For the good of Hutoriane, I hope it works."

ABOUT THE AUTHOR

Jimmy Eaton is a life-long creative artist: author, illustrator, singer/songwriter. He craves the outdoors, especially the mountains and the beach. Jimmy has earned a BA degree from Brigham Young University, and a Masters degree from Westminster College. His formative years occurred in the northwest suburbs of Chicago, Palatine and Barrington. A big sports fan, Jimmy's teams are the Cubs, Bears, Bulls, Blackhawks, Jazz, Cougars, and Tigers. He actually lived in Caracas, Venezuela for two years on a service mission. Most of all, Jimmy adores his wife, children, family, and close friends. He hopes to always follow Jesus Christ and seek God's will in his life. He resides in Utah Valley, at the base of the majestic Wasatch Mountains.

Follow him on Instagram: @thejimmyeaton
www.facebook.com/authorjimmyeaton
www.Hutoriane.com

Made in the USA
San Bernardino, CA
26 September 2018